HALCYON

HALCYON

A NOVEL

Elliot Ackerman

ALFRED A. KNOPF,
NEW YORK 2023

THIS IS A BORZOI BOOK
PUBLISHED BY ALFRED A. KNOPF

Copyright © 2023 by Elliot Ackerman

www.aaknopf.com

Library of Congress Cataloging-in-Publication Data
Names: Ackerman, Elliot, author.
Title: Halcyon : a novel / Elliot Ackerman.
Description: New York : Alfred A. Knopf, 2023.
Identifiers: LCCN 2022049908 (print) | LCCN 2022049909 (ebook) |
ISBN 9780593321621 (hardcover) | ISBN 9780593321638 (ebook)
Classification: LCC PS3601.C5456 H35 2023 (print) |
LCC PS3601.C5456 (ebook) | DDC 813/.6—dc23
LC record available at https://lccn.loc.gov/2022049908
LC ebook record available at https://lccn.loc.gov/2022049909

This is a work of fiction. Names, characters, places, and incidents
either are the product of the author's imagination or are used fictitiously.
Any resemblance to actual persons, living or dead, events, or locales is
entirely coincidental.

Jacket image: *Gettysburg, The First Day, 1863* (detail)
by James Walker. IanDagnall / Alamy
Jacket design by John Gall
DNA strand on title page by Mister Emil/Shutterstock,
DNA model on part titles by Neokryuger/Shutterstock

Manufactured in Canada
First Edition

IN MEMORY OF

Edmund N. Carpenter II

1921–2008

"And what does it mean—dying?"

—ANTON CHEKHOV,
THE CHERRY ORCHARD

ONE

DISCOVERY

News of the great discovery trickled out: resurrection, new life, had become a scientific possibility. The story ran below the fold in the *Richmond Times-Dispatch* on an unseasonably cold Sunday in April. The two narrow columns of text described how a team of government-backed geneticists had leveraged findings from the recently mapped human genome to regenerate cells in cryo-preserved mice. Weeks and even months after death they were resurrecting these mice.

I had read about the "Lazarus mice" in a rented guest cottage nestled in the foothills of the snowcapped Blue Ridge. My reason for coming here was to escape, among other things, the relentless binges of breaking news that over the years had quietly subverted and replaced what was once known as "the national conversation." The history department at Virginia College, where I taught (but have since left) had granted me a semester's writing sabbatical along with a healthy allowance.

After finishing the *Times-Dispatch* that morning, I pitched it into the stone hearth at the cottage's center where a half-burned back log still glowed; that is, I pitched all of it except the story on the Lazarus mice. I held on to that, choosing to save it for later that day, when my landlord, Robert Ableson, would come around for one of his early-evening visits. These visits proved a pleasant inter-lude after tedious, unproductive hours spent alone at my desk. I had rented the cottage from Ableson's wife, Mary, who was more than twenty years his junior. This age difference, he admitted, had proven quite the scandal amidst the prudery of decades past— less so now. Mary was an old soul and Ableson was anything but, which caused her to joke that he was, in fact, her younger man. Handsome in a minor key, with clear bluish-gray eyes and carefully groomed hair still flecked with strands of reddish brown, his appearance belied his ninety years. His face was high-boned, his cheeks rosy and vital, his features distinct. He would have been a natural for a caricature except caricature freezes, and his face was a paradigm of fluid expression. He was possessed by a vigor that he insisted was the result of his daily walks. He called these his "constitutionals."

It was after these constitutionals that Ableson would typically pay his visit, mixing us each one of his signature four-olive martinis, and we would settle in on the cottage's lumpy furniture. Our talks would range in topic, animated by a collision of interests. My work: a study of postbellum attitudes on the Civil War. His life: service in the Second World War, a career as a prosecutor, and the behind-schedule and above-budget renovation of the property's main house, a white brick neoclassical with a wraparound porch they called Halcyon, the name itself linked to the estate for as long as anyone could remember and conjuring a nostalgia for better days. We'd drain our glasses and the hours would pass while we exchanged our drink-inspired truths. Inevitably, the conversation would turn to the headlines, which was why that evening I had saved the story about the mice.

Before I get to Ableson's reaction to those mice, the year itself, 2004, is a necessary digression; that year and the confluence of forces harnessed to create its zeitgeist are as much an actor in Ableson's story as any one person. For those of us who lived through it, we can remember that it was a time when a frenzy pervaded our national psyche, with its liberal and conservative personalities conspiring against our collective sanity. From the political left and from the political right, America had learned over the years to binge on scandal (the Clinton conviction), on piety (September 11th), and on wrath (bin Laden's body dragged from a cave in Tora Bora on Christmas Day). We had lost our ability to disaggregate our values from our rage. Opinion mattered. Accusation mattered. In recent memory had there been a greater epoch of either? Had there been a time when a single word (anonymous or otherwise) possessed greater potential to undo the old order on which we'd once relied? Destruction and creation were in the air, and so had there been a greater time of freedom? Didn't our flawed society need to evolve? And, if we did evolve, would any of this associated destruction have been wrong? We didn't know. Anything could happen. Nothing was sacred. All thinking became absolute. We congregated to the poles of leftward and rightward consciousness. We hollowed out the center of our political life, unraveling the braid of our societal obligations to one another only to awaken and realize with wonder that none of those obligations were—or ever had been—any stronger than a single strand of thread.

It was on those threads that Ableson's life would come to depend, but that night the story of the mice was foremost in my mind. Had it appeared in the paper five or even ten years earlier—in a different time, which is to say a saner time—I wonder whether Ableson would have regarded it with such hostility. Once he'd finished reading, he handed me back the page with a flick of the wrist. "Utter nonsense," he'd said as I took it from him. Did he think the report was a fabrication? "Martin," he added, "I haven't survived the better part of a century by believing every word put into print." The doubt he'd introduced into something I had so readily believed left me feeling a tinge inferior. He went on, "You have to be careful with these scientists. They get their jollies playing God."

I knew from our other conversations that Ableson wasn't a particularly religious man. On a different night, after he'd lingered over too many martinis, that weighty subject had come up. I had confessed to Ableson that although I was born Jewish, I no longer practiced and wasn't sure I even believed in God anymore. But I also knew it felt wrong to say God did not exist. "When people cease to believe in God," he had answered, "they come to believe not in *nothing* but in *anything*." For Ableson, God wasn't a belief so much as a defense mechanism against other, more frightening forms of belief. Also, he thought he had little to lose by believing in God. If the other side of death was, truly, nothing, what did it matter if he believed. But if there was something on that other side, he had everything to gain. This was Ableson's logic of heaven.

And now, gently, in service of the present conversation I reminded him of our previous one and its logic. "Is it so bad," I asked, "if some scientists want to play God with mice? You've said it yourself: we've got nothing to lose and everything to gain."

Ableson brooded by the fire. In the weeks since I'd met him, it was the first time he'd seemed uncomfortable furthering an argument. Eventually, he rose from his seat. He announced it was time for him to make his way back to Halcyon. The evening had turned overcast. The thermometer dipped below freezing. I offered Ableson a thicker coat for his return; however, he declined. He passed through my front door and made fresh tracks home through a curtain of steadily falling snow. As I watched him go his breath rose in a fine mist, crowning his head, and I marveled at his resilience to the cold.

Inches turned to feet as all night long the snow came down. I had finished off the shaker's worth of martinis left behind by Ableson and this led to an obliterating sleep followed by an equally obliterating hangover the next morning, and when I finally awoke it was to a landscape transformed. The sky was a bracing chlorine blue, featureless and sublime. The snow was pristine, without a track—animal or human. Standing at my kitchen window, mug of coffee in hand, I felt as if I were witness to the very dawn of creation. This reverie, however, was interrupted by the realization that the single-lane dirt road connecting my guest cottage to Halcyon had vanished entirely.

I headed upstairs and sat at my desk, which was pushed to the gabled attic window. My vast, unfinished work was spread before me. My eyes ranged over it, and this only added to an intruding sense of isolation. Regrettably, this isolation had done little for my productivity. My project—a book, which that spring I was considering abandoning altogether—had to do with the Civil War and what the historian Shelby Foote termed "the great compromise," a cultural reconciliation between North and South that followed those blood-soaked years. Before departing on sabbatical, my department chair had called me into her office to express "certain reservations," as she'd put it. Foote's interpretation of the war had fallen from favor, and she felt that the selected topic—particularly for a lapsed-Jewish divorcé of Ukrainian descent, like me—was problematic. I listened and, after giving her concerns the consideration they merited, replied: "How is my being a divorcé *problematic?*"

The idea of writing closer to my own experience had once occurred to me, but it'd proven a non-starter. As an undergraduate, when I'd asked my great-uncle Seymour the name of our family's ancestral village in Ukraine, he'd said it was "Anatevka," whistled a few bars of "If I Were a Rich Man," and told me to focus on being American. So I'd chosen to study the Civil War and Foote had become my fixation. On C-SPAN Book TV, in a July 26, 1994, interview, he had said, "In the Civil War, there's a great compromise as it's called. It consists of Southerners admitting, freely, that it's probably best that the Union wasn't divided. And the North admits, rather freely, that the South fought bravely for a cause in which it believed. That is a great compromise and we live with that and it works for us."

How, at times, I wished I could un-see that clip.

It had become the contentious seed from which my tangled work germinated. I had become obsessed with the role of compromise in the sustainment of American life, as well as our relatively recent departure from it as an American virtue. I had my theories on what contributed to our current plague of polarization: gerrymandering, the shifting media landscape, campaign finance laws; however, identifying the causes wasn't enough, it would do nothing to ease our grim national mood, which I would have diagnosed as *rage-ennui*. I had once shared these views with Ableson, who through the wisdom of his many years identified a different source of America's blight. "Sex," he'd said, "the conflict between the male and the female, it is the conflict from which all others derive." He was, of course, referring to our recently disgraced president. When I said as much, he made a little negative wave of his hand. His reference went far deeper than that, traveling backward well beyond Clinton or even my specialization, the Civil War. "The ancients fought about Helen of Troy. We fight about Monica Lewinsky. It's all the same; it's all sex."

In my own work, I was, admittedly, searching for a theory as universal as what Ableson prescribed. However, no such theory had presented itself as I plowed through thousands of pages of nineteenth-century American history and increasingly found myself haunted by the ghost of Shelby Foote. If American life was in the past defined by the reconciliation of its divergent parts— "to form a more perfect Union" as the Constitution framed the endeavor—today American life had become defined by absolutes, and an absolute theory of this blight would, likely, forever elude me.

Below came a knock. Out my window, a string of footprints disturbed the otherwise unblemished snow and led to my front door, ending at the stoop. With my forehead pressed to the cold, mottled glass, I tried to see who stood there, but the angle wasn't quite right. I could only make out a single set of diminutive shoulders no wider than the handles of a child's scooter. Again, there was the insistent knocking. Whoever was at the door knew I was inside; and so I resigned myself to answering, taking the stairs carefully as my head continued to throb from last night's martinis. "Be right there," I called out; still the knocks came, a percussive torture. When I finally swung open the door, I was met by my landlady, Mary Ableson. "Mind if I come in?"

Whether I minded or not, Mrs. Ableson crossed the threshold, taking off her fur-lined parka and tossing it over the arm of a recliner as though she owned the place (which of course she did despite my rent being paid through August). As she entered—giving me a bit of her shoulder in the process—I once again noticed her height, how the top of her head ended exactly where the bottom of my chin began, as though we fit into each other in some way, like nesting dolls. At six-feet (five-foot-eleven-and-three-quarters, if we're being stingy), my proportions are that of an unremarkable man of this new century. Mrs. Ableson, a tiny doll-like woman, was smaller but not in the normal way, and her miniaturized silhouette suggested another time, like those of mannikins in a museum's display of costumes from one or even two centuries past. Her silver hair pulled back into a chignon retained a metallic luster. It was the hair of a woman determined to age gracefully and I doubt very much if she'd ever colored it in her life. She took off her leather gloves finger by finger, while rotating her neck in a panoramic arc as she examined the cottage. Her eyes, narrow and bright, pointed to the kitchen. I had left out the shaker and martini glasses from the night before. Her vision traced a direct line from the glasses to me. "Chilly in here, isn't it?"

I nodded, crossed to the hearth at the center of the room, and began knotting pages of newspaper as I built another fire. Two sofas flanked the hearth with a coffee table between them. She sat on one and, having lit the fire, I settled down companionably on the sofa opposite hers. Observing her red-burnished cheeks and the continued heavy rise and fall of her chest plus a rapid succession of sniffles, I understood how she'd exhausted herself to reach me through the heavy snow. The subject she'd come to discuss must've been urgent.

"Was it much trouble walking out here?" I asked.

Mrs. Ableson stared vacantly at the purring fire, fingering a pendant around her neck. I could see it was a dime. But it wasn't Roosevelt's profile minted on the coin. This dime was of an older vintage, set on the pendant in what looked like platinum. Her eyes diverted from the fire to me, and they were wide and brown but not brown in a plain way; rather, in the way any collection of vibrant colors when blended together turns to brown. If you looked closely—as I was drawn to do—you could detect blues, greens, even hints of red in her gaze. "We need to discuss my husband," she began. "I understand he's been paying you visits." She paused, employing a single beat of silence as an accusatory tool of rhetoric. She was, after all, the wife of a litigator. I could imagine a younger Mr. Ableson sequestered in his bedroom with Mary rehearsing his closing arguments, which she would edit down to the last gesture. With a similar precision, her gaze returned again to the martini glasses in the kitchen. "It's not the drinking that worries me," she said, her tone softening, from that of inquisitor to concerned wife. "What worries me is the newspaper story you showed him last night."

"Newspaper story?" The day had yet to come into focus. I placed a fingertip to a sudden ache in my temple. Last night's conversation with Ableson blurred with those of other nights.

"Yes, the story about the mice," she said impatiently. "I'd like to see it."

I glanced at the fire. Had I already taken a match to yesterday's paper? I then recalled that I'd left the story on my desk before heading to bed. When I went to the attic to retrieve it, Mrs. Ableson followed.

"It's here . . . somewhere," I muttered, ransacking my things.

Mrs. Ableson seemed in no rush. She leaned against the window frame, gazing out at her property, her eyes following the tracks of her journey here. I was prepared for her to comment on my books, my notes, on the clutter that I would—if asked—assure her passed for serious academic work. But she proved incurious. Spread face down on my desk was the first volume of Foote's three-volume *The Civil War: A Narrative*, subtitled *Fort Sumter to Perryville*. When I picked it up, I found the article about the mice beneath.

"Here we are." I spread the crumpled sheet of newsprint flat on my desk, as though Mary and I might read the story together. She had no such plans and plucked it up by the corner like a tissue from its box. She returned downstairs, seemingly unconcerned whether I might follow, which of course I did. She stood by the edge of the fire and, leaning against the mantel, silently mouthed the words of the article as she read. I sat on the sofa, watching her. Then she sighed, saying, "Remarkable, isn't it?" and crumpled up the story, pitching it into the flames. "I guess now it's only a matter of time."

I offered my uninformed opinion that resurrecting lab mice from the dead was one thing but performing a similar feat on a more complex organism—like a human—was a task of a different magnitude, one that if ever plausible would be decades away and fraught with unforeseen complexities. However, while I was speaking, Mary had reached into her pocket and removed another article. It was preserved in a plastic sheath and the paper had yellowed with age. This was also from the *Times-Dispatch*, an obituary: *Beloved husband, father, veteran of the Second World War and renowned litigator Robert Ableson passed away in his sleep last night.*

The cause of death was complications from pneumonia. He is survived by his wife, Mary, as well as their daughter and two stepsons. In lieu of flowers please send . . .

"I don't understand . . . but he's not . . . ?"

Arms crossed, chin slightly elevated, Mary interjected, "He's not what? . . . dead?" She offered a look of slight disappointment, as though inviting me to be more intrepid with what I imagined possible. She continued, "These scientists and the government agencies that fund them can't simply announce what they've discovered. They can't hold a press conference and say they've conquered death. They need a rollout plan, a media strategy. The public has to get comfortable with this breakthrough, has to evolve into it, so it feels more like an inevitability. Hence the first article about the mice. The rest will follow."

I struggled to comprehend what she was telling me, muttering only "But Mr. Ableson *is* alive . . . I saw him last night."

She inhaled deeply and then, very slowly, with special emphasis on each word, said: "They've—brought—people—back. They've already done it. Robert was one of their . . ." and she fished for the phrase to describe what he was to them ". . . was one of their test cases. My husband has spent the last year under social quarantine until news of the discovery becomes public. I suppose he couldn't take being cooped up with me anymore, that's why he sought you out."

Whatever minor hostility I felt from Mary wasn't specific to me. Her husband had hurt her by breaking the rules of his quarantine. He had needed someone that wasn't his wife to talk to, a confidant of sorts, and this idea wounded her. I interrupted: "Mrs. Ableson, so you know, when your husband visits it's only because he wants to chat. My work, stories of his old court cases, his time in the war, even your renovation of Halcyon. Stuff like that."

She nodded appreciatively, saying, "Last night, after you showed him the article about the mice, he thought we needed to tell you the rest before someone else did. Since his"—and she stumbled in choosing her word—"since his *return*, the isolation has been hard on him. There is, however, one other person we've both been able to confide in." She crossed the room, to where she'd placed her coat over the chair. From its pocket, she removed a business card: *Dr. Charles Shields MD*, with a listing at the University of Pennsylvania's Abramson Cancer Center. "I'd like you to pay him a visit. It's important you hear his take on our situation."

I was behind in my writing, having already blown past several self-imposed deadlines. I did, however, have a trip to Gettysburg planned for later in the month. I could visit Dr. Shields then.

"Or perhaps you could move up your trip?" She wasn't asking but telling me this was what I should do. Although I needed the time at my desk, I was paying a very reasonable rent for her guest-house and felt I shouldn't disappoint. I'd visited the battlefield many times before so wasn't in search of any new facts. I simply enjoyed making the pilgrimage. The ground there hummed. The Peach Orchard. The Devil's Den. The Bloody Angle. Each was like an instrument's string pulled long ago that continued to emit a note.

Mrs. Ableson had begun to gather her things. My audience with her was at its end. As we walked to the door, I assured her that I'd make the detour to Philadelphia to meet with Dr. Shields. She thanked me as she finished buttoning her coat. Before she stepped into the snow-covered meadow to pick her way back to Halcyon, I noticed that she'd left the copy of her husband's obituary inside. When I offered to retrieve it, she said, "Don't bother. Do me one last favor, will you? Pitch that thing in the fire."

The snow didn't let up for the next week. I considered postponing my trip north but couldn't stand the thought of Mrs. Ableson discovering me hunkered down in the cottage after I'd assured her I'd pay Dr. Shields a visit. My Volvo station wagon was a reliable all-wheel drive, so the next afternoon I loaded it with everything I'd need for the excursion and dug it out of the snow. The Volvo was one of the few items of value I'd fought for and won in my divorce. The apartment, the dog, the savings account, these were all battles lost. Perhaps this is why I took such pride in the Volvo's performance, the way it handled on the ice, the way it got me anywhere that I needed.

Amid the darkening fields, down the freshly shoveled road, I drove past the Ablesons' house. A light in the top corner was softly burning. I had only ever spent time with the Ablesons individually. I wondered what they were like together. I also wondered about the other rooms in the house, the unlit rooms where he and Mary had raised their children. Over our martinis, Mr. Ableson had mentioned stepsons. There was Doug, a Manhattan-based financier who "likes to be very helpful to his mother," as Ableson put it with a trace of judgment. There was also Bobby, a Boston-based lawyer who "always has plenty of sound advice." Ableson told a story about a day spent sipping Cokes by the swimming pool when they were little boys, how Bobby (the future lawyer) compulsively got out of the water to use the bathroom and how Doug (the future financier) never once got out, only interrupting his fun to give Ableson an occasional, guilty look from the shallow end.

Youngest of all was his daughter, Elizabeth. His only biological child was born more than a decade after her two half brothers. Ableson called her "Caboose" or simply "Boose" for short. Of the children, she was the only one he'd shown me a photograph of. "That's about six years ago," he'd said with some pride of this girl in her cap and gown. The recessed brown eyes, which you could read and then reread for a different meaning, the high cheekbones that mimicked her mother's, and her hair—a reddish brown—like those hints that remained in Ableson's hair, despite his ninety years. "Who's that man she's with?" I asked. Beside her in the photo, clutching Elizabeth's hand like a cane, was an ancient and sickly looking fellow with prune-dark eyes, their lids pouched and houndlike, and white hair that was merely a suggestion blown across his pockmarked scalp. "That's me," said Ableson defensively. He made a second, examining glance at the photo and added, "I wasn't well back then," before tucking it away. "And what does she do?" I asked, changing the subject. "Boose?" Ableson had said fondly, as if his daughter's occupation infrequently occurred to him. "She's still figuring it out."

As I passed by Halcyon, I wondered whose room was whose. I also got another look at the scope of the renovation, which seemed a stop-and-start effort. The backhoe parked on the front yard hadn't moved since weeks before when I'd last driven past; neither had the pallets of roofing materials, the stacks of plywood, or the sacks of cement. If what Mary had told me was true, and her husband had quarantined all this time, that meant "helpful" Doug and Bobby with the "sound advice" likely didn't know about the renovation of their childhood home. Neither did Boose. To say nothing of what they didn't know about Ableson. As far as they knew, their father was still dead.

I reached I-81, that six-lane monstrosity which runs up the Shenandoah Valley, the onetime breadbasket of the Confederacy. This is some of the most beautiful country. It is also some of the most haunted. Although both blue- and gray-clad ghosts certainly stalk the valley, what it is really haunted by are alternate histories. Take for example May 2, 1863. It is the end of the first day of the Battle of Chancellorsville, which Southerners will come to refer to as the Miracle of Chancellorsville. Stonewall Jackson, the architect of that "miracle," has repelled a Union army twice the size of his own. He is now considering a night counterattack. After making a reconnaissance of the Union lines, he is reentering his when a Confederate sentry fires on him, knocking Jackson from his saddle. Eight days later, after having his left arm amputated, pneumonia sets in and kills Jackson. But what if that sentry hadn't fired? Jackson then would've been at Gettysburg the following July. Jackson, aggressive as he was, would have known to seize the high ground on Culp's Hill on the battle's first day. With Culp's Hill in Confederate hands, Gettysburg might have ended very differently, a conclusion acknowledged by both Foote and his contemporary, the historian James McPherson, a century later. And if Gettysburg had ended differently, if the Confederates had successfully invaded Pennsylvania, European powers like Britain would have likely intervened. Lincoln's government wouldn't have survived the debacle. George McClellan, Lincoln's old rival and the Democratic nominee of 1864, would have swept into office with promises to end the war. This would have involved recognizing the Confederacy. The nineteenth century would have been transformed. As would the twentieth. And the twenty-first, even now only at its inception. All because of an accidental gunshot. What's more remarkable is that you can stand where that shot was fired. This pivot point in the history of mankind is situated right after a rest stop with both a Dunkin' Donuts and a Subway franchise. Exit 130B off the interstate.

I drove by exit 130B lost in these strange imaginings. What, I wondered, were the minor events of today that would forever change the trajectory of the future? Was some other sentry firing an equivalent gunshot at this moment as I drove north? Likely so. Twenty-first-century life far outpaced that of others, and so it followed that events like the gunshot that killed Jackson occurred today with greater frequency. Identifying those moments usually required the maturation of time and the work of historians. However, certain recent events needed no such distance. This was where my thoughts now turned.

Specifically, I was thinking of Bill Clinton. What if he hadn't installed a recording device in the Oval Office like Nixon did? Then the tapes of him with Ms. Lewinsky never would've surfaced. How did Clinton think he'd be able to control those tapes when Nixon couldn't? How did he expect a different outcome? Those tapes, his heavy breathing as he told Ms. Lewinsky what he wanted, her halting consent—it's what assured his conviction in the Senate. Clinton's resignation, which jubilant Republicans believed assured them the next election, allowed Gore to fill his presidential shoes for a year before his own candidacy. It's difficult to imagine how Gore would've narrowed out Bush in Florida had he not possessed the advantages of an incumbent. It seemed the dust on the recount had hardly settled when September 11th hit. Our response was swift and decisive, bin Laden dead by Christmas and our troops home by Easter. Would Bush have possessed Gore's forbearance in the Middle East? I've often wondered.

At last my headlights crossed the exit for Gettysburg. Outside of town, I passed the sprawling campus of Gettysburg College. Inside of town, snow clogged the unplowed roads. I crept past the redbrick David Wills House where Lincoln had crafted his famous address. I parked my Volvo in a backlot of the historic six-story, forty-eight-dollars-per-night Gettysburg Inn. I grabbed my duffel and headed into the hotel. The lobby's tasseled draperies, paisley upholstered wing chairs, and polished oak tables were a paean to the Civil War era's Victorian aesthetic. Historical accuracy aside, the décor was kitsch—in much the same way battlefield reenactments are kitsch and selling cap guns and blue and gray uniforms to kids is kitsch; however, when I searched for last-minute reservations, the Gettysburg Inn posted the best rate.

The off-hours receptionist—a kid with acne scars in the hollows of his cheeks and greasy black hair—offered to upgrade me to a corner king-sized room on the sixth floor with a view of Lincoln Square. He needed a moment to modify my reservation but assured me the upgrade was well worth it. While he clacked on his keyboard, he asked what I'd come to town for. Exhausted from my drive, and still without a room key, I had an inclination to reply sarcastically but could think of nothing to say. I noticed an open textbook spread next to the receptionist's computer, its title: *Principles of Business Management*. That combined with the dark circles beneath his eyes, and I could easily imagine this kid working the hotel night shift, making do with two or three hours' sleep, before trudging off to his first morning class at the college; and so I answered, "To visit the battlefield."

"Have you got a tour planned?"

"I know my way around," I said, and was about to add—obnoxiously—*I'm a historian*, when the receptionist pointed to a framed notice on the counter. The National Park Service, it seemed, had closed the battlefield because of the heavy snow. "Unless you have a guide registered with the NPS, they won't let you in," and then he asked, "Will you need one or two room keys?"

I sat on the edge of the bed. Through the sheer drapes I could make out the vague lamplight of Lincoln Square. This was one of the nicest rooms in the hotel, which must have been empty, or next to empty. The digital clock on my bedside table read 10:04 p.m. I needed to place a phone call if I was going to be able to tour the battlefield the next day. It was already late and the longer I waited the more impolite that call would be. I half hoped my old friend Lucas Harlow wouldn't answer, then my decision would be made for me and I could drive on to Philadelphia and this curious appointment with Dr. Shields. Instead, Lucas Harlow answered on the first ring.

"Wait, you're here?" he asked after an exchange of hellos.

"It's last minute, I know, but I wondered if you wanted to tour the battlefield tomorrow. I thought we could catch up."

"You're asking because you need a certified guide."

I said nothing.

Then he laughed. "That's okay. I'll take whatever time we can get. I'm teaching an eleven o'clock class. Could we meet at your hotel at seven? How's your car handle in snow?"

"I've got the Volvo."

"Still? How haven't you scrapped that thing?" He kept laughing, and behind him I could hear his wife, Annette, ask who he was talking to. "Tomorrow at seven then," he said and hung up. No goodbye.

My trip to Gettysburg had not only given me a reason to visit Dr. Shields but it had also given me a reason to spend a morning with Lucas. Although I had never heard of the National Parks Service restricting access to the battlefield, a part of me that I didn't want to acknowledge—something in my subconscious, perhaps—must have known that coming here in the aftermath of a blizzard would force me to call Lucas, who I hadn't spoken to in years, not since my divorce.

His wife, Annette, and my ex-wife, Virginia—or Ginny as everyone called her—were cousins. And so, when my divorce went through, Lucas's loyalty to his wife and her family eclipsed our friendship. There were no hard feelings on my part, but this explained why he'd hung up so abruptly; his wife likely wouldn't have approved of us rekindling that friendship. Lucas and I had met nearly two decades before as graduate students at Tufts, in a snobbish history department that was keenly aware it wasn't Harvard (a fifteen-minute drive south on Massachusetts Avenue). Among the doctoral candidates in the department, Lucas was perhaps the most promising and the only Southerner. Broad-shouldered, auburn-haired, he had been a nose tackle of some distinction as an undergraduate at the University of Mississippi, where in a team photo he stands a head taller than the other players with two lines of eye black concealing a smatter of boyhood freckles across his cheeks; the reputation that followed him to

Tufts was that he was the biggest nerd who ever played Ole Miss football and the coolest guy to ever step into its undergraduate history department. His graduate work, which was a thoroughly investigated study of former Confederate soldiers who'd gone on to prominent postwar careers in the Union, was well received by the coterie of professors at Tufts who—guided by their prejudices against Southern scholars of the Civil War—had first underestimated him. When his dissertation was published, it won him a departmental medal, a book deal with an academic press, and eventually a tenured position at Gettysburg College. Despite these accolades, his intelligence at times made him insufferable, like a man who sits beside you on the morning train and looks over your shoulder to solve your crossword puzzle.

The morning after checking into the hotel, I was down in the lobby with minutes to spare. Seven o'clock came and went. It was nearly half past the hour when Lucas finally barreled through the double doors. As we loaded my Volvo, he was tripping over himself with apologies. He could've easily blamed his late arrival on the snow-clogged roads, or on any one of his three small children. But he was honest with me, as he was with most everyone. "Annette asked where I was going so early and I told her to meet you and we had a fight."

I nodded grimly.

"So," he began as we pulled out of town, "where to first?"

We passed through a checkpoint manned by a single park ranger slumped drowsily in her police cruiser. Lucas flashed her his guide certification and we were on our way. The first spot I wanted to visit was Little Round Top. With the vast expanse of snow-blanketed battlefield completely to ourselves, we took Sedgwick Avenue (named for one general) to Hancock Avenue (named for another), which remained unplowed. The Volvo lost traction and began to stutter on the ice, so I suggested that Lucas and I walk the last couple of hundred yards. He shouldered his backpack and we made fresh tracks through the calf-high snow. Neither of us spoke as we climbed the mellow hill, weaving our way through granite boulders, some of which still exhibited the gouges and nicks made by fifty-caliber minié balls on that July day in 1863. Even at its busiest, when the battlefield teemed with tourists, the crowds would intuitively fall silent after arriving at this hillock, where the 20th Maine Volunteers held off the 15th Alabama Infantry, securing the left flank of the entire Union army.

"Holy of holies," said Lucas as we stood where Chamberlain, the commander of the 20th Maine, had staked his regimental colors. We both knew the spot, though the granite marker commemorating it was blanketed beneath the fresh snow. That Lucas could come here, Mississippian that he was, and declare in a southern drawl that the place where the Union held was "holy" proved in my mind the efficacy of Foote's great compromise.

Lucas pulled a thermos of coffee from his backpack. Perched on a twin pair of boulders we sipped from two steaming cups. Above us the wind passed through the high, heavily whispering trees. Had either of us been here with a group of students, or even tourists, we would have had much to say. We could've traced Chamberlain's defenses on the now vacant ground. We might have mentioned that if you drew a straight line from the logging towns of central Maine—where most of the defending 20th was recruited—to the rural counties of southeastern Alabama—where most of the attacking 15th was recruited—the midpoint of that line was the summit of Little Round Top. However, Lucas and I already knew these things. There was no point in speaking them to one another. Eventually, he asked about my sabbatical. He'd heard from his wife, who had heard from my ex-wife, that I was living in seclusion in a cabin.

"It's a cottage," I said defensively. "I'm renting it from an older couple."

"A cottage . . . well, that sounds nice. Who's the couple?"

I didn't quite know how to categorize the Ablesons, so after mentioning their name and some vague details, I changed the subject. I asked Lucas if he had seen an article in the paper a few days ago, one about a certain experiment that had resuscitated some dead mice.

"Those Lazarus mice, right?" he answered. "Yeah, I read about them. My colleagues in the philosophy department are pretty worked up about it."

"Why the philosophy department?"

"It's the ethics behind this, it's all new and has caught them off guard. The geneticists, the biologists, they've seen this coming for a while, ever since we mapped the human genome." Lucas took another long pull on his coffee, which he clutched between both hands. "What was that? Five years ago? If you can map out genetic structures, then you can map out cellular ones. Which means it isn't so big a step to go from engineering to *re-engineering* cells. The building blocks have existed for years. Someone's finally put it all together. Geneticists, cytogeneticists, even oncologists, most weren't too surprised to hear about the mice. It's the ethicists—those dinosaurs in philosophy departments—they're the ones who hadn't been watching. They've got no idea how to respond. One day you're resurrecting mice, the next day people. What are the ethical implications? They don't have a clue."

I didn't say anything. Lucas allowed the question to linger as we continued to gaze out over the battlefield. The sky had turned a profound and thoughtful blue. The snow shone with a particle glitter. "Where to next?" he eventually asked, glancing at his watch. It was a little after nine o'clock. I suggested we drive over to Seminary Ridge, to the woods where the Army of Northern Virginia had staged before Pickett's Charge. Lucas shook his head. "Those roads are in bad shape and probably snowed in. The monument's in bad shape, too." The monument to which Lucas referred was the Virginia Monument. Four stories in height and funded by the state's General Assembly in Richmond, it featured a mounted General Lee atop a granite pedestal with seven soldiers of the Confederacy deployed at its base. For decades—to include the years of my study—it was one of the most venerated sites on the battlefield. Of that ground where the monument stood, no less than Faulkner had written:

> For every Southern boy fourteen years old, not once but whenever he wants it, there is the instant when it's still not yet two o'clock on that July afternoon in 1863, the brigades are in position behind the rail fence, the guns are laid and ready in the woods and the furled flags are already loosened to break out and Pickett himself with his long oiled ringlets and his hat in one hand probably and his sword in the other looking up the hill waiting for Longstreet to give the word and it's all in the balance, it hasn't happened yet, it hasn't even begun yet, it not only hasn't begun yet but there is still time for it not to begin against that position and those circumstances which made more men than Garnett and Kemper and Armistead and Wilcox look grave yet it's going to begin, we all know that, we have come too far with too much at stake and that moment doesn't need even a fourteen-year-old boy to think This time. Maybe this time with all this much to lose than all this much to gain: Pennsylvania, Maryland, the world, the golden dome of Washington itself to crown with desperate and unbelievable victory the desperate gamble, the cast made two years ago . . .

When I mentioned the Faulkner, Lucas shrugged. "Too much has changed. People hardly visit there anymore." He spoke to me gently, as though revealing the terminal sickness of a mutual friend. He went on: "There's a movement among some of the students and faculty at the college to petition the Virginia state authorities for a replacement monument that's, well . . . more appropriate."

"More appropriate?"

"Less grandiose."

"What does that mean?" I asked. "That monument is one of the most—if not *the most*—significant on the battlefield. You know that better than anyone. Did you tell them about the battle's fiftieth anniversary, when Pickett's veterans set out from the monument's site to re-walk their charge? Have they seen the photo at the stone wall from that day? When the Confederate and Union veterans shook hands across it, right at the Bloody Angle? Destroy the monument?"—I had become exasperated—"They should be mobilizing to renovate the monument, not tear it down. You're one of their top professors. Aren't they listening to you?"

Lucas hunched his massive shoulders and stared down at his hands, his face wore a look like prayer. He offered to take my now empty cup. "Whaddya say we go. I'm getting cold. Coming up here was nice, though . . . I'm glad we had a chance to catch up."

"Why don't you and I both weigh in?" I offered, as Lucas was already finding his way back to my car. "These ideas of reconciliation, of compromise in American life, this is exactly what my work is about. We could partner on this."

Lucas remained with his one hand on the car door handle as he waited for me to unlock it. "It's me," he finally said. "I'm the one petitioning to take it down . . . C'mon, Martin . . . our thinking on this needs to change. It has to evolve past Lee on his horse and Pickett waving his saber on his doomed but glorious charge." Lucas sighed, and the noise of that exhale carried like wind through a chasm. "It's the same as those Lazarus mice and the reason the philosophy departments are up in arms. Every ethicist knows that death isn't such a bad thing. For mice. For people. Or for certain ideas."

Lucas climbed into the car. We drove back toward town. At

the crossroads on Cemetery Ridge, he began telling me about one of his students, a brilliant young woman double majoring in both pre-med and history who'd chosen to write her senior thesis on the aftermath of the battle, instead of on the battle itself. "It's energizing," Lucas said, "to see young people pushing past the traditional narrative. Before the battle, Gettysburg's population wasn't even three thousand. After fighting, the two armies left behind seven thousand dead. The public health implications proved profound, yet there's hardly anything written about it. We might even get her study published in . . ."

But I'd stopped paying attention to Lucas. My stare lingered in the Volvo's rearview mirror. Hovering at the jagged border of the leafless treetops, I could discern the Virginia Monument, specifically the bronze crown of Lee's head caught in a spread of light cast by the late morning sun. Then, with total clarity, I could imagine a wrecking ball flung back on its chain, hurtling toward Lee, poised to deliver the decapitating blow Lucas was advocating for, when his voice interrupted my daydream, as if he were speaking from down a tunnel: ". . . people had to abandon their homes. For years they couldn't come back. Can you imagine what it was like?"

"What what was like?"

"Gettysburg, after the battle. The dead in the fields. The townspeople left to clean them up."

I then imagined the carnage, my mind fixating on a single image among the vast ruin of bodies: mice, a frenzy of mice.

When we returned to the inn, Lucas didn't get out of my car right away. "It's not that I don't agree with the premise of your work," he said, sitting in the passenger's seat as we idled curbside. "Foote has influenced me as well, and I still assign certain of his writings to my students. But when you commemorate Southern courage, who is asking who to compromise? Who is benefiting? And who isn't? You just want to be cautious. The study of history shouldn't be backward looking. To matter, it has to take us forward. You understand?"

Did I understand? No, I didn't. By definition history *was* backward looking.

By this point in the morning, I could hardly contain my frustration with Lucas and what I felt was, through equivocations, the corruption of a thinker I'd once so admired. As of yet, I didn't say any of this to him, or agree with his seemingly absurdist assertion that the study of history should be forward looking, and so answered, "Please give my best to Annette." He nodded once disappointedly and stepped out of the car.

After packing my bag at the inn, I traveled east on I-76. A low sky weighed on the earth, gradually absorbing the distance into a fog. After a couple of hours in the car, the rolling Pennsylvania countryside yielded to the gritty outskirts of Philadelphia, this old city of our Republic. Slick high rises confronted one another across the humped and uneven sidewalks. Filth-encrusted slush replaced pristine meadows of snow and this transition mirrored what felt like a transition in time, from the pastoral life of other centuries to the urban life of this new one. While on the road, I had received a voicemail from Mrs. Ableson. She'd arranged a room for me at the Four Seasons on Arch and 19th Streets. At nearly four hundred dollars per night, it was a gesture of extreme generosity.

The hotel receptionist, a well-groomed and pomaded gentleman—a facsimile employed by five-star hotels the world over—checked me in. When I offered my debit card for incidentals, he waved it away. "It's all covered," he insisted. Unlike the Gettysburg Inn, there was no complimentary upgrade; however, when the bellman led me to my room, I struggled to conceive of a way that any upgrade could have possibly improved my accommodations; these included a panoramic view of Logan Square, a bath and waterfall shower, sitting area and stocked mini fridge with a complimentary bottle of seven-year-old Château Haut-Brion.

My appointment with Dr. Shields wasn't until the following morning. I settled into the couch, poured myself some of the wine, and began to scroll through the pay-per-view selections. After drinking deeply from my glass, an unsettling—if obvious— thought occurred. What service was I doing for the Ablesons that necessitated such a display of generosity? Had I, perhaps, gotten in over my head? And was this room evidence of that? Before I could follow this strand much further my phone rang. It was my ex-wife, Ginny.

"Annette called. She says you're in town."

"Hi, Ginny."

"Well, are you?"

Even though I was Ginny's ex, she was competitive and didn't like that Annette knew I was in town before she did. I checked my watch. It was nearing three o'clock. On her side of the line, I could hear voices in the background. Ginny must have been at her law firm's downtown office. When we'd met, she'd been a public defender. By the time we split, she'd transitioned to matrimonial law. Which didn't work out well for me. The judge had awarded her everything that two twenty-somethings with pristine credit who'd convinced themselves they were in love could accumulate. In acknowledgment of the disparity between our future earnings potential, the judge had ordered Ginny to pay me one year of alimony—"occupational rehabilitation" was the euphemism—but that had backfired, hurting my dignity far more than it ever hurt her pocketbook. I suggested we meet that night for a drink, "just to catch up."

"Sorry, I've got plans with Daryl." This was her latest boyfriend, an associate at the law firm where Ginny had already made partner.

"Then why'd you call me?"

"Annette said you paid Lucas a visit and that you're working on a book."

"What else did she say?"

There was a pause. "Maybe that it wasn't going so well."

Lucas was one of those friends who had the annoying habit of telling his wife everything, which was only a problem if that wife had the habit of passing along the information—which Annette did. A familiar tension settled in my jaw. I took a deep breath and again became aware of my surroundings: how beautiful this room was and that the entire reason I'd traveled to Philadelphia had nothing to do with my academic work (increasingly I believed myself to be the only one persuaded of its merits). "Things are going well," I said, "great actually," making an effort not to overdo the enthusiasm. "Come by for a drink. Bring Daryl."

There was a pause on the line. "Where are you staying?"

"The Four Seasons downtown. Meet at the bar at seven?"

"The Four Seasons—very nice."

"I told you. Things are going well."

I arrived at six thirty to make sure we got a decent table. I sat facing the door, in a corner booth reserved for guests of the hotel. Blue clouds of cigarette smoke rose in slow drifts. Every corner hummed with indistinct shreds of conversation. Above a mirrored bar lined with backlit bottles, a television played the news on mute with closed captions. Unnamed sources had recently reported that President Gore was on the cusp of issuing a pardon for Bill Clinton, a prospect that polled poorly. Two political commentators on the screen—one Democrat, the other Republican—were debating this eventuality so soon after Clinton's conviction. The Republican, a silver-haired and dandyish gentleman with a shotgun blast of patriotic lapel pins above a neatly folded silk pocket handkerchief the color of his tie, spoke of the severity of Clinton's crimes and how he had *debased the office of the presidency*, and then, smirking, so a finely engraved parenthesis framed his lips, he asserted that his objection to a Clinton pardon was based on principle alone because it ran counter to his own best interests, seeing as a pardon by Gore would assure the Republicans the next election. The Democrat, a woman—simply yet impeccably dressed—stared down the camera as though she were a sprinter staring down the track. When the Republican finished, she fired off a list of suspect Republican pardons under their last president, H. W. Bush, to include those for the perpetrators of Iran-Contra. *If selling illicit arms to the Iranians merits a pardon, doesn't a blow . . . bob?* The censorious close caption wouldn't form the entirety of the phrase, editing out the final word so clearly formed by her mouth; however, it hardly mattered. I could see those two words vault off her lips, as well as the other commentator's expression, as if a flashbulb had gone off in his face when she said the words live on national television.

The camera cut back to the anchor, who led into the next segment: *. . . which is a story we've been tracking the last few days: A team of scientists has managed to bring lab mice back from the dead. Could human application be closer than we think? Our correspondent investigates . . .* The program cut to a commercial and Ginny walked into the bar.

We hugged awkwardly. A divorce without children is really little more than a very bad breakup. Through the experience of our failed marriage, the two of us had inherited each other. Ginny, despite our history—or perhaps because of it—had come to feel like a sister.

She ordered us another round of drinks and then got right to the point. "What's with all this?"

"With all what?"

"The fancy hotel. The eighteen-dollar drinks."

"I'm here for work," I said evasively.

"You mean your book?" She crossed her arms and leaned

slowly back into her seat, daring me to lie to her, which of course I couldn't. Instead, I stammered away not only about my book, but also my trip to Gettysburg and Lucas's evolving views on the appropriateness of certain monuments. But the evaded point was swelling. I relented, explaining that I'd really traveled all this way as a favor to a friend, the one who had arranged for this hotel. "That's some friend," she said as the waiter brought over our brightly colored drinks. "Who is it?"

"My landlady."

"Annette told me about your landlady," said Ginny. "You know, her husband, Robert Ableson, he was a big deal in the legal world. What's the favor you're doing her?"

Not wanting to answer, my eyes wandered to the television behind Ginny, where the segment on the Lazarus mice was playing. I pointed up to the screen. "Have you seen this?"

She turned in her chair. "The Lazarus mice? Yeah, I saw. Pretty amazing." We sipped our drinks and watched the remaining seconds of the segment, in which a geneticist explained that the team working on resurrective technologies was making vast strides, and at an unprecedented pace. *The one certainty of life is death*, read the closed caption beneath the geneticist. *And now?* came the correspondent's question, to which the geneticist shrugged, only to answer: *Now, nothing is certain.*

The segment ended. Ginny and I were left sipping our drinks. "Pretty amazing," she said again, though her tone was flat, as if she weren't quite sure. "If we're able to bring more than mice back from the dead, Gore deserves a lot of the credit. The ultra-conservatives on the religious right would've killed this research. Imagine if Bush had become president in 2000? His judges would've blocked all of this from the bench. You still haven't answered my question. What's this favor?"

"A meeting with a doctor."

"Are you sick?" I detected a hint of panic in her voice, one which flattered me and which she must have noticed too because she grew silent, as though momentarily embarrassed by her concern. "No, nothing like that. The doctor is a friend of Mrs. Ableson . . ." I came slightly forward in my seat and, taking a sip of my drink, hid my mouth with the glass. Ginny had always been able to get whatever she wanted out of me, which was one of the ways she'd convinced me to confess to the minor infidelity that had led to the dissolution of our marriage. I could feel my resolve slipping, as if the segment I'd seen on television with the mice might even have been a sign that confiding in her about Robert Ableson could be the right decision. I would explain everything to Ginny and she, with her good judgment, could advise me what to do next. I had no idea what Dr. Shields would tell me at our meeting but felt as though I would want Ginny to help me make sense of it, whatever the *it* was. I was thinking of ways to convince her to stay for dinner when her phone rang.

"You're where?" she said, her free hand cupping her ear. "We're in the bar, not the restaurant . . . Wait, you're in the bar? . . ." Then she stood, squinting out at the crowd. "Hold on, I see you," and she waved overhead toward a tall, broad-shouldered guy in a charcoal suit with a flop of blond hair. His back was toward us. "Daryl, I'm behind you. Turn around." He executed a full pirouette. "No," she said. "Turn halfway around." He was looking straight at us now, but Ginny didn't seem to register to him, and so he dumbly stood there. She exhaled sharply, flipped her phone shut, and marched toward the door. When she touched his arm, he still hadn't seen her. Then, with a big stupid smile on his big stupid face, he threw out both his hands in a gesture that said *Taddah!* as though he himself had made her appear. What did it say about me that she had chosen to be with him? Which is another way to say that I hated him before he'd even sat down.

He scooted up an extra chair to our table. "Really good to finally meet," he said magnanimously, as though he was the one who'd stolen Ginny from me and welcomed this chance to clear up some imagined rivalry between us. The reality was I possessed no greater rival than myself and had long ago ruined my marriage without his help and didn't appreciate any insinuation to the contrary. "Ginny mentioned you're in town for work," he added. "You're a history teacher, right?"

"Historian," I said.

His confused expression mimicked that of a moment before, when he was looking straight at Ginny but still couldn't find her. He glanced at his watch. "I hate to break things up," he said to Ginny, "but we should probably get going." He turned to me. "Wish we had more time, but Virgie and I got an eight o'clock reservation at the Hungry Pigeon." I shot Ginny a look—no one called her "Virgie"—but she dipped her eyes away, as if too embarrassed to acknowledge Daryl's pet name. The two of them stood. When Ginny offered to pay, I refused. She thanked me with a dry kiss on the cheek, and I could feel Daryl monitoring us. His response was a crushing handshake as we parted. The two left and as I sat back at my table, I wished that I'd told Ginny about Mr. Ableson. Everlasting life had become a reality—or at least it seemed so—and the burden of that knowledge had become too strange to carry on my own.

I ordered dinner, ate alone, and continued to watch television from across the bar as I sipped my coffee. The segment on the Lazarus mice ran once more on a different news channel. People entered and exited, slowly filling the tables, unaware that the fabric of their existence had forever altered. Eventually, a woman approached. Her eyes shined like new coins and her smile was kind, the type a good-natured stranger offers to a lost child. As she covered the half-dozen steps between us, I imagined possibilities. Could the kindness of a stranger be what I needed? "I am so sorry to bother you," she began, to which I answered hopefully, "No bother at all," and added my own smile, gesturing for her to

sit down if she wanted. She shook her head with awkward hesitation, and then asked if I was using the extra chair. I wasn't. "Would
you mind?" "No." And she took it.

Finally, I went back to my room. That night I had perhaps the
worst sleep of my life in the most comfortable bed I'd ever known.

At a little after nine a.m. the next morning, I found myself sitting
on a leather tufted sofa across from Dr. Shields. Aside from wel-
coming me, he had yet to say anything. We shared the silence as
he glanced down at the inches-thick manila folder spread across
his immense desk. Photographs of his wife, his children, and his
infant grandchildren rested on the console behind him. Framed
degrees crowded two walls of his corner office. On the other two
walls, floor-to-ceiling windows boasted views of the ambling
Schuylkill River.

"You'll have to excuse me," he said. "I'm not sure where to begin."
He steepled his hands together. His fingers were thick and stubby,
akin to a butcher's, not a surgeon's, and his skin bulged around his
wedding band, the only jewelry he wore. His jaw was square, long
and flat of the nutcracker type, and his white eyebrows formed a
ridge above his eyes; these were dark and dense with thought like
a marksman sighting down a rifle barrel. "Why don't you tell me
what you know." This I proceeded to do, explaining how I'd come
to rent the guest cottage, the nature of my academic research, and
my visits with Mr. Ableson.

"What do the two of you talk about?" he asked gently.

"My work, his renovation of Halcyon, his work, a bit about
the war."

"The war," answered Dr. Shields. "Let's start there." From the
back of the console, he lifted a sepia-toned portrait in a silver
frame. It was of a man in uniform wearing a garrison cap tilted
jauntily back to reveal a bristly military-style haircut. Uniform
and haircut notwithstanding, the man appeared to be a younger

version of himself. "That's my father, Jim Shields. Have you heard about him?"

I had.

By this point, Robert Ableson and I had shared enough drinks on enough evenings in the guest cottage that I had heard most—if not all—of his war stories. This chapter of Ableson's life began in 1941, in those feverish days after Pearl Harbor ("feverish" being Ableson's adjective, not mine), he had through his extensive and WASP-ish family connections earned a commission in the infantry despite the fallen arches in his feet which should've disqualified him. At first, his war proved uneventful. He had rotated between stateside training camps and clerical duties on large staffs. Soon enough, however, bloody campaigns in North Africa, Italy, and the Pacific had ground up the ranks of combat officers and he eventually found himself on a landing craft, sea spray hitting his face from over the front ramp, at the head of a rifle company on June 14, 1944, as it crossed Red Beach 1, onto Japanese-held Saipan. That island—a speck on the map in the vast Pacific— would come to haunt Ableson for the remainder of his life. The troops he led were mostly down-and-outers from hick towns and ghettos (as Ableson put it), none of whom he would have ever known without his fallen arches, had he served as a captain in the Marines or the Screaming Eagles, or any outfit with a pedigree more illustrious than that of the 27th Infantry Division.

They had loaded ships in San Francisco Bay and their journey had lasted five weeks as they bounced between transports and staging camps. Ableson would explain that the deep bonds forged by fighting men only solidified after the events themselves, often through a process of tearful and boozy reunions, so that during the fighting your comrades were barely known to you, strangers really. They died as strangers too. It was only if they lived that they became friends. This was how Ableson found himself crouching in a foxhole on the third day of the fighting alongside Jimmy Shields, the company medic, whom he hardly knew at all.

Before then, Ableson had only one other interaction with Shields: his physical aboard the transport as they steamed westward. This requirement of a physical before a battle—in which being maimed, crippled, or killed were all likely outcomes—was one of many such contradictory requirements imposed by the military bureaucracy, and it involved Shields drawing several vials of his commanding officer's blood. "Relax, Doc," Ableson had said when he noticed the tremble in Shields's hands as he searched for a vein. In an effort to calm this nervous medic armed with his beveled needle, Ableson had tried to talk with him about something else—anything really—and noticed his gold wedding band. He asked whether the young medic had children. "One," said Doc Shields, "a little boy." Then he stuck Ableson, missing the vein entirely and painfully hitting muscle. Ableson winced and then calmly took the needle from Doc Shields. In a gesture of incredible competence, which shocked the medic, his commanding officer stuck himself, piercing the vein and drawing a gusher of his own blood that he emptied expertly into a first and then second vial, until Doc Shields composed himself enough to take over. More than a month later, when the pair found themselves sharing a foxhole, Ableson still had a bruise on the tender inside of his elbow given to him by Doc Shields.

Ableson had once before told me the story of the medic who had fumbled taking his blood, with the punch line being how he'd wound up taking his own blood instead, a neat trick. He hadn't given the story any greater context than that, and now Dr. Shields, renowned oncologist and son of that very same army medic, filled in the rest. That night, Ableson's company was holding a portion of the defenses around Alito airfield, a strategic objective on the island. The 27th Division along with the Marines had pushed the Japanese into the jungle earlier in the day and were waiting for the inevitable counterattack. At a little after midnight, from the canopy of trees beyond the runway, came the noise of bugles followed by shouts and jeers from the opposing Japanese. This was the overture to the inevitable banzai charge. A dense human wave then broke on top of them, isolating each defending pair within its foxhole. The battle proved an intimate affair, like a series of knife fights settled in individual telephone booths, their dozens of outcomes across the defensive line ultimately determining which side would hold the airfield by morning.

Doc Shields and Ableson fired at the onslaught of muzzle flashes and voices that surged toward them (by morning Ableson would preside over a carpet of bodies). Soon both had emptied their rifles, so they fired their pistols into the black night. When one of the charging Japanese leapt into their foxhole, Ableson caved in his face with the flat side of a rock. Then, amidst this ever-heightening chaos, a grenade landed at their feet, a stem of acrid smoke uncoiling as its fuse fizzled down. Thousands of rifles were firing at once but Ableson and Shields heard it land with a hollow thud. As Ableson remembered it, Shields gave him a reckless look, an insane look. In the glare of the fires that burned around them, Ableson recognized it as the look of a man who was about to give everything away and couldn't be persuaded otherwise.

Doc Shields flung himself belly down on the grenade.

Ableson, stunned by the gesture, didn't dive to the ground to protect himself; instead, he stood frozen over Shields, whose body lifted in the air as if it were tied at the waist to an invisible, upward raised tether as it absorbed the blast.

This part of the story was new to me. I didn't know quite what to say, so after an extended silence settled on "Did they award your father a medal?"

Dr. Shields shook his head, no. Ableson had filled out a recommendation to that effect, specifically the Medal of Honor; but, when Doc Shields's wife got wind of it, she asked him to withdraw her husband's name. "She was upset at my father," Dr. Shields explained. "She didn't think he'd needed to do what he had done. Maybe she thought he could've jumped in one direction and Ableson could've jumped in the other and they might have escaped with little more than some cuts and bruises. Truthfully, I don't really know what my mother thought as she didn't like to discuss my father, at least not with me. My father sacrificed everything, tossed it all away on a gesture. In her mind, I think she believed my father had chosen Ableson over her. To the day she died, I don't think she ever forgave my father."

"Did you feel the same?"

Dr. Shields returned the photograph to the console. He placed it in its spot among the family he himself had created, the children and infant grandchildren of a man whose own father had been too frightened to take a vial of his commanding officer's blood but who had possessed enough courage to jump on a grenade for that same person. "Robert Ableson is the best man I know," answered Dr. Shields. "I don't think my father would mind me saying this, but he probably did a better job helping raise me than my father would have done had he lived. In that way, I sometimes wonder if my father knew exactly what he was doing when he jumped on that grenade."

As I sat across from Dr. Shields, admiring the view from his corner office, surrounded by his impressive and calligraphed credentials, it was obvious that without Ableson's support and guidance the son of an army medic never would've ascended to these vaunted heights within the medical establishment. Dr. Shields owed his life to Ableson just as Ableson owed his life to Doc Shields, whose single, selfless act precipitated everything that followed. This is why Dr. Shields had begun our conversation by speaking of the war.

"After what my father did," Dr. Shields explained, "I don't think

Robert ever again felt that he was living simply for himself. Every day he believed he had to earn what my father sacrificed. Look at his career as a litigator. Robert managed nearly twice the caseload of his peers, to say nothing of his pro bono work and the role he played as a surrogate father in my life. Mary's always believed his career is why he waited so long to start a family of his own. Have you met his stepsons, Bobby and Doug? If you get a chance, ask those two about his work habits, his impossible standards. What I'm trying to say is, knowing him as I did, knowing how he'd lived his life after the war, always trying to make good on my father's sacrifice for him, I shouldn't have been surprised that he'd do anything to gain himself a little more time. The only part of this that's surprising is that it has worked."

Dr. Shields described in some detail how a decade before, when Ableson's health had begun to deteriorate and it became obvious his years were dwindling to their end, he'd taken a great interest in a specific series of legal briefings. These arguments, submitted by attorneys within the Clinton Justice Department, and thus discoverable by a simple Freedom of Information Act request, explored the implications of the Human Genome Project's research across myriad fronts, from cloning to cellular restructuring to cryonics. Contemporaneous to the scientific work done by the NIH, HHS, DOE, and an alphabet soup of other government agencies, was the administration's legal work. Clinton wasn't going to allow the application of these scientific breakthroughs to become stalled in the increasingly right-wing, conservative courts. By following the progress of these legal arguments, Ableson could follow the progress of the geneticists' work. This is what led him into Dr. Shields's office a year before his death with a somewhat obscure legal briefing on cryonics.

On that visit, Ableson sat on the very same sofa where I now sat, the two of us divided by a decade but facing out toward the

Schuylkill River that churned toward the Atlantic. It was obvious Ableson wasn't well, and as he reached across the desk to show Dr. Shields the legal brief, his suit was baggy at the shoulders from where he'd begun to lose weight, as if with more time he might vanish entirely into its folds. Ableson had highlighted whole sections of the brief and his cramped notes assiduously crowded the margins, often in different colored pens, as though he'd read the document many times over. "Cryonics . . . the possibility of cellular restructuring through reverse biochemistry . . . resurrection . . ." Dr. Shields became increasingly agitated as he read. "This is pseudoscience garbage," he told Ableson. "I hope you don't believe a word of it." He swatted the paper down onto his desk as though killing a fly with it.

"Why would attorneys at the Department of Justice put together this briefing at great energy and expense if this wasn't a possibility?" asked Ableson as he returned the brief to its folder.

"What are you suggesting?"

"I want you to help me make the appropriate preparations . . . in case the breakthroughs in these pages actually happen." Ableson already had most of his plans figured out. He'd selected a reputable cryonics carrier. He'd arranged the recurring payments. He'd even drafted and signed a hidden provision in his will, which outlined his wishes in the event that he was at some later date "resuscitated." He simply needed Dr. Shields to act as his executor.

"But why go to the trouble?" Dr. Shields asked. "The chances are infinitesimal." Ableson coughed thickly into his handkerchief, bending at the waist. He glanced into its center and then returned the handkerchief to his pocket, whatever he'd coughed up having troubled him. He crossed Dr. Shields's office and removed a single volume from the shelf . . .

In recounting this part of the story, Dr. Shields went to that same bookshelf and removed that same volume, the *Pensées* by

Pascal. Ableson had given him the treatise on his graduation from medical school. Dr. Shields now turned to a familiar page. "This is Pascal's wager," he explained, and began to read:

> God is or is not.
> A game is being played where heads or tails will turn up.
> You must wager, it is not optional.
> Let us weigh the gain and the loss in wagering that God is. Let us estimate these two chances. If you gain, you gain all; if you lose, you lose nothing.
> Wager, then, without hesitation that He is. There is here an infinity of an infinitely happy life to gain . . .

This brought to mind a conversation I'd already had with Ableson over one of our martinis, where he'd explained the nature of his belief, which was that he believed because he had nothing to lose and everything to gain; this was not only his logic of God but of heaven and the afterlife, and I now understood it was why he'd made not only religious arrangements for his death but also scientific ones. And it seemed the scientific arrangements had paid off. "Remarkable, isn't it?" I said to Dr. Shields.

He slotted the copy of Pascal back onto the shelf, returned to his desk, and grew silent, as if he were for the first time considering whether or not Ableson's resurrection was remarkable, and, as Pascal put it, "an infinitely happy life to gain."

Dr. Shields explained how not long after Ableson's death, a pair of representatives from the Division of Medical and Scientific Research at the National Institutes of Health had arrived at his office. They alerted him that Robert Ableson was a prime candidate for a series of groundbreaking trials on cellular restructuring and regeneration. Because cryonics had so long been relegated to a pseudoscience, the pool of suitable applicants was relatively slim. And so began Ableson's resurrection.

When I asked how much longer Ableson would live, or if there were any side effects to the treatments he'd undergone, Dr. Shields seemed to possess little insight. He wasn't being evasive; instead he explained that his role in this wasn't as Ableson's physician but rather as the executor of his will, nothing more. I had assumed— falsely, I now realized—that Mary Ableson had asked me to visit with Dr. Shields so he might reveal some secret of her husband's condition. When I mentioned this to Dr. Shields, he laughed. "No," he said. "I'm afraid it isn't anything like that."

"Then why?" I asked. "Why did she want me to see you?"

Dr. Shields once again steepled his hands together on his desk. "When Mary and Robert met, he was in his early fifties and she was in her late twenties." He reached behind him to the console, plucking out another framed photograph, in which a college age Dr. Shields stands flanked between the two of them, his hands brooding in the pockets of his flared jeans, while Ableson has his well-muscled arm draped paternally around this young man, and although Ableson's hair is flecked with gray, it's mostly that recognizable shade of reddish brown. He's wearing a pair of Persol sunglasses like the ones Steve McQueen wore in *Bullitt*, and Mary, his much younger wife with the feathered hair and beaming smile, looks like any one of the ingénues who graced that film set. While I examined the photo, Dr. Shields continued, "Because of the age difference, Mary had thought they'd only get two good decades together. Instead, they got three. She used to say that Robert was fifty until he turned eighty. Those last ten years his deterioration was hard on her, but ultimately it's what she'd signed up for. Their relationship was based on an agreement. When they'd met, she was a young single mother struggling to raise two little boys. Robert took care of her. When he got older, she would take care of him. Now that he's back, that balance has again shifted."

I didn't understand. "But she's not even seventy?" I said. "And he's—" How old was Ableson? I would've said ninety, but his age could no longer be calculated by adding up years, and so I settled on "—he's healthy. They're both healthy, so why can't they just enjoy this time together?"

"Because, Martin, both of them aren't healthy."

Ableson not healthy? His vigorous constitutionals came to mind, him standing at the guesthouse door, the steam pouring off his body as he'd marched however many miles across his property, only to demand an hour or more of drinking and conversation. I could see his hair, which held a stubborn line against the advance of gray. Could it be that death was overtaking him even as he appeared to possess the stamina of a man two or even three decades his junior? It was like Mary used to say, "He was fifty until he was eighty."

Incredulous, I described to Dr. Shields this robust figure I had come to admire.

"It's Mary," he said, interrupting me. "She's the one who's sick."

"Sick?"

"Cancer," he added. "That's why she asked you to come see me."

TWO

DISEASE

The drive back to Halcyon would take five hours. I traveled the interstate lost in thought, radio off, cars passing me as I hovered at or below the speed limit. I kept replaying the end of my visit with Dr. Shields. I couldn't even recall what specific type of cancer he'd said that Mary had, only that after he'd explained where it had originated in her body—and the grim itinerary of everywhere else it had traveled—I could no longer remember where he'd started on that journey. "But she doesn't look sick," I kept muttering. He said not yet, and when I asked how much time she had left his answer was a vague "months, not years."

And so, the purpose of my visit had had little to do with Ableson's condition. He was as he appeared: youthful, energetic, a man of reclaimed vitality in complete possession of his health. It was Mary who was in crisis. Why, I wanted to know, had she asked me to see Dr. Shields instead of simply telling me herself? "She hasn't told her husband," he'd explained, "and she doesn't plan to, at least not yet. In her mind, it's important that he be the first person she tells. Also, I don't know if she could've told you without getting emotional in a way that's unacceptable to her. Eventually, though, she won't be able to keep hiding her condition from him. She mentioned that you've become a confidant of Robert's, that he's broken his social quarantine to spend evenings with you. When the time comes, Mary didn't want you to be in the dark about her disease. For Robert's sake. So that he'll have someone around to talk to, someone who understands."

As I continued south down the interstate replaying our conversation, I couldn't help but conclude that Mary's keeping her cancer from her husband was a misguided yet generous gesture. Despite Ableson's vigor—his martinis, his daily constitutionals—and all I'd learned of his life, to include a coda of having defeated death, his wife understood that he was too fragile to carry the burden of her sickness. The time they had remaining together was no longer defined by him, as he had always assumed—but by her. Because she loved him, she would keep her secret as long as she could, to grant them both this last unfettered bit of time.

Before leaving, I had asked the other obvious question, which was about her children. Ableson's social quarantine meant they didn't yet know about his return and, as Dr. Shields explained it, they also didn't know about Mary. And so, the two great secrets of this woman's life—who until a few days ago I knew only as an acquaintance—now resided with me. When I made this observation to Dr. Shields, he acknowledged the unique circumstances but then reached into his briefcase, where he removed that morning's newspaper.

"The children will know he's back soon enough," and he handed the copy to me. On the front page—above the fold this time, the story having seeped up like a stain—it seemed an enterprising investigative journalist, spurred on by the disclosure of the Lazarus mice, had through carefully placed sources uncovered what they termed "a detailed accounting of the contemporaneous resurrection of individuals," of which Robert Ableson was one of over one hundred names listed. Dr. Shields had allowed me to keep his copy of the newspaper (he'd bought a dozen that morning) and it sat in the backseat of the Volvo as I drove. Had I turned on the radio, I might have listened to what was now blanket media coverage of the story. I preferred the silence instead.

I wondered who the others were. Who aside from Ableson had been resurrected? He was one of a larger group. This would prevent any single person from becoming sensationalized and would, hopefully, assure Ableson a certain modicum of anonymity. What would it be like for a person near the end of their life—either elderly or sick—to read this story? How many would scramble to become participants in the next round of clinical trials when death ceased being inevitable and instead became treatable. Who a society brought back would say a great deal about it. Would ours, with its split personality, be able to agree on which minds merited eternal preservation?

Pondering who those minds might be, my thoughts turned to my academic hero, Shelby Foote, who had stopped writing years ago due to poor health. I had met him once, at the height of his powers, shortly after he'd achieved celebrity as the star commentator in the Ken Burns–directed PBS documentary *The Civil War*. That long ago evening, he'd delivered a ninety-minute lecture to a filled auditorium at Tufts. Lucas and I had arrived early, brimming with enthusiasm like two kids traveling to the ballpark to watch their favorite big-league slugger. Foote had spoken without notes, standing not behind but bestride the lectern, his bent elbow resting casually on its edge and his spent pipe cradled in his palm. A slide show of photographs and maps projected behind him, though he never glanced back for reference. He wouldn't think to, in much the same way a dancer would never think to mouth the count of his steps; Foote was balletic in that way.

He lectured about Stonewall Jackson, his death and the cottage industry of alternate histories that hinged on what if he'd lived. Foote traveled the familiar terrain of events: Jackson's reentry into his own lines at Chancellorsville after a night reconnaissance; how when he and his staff had identified themselves, Major John Decatur Barry, the commander of the sentries, took them for Union soldiers and replied, "It's a damn Yankee trick!" firing a fatal volley at Jackson. Foote noted as an aside that Barry would fight on for the remainder of the war, dying in 1867, two years after its end, at the age of twenty-seven, of what his friends called "a broken heart" for what he'd done to Jackson. Foote theorized that what Barry died of was in fact an alternate history. What if Jackson had lived? That very question tortured Barry into an early grave.

"Had Jackson lived," Foote explained to the auditorium in his languorous Mississippian drawl, "he would not have been Jackson." The Confederate leadership, according to Foote, had immediately rendered that evening's debacle into a *kalos thanatos*, a Greek term of exaltation meaning *beautiful death*. A mourning public received every detail of Jackson's final moments from a newspaper account that sold out within minutes on the streets of Atlanta, Charleston, and Richmond to name but a few places. The recollection in print was that of Jackson's attending physician, a Dr. McGuire: *". . . before he died he cried out in his delirium, 'Order A.P. Hill to prepare for action! Pass the infantry to the front rapidly! Tell Major Hawks—' then stopped, leaving the sentence unfinished. Presently a smile of ineffable sweetness spread itself over his pale face, and he said quietly, and with an expression, as if of relief, 'Let us cross over the river, and rest under the shade of the trees.'"* In his lecture Foote had asked us to imagine this scene splashed across the Confederate newspapers. We're only two months before Gettysburg, the "desperate gamble" as Faulkner had written of it, a battle that would prove the high-water mark of the Confederacy. Jackson's death ceased to be tragic but rather became aspirational for the tens of thousands of Southerners who, as I recall Foote wryly putting it in the auditorium that day, "would soon follow him into the shade of those very same trees."

The lecture ended and a vast, out-the-door line formed in the direction of the table where Foote signed books. Through snippets of conversation, I could hear how Foote's remarks had riled those listeners who had become invested in a certain mythologized version of Jackson. "What did you think?" I asked Lucas as we took our place on the sidewalk that night, toward the back of the line. "I still think Jackson would've known to take Culp's Hill. And if he had, Gettysburg would've turned out differently." I didn't disagree with Lucas but also couldn't shake the nagging idea that Foote had a point. Where did the myth end and the person begin?

The line was crawling. Lucas had a dinner plan with Annette, who was then his girlfriend. He kept glancing at his watch. If he wanted to leave, I offered to get his books signed for him. Lucas couldn't quite decide, and years later, when I thought Lucas had compromised himself as a historian, when he would deal in platitudes about history's need to be "forward looking" to matter, I would always—whether fairly or unfairly—trace the genesis of my disappointment in his methods to the decision he made that night to prioritize dinner with Annette over meeting Shelby Foote.

"I owe you one," he said, as he handed me his three volumes of *The Civil War: A Narrative*, which I now cradled along with my own, a total of six thousand pages.

The line in front of me moved slowly and the line behind me dissolved as others, like Lucas, gave up on the idea of having their books personalized by Mr. Foote. After nearly an hour, I was the last one. When I lifted my copies onto his table, Mr. Foote— tired though he must have been—seemed intrigued by their worn spines, running his finger along the heavily creased bindings. "You've read this?" he asked, speaking of the work as though it weren't his own. I told him that I had. He made a slight, respectful nod. "And who is this other copy for?" he asked, removing the cap from his signing pen.

"A friend of mine. He had a dinner date," I said, self-consciously adding, "He really enjoyed your remarks."

"Does this friend have a name?"

"Oh, sorry. It's Lucas Harlow," and Mr. Foote began to sign, while I told him how much I also enjoyed his lecture.

"And which part of it did you enjoy?" he asked, again with his Mississippian drawl.

"We don't think enough about the myths we create around people."

"Are you a student at the university?"

I told him that I was.

"In the history department?"

I nodded.

"Very good," he said, offering a thin, conspiratorial smile. He got back to work on the books, his whole arm moving as he signed his name to each volume. "When considering Jackson," he continued, "or any of the dead, it is important to remember that had they survived life itself would have proven their faults, as it does with each of us." He arrived at the final volume of his series, *Red River to Appomattox*, which was at the bottom of the pile. He glanced at me once more, and instead of simply a signature I could tell he was crafting a longer inscription. He then shut the volume, ran his fingers down its worn spine a final time, and, passing it back to me, said, "Best of luck with your studies."

The inscription he'd made was on my mind as I took the exit off the interstate toward Halcyon. It was a little before midnight as I drove past the darkened main house. I then turned onto the single lane road banked with chest-high snow drifts that led to the guest cottage. A car was parked by the front door and the desk lamp glowed softly in the attic. The same desk where I'd left the volume of Foote's work, the one he'd inscribed:

For Martin,
Never forget, history is what the living think of the dead.
                                        Yours truly,
                                        Shelby Foote

.   .   .

I knocked on what I believed until that moment was my own front door. The single lamp in the attic went out. I heard a half-dozen footsteps inside followed by a minute or more of deliberate silence. I knocked again and this time the downstairs light switched on. Someone peeked through the vestibule blind, a set of eyes appearing and then vanishing. Still, they didn't answer the door. Despite paying rent, I considered myself a guest of the Ablesons, so didn't want to barge inside. But it was cold and this person—whoever they were—seemed determined to ignore me.

I slotted my key into the lock.

"Who is it?" came a woman's voice.

When I pushed the door open, this woman had levered it shut with her shoulder. I gave my name and announced that I had a lease on the cottage. A pause followed, as though she were considering the plausibility of my claim, and I added, "Those are my books about the Civil War on the attic desk ..."

The door opened and her silhouette appeared in the lighted rectangle. She introduced herself but hardly needed to; the dark hair, the heavily lidded brown eyes, the long neck and straight back aligned with finishing school precision—the resemblance was apparent. "I didn't know my parents had a renter," she said, and what also became apparent in that brief exchange was that Elizabeth Ableson knew about her father's return; it was her use of the word "parents."

I told her that they were both up at the main house. No further explanation was required, no acknowledgment on my part of the great experiment in which Robert Ableson had participated. I simply added, "May I come in?" and she nodded apologetically, stepping away from the door. The house was cold, and I was now very awake so offered to start a fire. Elizabeth—or Boose as I couldn't help but think of her after my many conversations with her father—joined me in the living room, sitting on the battered cushion of the same chair where Ableson typically sat.

I noticed her bag by the door and surmised she'd planned to spend the night at the guest cottage before going up to visit her parents in the morning. "I couldn't quite figure out who was working in the attic," she explained. "After I saw your books, I thought it might be my father." When I asked how she'd heard the news, her answer was "the paper" but then added that it was something she'd already suspected through her mother, who "hasn't been herself for a while now." Boose crossed the room, glancing out the night-dark windows in the direction of Halcyon. "I suppose I'll head up first thing in the morning. It's going to be pretty busy around here by breakfast."

She was right. The next morning, not long after sunup, I heard the first set of tires crunching down the snow-covered drive. I had slept the night on the futon in the attic, having offered Boose my own bed. When I climbed down the stairs, the door to my room was open but she was gone. Instead of moving her things up to the main house, which was more comfortable, she had left her suitcase in my room, its contents exploded across the floor in the way a child might unpack themselves. I shut the door.

For the remainder of the day, I sat at my desk trying to forge ahead in my own work from which I'd now taken a nearly week-long hiatus. Progress proved frustratingly slow. I couldn't help but imagine the reunion taking place up the road. I assumed Ableson's stepsons, Doug and Bobby, had by now traveled in from their respective homes in Manhattan and Boston. Did they bring their children with them, so that Ableson could see how the next generation had grown over the past few years? Ableson's return would be easier for a child to understand. Life, death, the levers of the universe, none of these are yet fixed ideas for a child. For an adult, however, it is a different matter. I could imagine Ableson's sons being angry at him, or angry at their mother for keeping this secret. Death is horrible, but might it be equally horrible to disrupt life's natural progression?

By the end of the day, I had little to show for the hours at my desk. I had only poked at my books. Stacked to my right were the three volumes of Shelby Foote's *The Civil War: A Narrative*. The one I worked from lay open, facedown, its margins annotated with a plumage of multicolored Post-it Notes. On my desk's left-hand side was *Battle Cry of Freedom: The Civil War Era* by James McPherson, whose Union-centric writings had aged far better than the writings of Foote, a Mississippi native, though it's a less compelling read and the guns don't fire on Fort Sumter until page 273. Tucked beneath the McPherson was Michael Shaara's *The Killer Angels*, the Pulitzer Prize–winning fictionalization of the Battle of Gettysburg, and beneath that rested firsthand accounts like the memoirs of Ulysses S. Grant and the diary of Mary Chesnut, a genteel Southerner who lived in Richmond through much of the war. There were, of course, other books, and scattered between them all were my yellow legal pads with whole pages written in jagged script, angled like a healthy cardiogram, only to be viciously scratched out.

Outside the attic window, the slanted light moved in a flow, receding quickly as the sun descended past the tips of the bare trees. Through those trees, I suddenly glimpsed a long shadow and then a silhouette. With its determined gait, I recognized the silhouette immediately. It was Robert Ableson, out for his evening constitutional.

"To your health," he said slyly, raising his glass.

I had welcomed Ableson inside and after mixing our drinks repeated his toast. We settled into our familiar positions in the guest cottage and one by one he ate the four olives off the single toothpick slotted into his martini. There was much to be said between us—too much, in fact—yet I felt certain I wasn't the one to begin. We lingered in silence, sipping our drinks, and I noticed how Ableson kept regarding himself, stretching out his legs, examining the bend in his arm, like a man who has recently purchased a very expensive new set of clothes. I wasn't halfway through my martini and he had already drained his first. He walked to the kitchen and poured a second. Reclining in his chair, he'd loosened up, and so began, "A complete disaster. That's how it went with my children today, in case you were curious."

"They must have been . . ."—and I struggled for the word but found it—"*overwhelmed* to see you."

He looked at me askance from above the rim of his glass, as if uncertain whether he liked that word. "*Furious* is more like it, the boys in particular." From our past conversations, I understood the contentious relationship Ableson had at times with Doug and Bobby. Surely neither had inherited as much of his estate as Boose had, which inevitably caused some resentment; however, I suspected their inability to celebrate Ableson's return ran deeper than that. Mary's first husband and their father, a drunken puddle of a human being, stood in stark contrast to Robert Ableson, war veteran, prominent litigator, a man revered. Ableson was the ideal that Doug and Bobby had measured themselves against since boyhood. His death—though they grieved it—had been liberating in its way. It had freed them from an existence in contrast to that ideal.

Since Ableson's funeral (which the boys now learned had been an empty casket affair) Doug had bought a ranch in Wyoming, where he planned to move off-grid with his family, and Bobby had divorced his wife and taken up with a woman he had yet to introduce to his mother and whom he had no inclination to introduce to Ableson, not because he didn't revere his stepfather but because he did.

When I asked about his daughter's reaction, Ableson extended his legs out in front of him, crossing them at the ankles while folding his arms. He studied his drink, his eyebrows knitting together as he considered the question. "Boose is more complicated," he answered. "She's still figuring it out." *Figuring it out.* This was the second time he'd described his daughter in this way, and I began to wonder what was involved in this process of figuring. He spoke about it deferentially as though it were her profession, or some higher calling. I remembered her suitcase in my room, with its contents exploded across the floor; this didn't bespeak a person who was in the business of meticulous figuring.

"There was a time when she had more direction, too much maybe," Ableson explained. "Right out of grad school, her older brother landed her a job in finance, in a firm with offices above the 90th floor of the World Trade Center's North Tower. Her first day would've been September 12, 2001, though she's had a hard time seeing that as a stroke of good luck."

"How does she see it?"

"Had she died, she believes she would've died for no reason. But having lived, she's often felt she lived for no reason too. What does anything matter when it can all be arbitrarily swept away? But, little by little, she's been figuring out her answer to that. I understand the two of you met last night."

"We did, briefly." I explained how I'd startled Boose when I'd arrived at the guest cottage unannounced.

"And how was your trip?"

"Fine," I answered, but guardedly. Like a tiger in tall grass, Ableson the litigator stalked the recesses of our conversation, which suddenly felt as though it might turn into a cross-examination.

"I understand from Mary that you met Dr. Shields, that he spoke to you a bit about my condition." When I nodded, Ableson added simply, "Good, I'm glad she set that up. He's quite a remarkable man," and I recalled Shields's office with its panoramic views of the Schuylkill River and his degrees hung against the wall. "Amazing to think," Ableson observed, "that a father and son might save the same life twice."

I agreed with him but had the secret of Mary's illness to keep and so wanted to change the subject away from Dr. Shields. "Can I ask you something more personal?" Ableson nodded, telling me that I was welcome to, and so out I blurted: "What's it like, dying?"

Ableson startled, blinking as though I'd clapped my hands in his face. "Hmmm . . . You know, I haven't really thought about how to answer that." He set his drink on a side table. "I guess the only thing I can really say about it is I have a suspicion that it is different for each person. So if I told you, it would hardly matter."

"And coming back?" I asked. "What's that like?"

He leaned forward in his chair and clasped his hand on my leg, giving it a good-natured tussle. "Who says I'm all the way back yet," he answered with a smile. "But you're going to help me with that."

Two days later, at a little after seven in the morning, I stood in the echoing foyer of Halcyon. Hazed light slanted in from the front door's transom. Motes of construction dust glittered and swirled. I was waiting for Ableson, who had asked me to drive him to the municipal records office in Richmond where he needed to present himself to have his death certificate annulled. While I waited, I could appreciate how grand the main house must have been in its heyday, despite the chaos of the current renovation. In a corner on the floor, blocking what appeared to be a coat closet, rested a chandelier. A few of its crystal pendants peeked out from beneath the white painter's tarp that covered it; they peeked out like the fingertips of a body concealed by a mortician's sheet. The foyer led to an airy two-story receiving room, with a trio of grand French doors. A vast garden descended beyond these doors, its environs enclosed with trellised redbrick walls gripped by knotty vines and its terraced four levels strewn with ancient stone planters.

I had come to the main house at the invitation of Ableson, but it was Mary who had let me in the front door. She wore her bath-robe tied tightly at the waist and a creaking silence permeated the house, as though its occupants remained asleep. I had wondered if she might broach the subject of my trip to Philadelphia, which she did in only cursory terms, thanking me for it and also for driving her husband to the records office today. What I craved, however, was an acknowledgment of the secret she'd asked me to keep; or, more specifically, of her intention for how and when I might divulge that secret to her husband. But that morning she wouldn't mention her own sickness. Her focus was—as I imagined it typically was—on Robert, who soon presented himself.

Outfitted in a gray chalk stripe suit and black leather oxfords and clutching his briefcase, Robert Ableson cut a striking figure. This had been his uniform over the decades that he practiced law, and seeing him attired in a uniform, I could detect something of the old soldier in him. In a final flourish, a white handkerchief poked from his breast pocket and Mary, after making her inspection, straightened it. She then kissed him on the cheek as I could've imagined her doing on countless other mornings. "Good luck," she called after him. She waved at us with one hand while the other remained snugly in the pocket of her robe as we headed out the front door. This trip wasn't merely a visit to the records office but also Ableson's first foray into the outside world since his return.

We passed our forty-minute drive with idle conversation, mostly regarding Halcyon's renovation. The topic proved familiar territory, though up until that morning I'd never seen this enormous undertaking of his from the inside. Casually, I observed that sometimes it was more difficult to renovate a home than to simply start from scratch. "Was that ever something you considered?" I asked Ableson.

His briefcase sat open on his lap as he rechecked a sheath of documents, which he now glanced up from. "Was what something I considered?"

"Starting from scratch, building a new home instead."

"Never," and he went back to his documents.

When we reached Richmond's outskirts, Ableson expertly guided me toward the records office, located down a warren of choked one-way streets in the old Shockoe Bottom neighborhood. I could imagine him, in his younger days, running documents between his law firm, the courts, and this records office whose architecture was centuries-old redbrick. Many of these buildings—Libby Prison, Lumpkin's Slave Jail, or the Stewart-Lee House—were familiar to me, the old Confederate capital of Richmond being a mainstage of the Civil War, and as is the case with any stage certain performances linger long after the actors have uttered their final lines.

When Ableson entered through the glass double doors of the records office, it was as if to an encore. The elderly security guard at the X-ray machine recognized him and Ableson shook his hand amply. When we loaded into the elevator, the young clerks inside turned their heads as we joined them. Unasked by us, one of them graciously pressed the button to the third floor, certain that our destination was the chief registrar's office. Ableson mouthed a good morning and basked in their attention. Everyone knew him here or knew of him, either through his work or through his return, which had made headlines in the local news.

The years seemed to bleed off Ableson as we ascended the elevator and by the time we'd arrived at the chief registrar's door, I felt as though I were in the company of a man my own age, or perhaps even younger. The registrar's name, Ms. Susan Templeton, was stenciled across the pane of frosted glass, which Ableson rapped on with his knuckle before entering. Ms. Templeton, who was flanked by a much younger aide, stood from behind a large desk piled with paper records as well as at least a dozen framed photographs that faced away from her and toward any visitors. She was handsome, of a pale complexion, with her fine dark hair combed upward, threaded with gray, and clasped in a way that drew attention to her long and graceful neck. "Suzie," Ableson said affectionately as he approached her with arms outstretched.

The two embraced, and by the time they were finished Ms. Templeton's gaze wavered through a lens of tears. Ableson removed his handkerchief with a flourish and offered it to her. "I can't believe you're standing here. . . ." she said, trying to restrain her emotions. She turned to me and added, "If it wasn't for Mr. Ableson, I wouldn't be here today. When no one—and I mean no one—would hire me, he took a chance."

"Suzie . . ." said Ableson, refolding his handkerchief. "It's good to see you."

"You too," she said, and struggled to say more as if telescoping deep into memory, but in the end she could only repeat herself. "I simply can't believe that you're standing here." She waved to her aide, who sorted through a large folder, expertly placing an elaborate collation of documents across the desk, each of which was feathered with adhesive *sign here* tabs. While the aide arranged the documents, Ableson casually commented on how lovely Ms. Templeton looked, how she hadn't aged a bit. Ms. Templeton, for her part, seemed to welcome the old-world flattery, even placing her hand flirtatiously on Ableson's arm and coyly threatening to call his wife if he didn't let up. "And how is Mary?" she asked with what seemed a genuine affection.

Before Ableson could answer, I caught Ms. Templeton's assistant, a woman who could've passed for her daughter, narrow her eyes to half-mast and—if I observed correctly—roll them. What was it that upset her, I wondered, and could only suppose it was Ableson himself, his outdated flirtation with Ms. Templeton and the way she permitted it, despite her station as chief registrar for the Commonwealth of Virginia. I felt suddenly protective of Ableson, which is to say I felt a threat in the room. Ms. Templeton's assistant had finished laying out the papers that would bring him back, but Ableson no longer understood the rules of the game he was playing. He was returning to life in a time that was not his own.

"Is everything ready?" Ms. Templeton asked.

The assistant nodded, her irritability having faded toward a schooled politeness, as she offered Ableson a pen.

"Thank you, but I have my own," he said, to which the young woman didn't reply.

Ableson placed his signature on one page after another, annulling his own death, while Ms. Templeton worked alongside him, notarizing the documents. Once they'd finished, Ms. Templeton placed her hand on his. "Welcome back, Robert." He turned toward me and there was more emotion on his face than I had expected. "Welcome back," I also said. Ms. Templeton's assistant, however, said nothing. Coolly, she gathered up the documents.

On the return drive to Halcyon, Ableson cracked the car window. This emitted a sharp breeze. Outside the sun held high and raw above the horizon, presiding over an expanse of coarse clouds. I waited until we pulled onto the highway to ask him about Susan Templeton. "You know, she was twenty years old and pregnant when she first came to work for me," he explained, "a single mom-to-be. I interviewed a number of girls, some really sharp ones. Most of them had been through college. But none wanted the job more than Suzie. I didn't care that she'd have her baby right after starting. The other partners thought it was a bad idea, that she'd wind up quitting. Suzie stayed on for ten years, won me some important cases. She's incredibly loyal—too damn loyal. Opportunities came for her that I couldn't compete with. But Suzie wouldn't leave. The only way to have her take one of those opportunities was to fire her." He laughed to himself. "I think she's since forgiven me."

"Did you notice the young assistant in her office?" I asked

Ableson in an effort to steer him toward the subject I hoped to delicately raise.

"You mean Suzie's secretary?"

"I'm not sure if you realized how she was looking at you."

Ableson seemed confused.

"It's just . . . What I'm trying to say is that no one calls them secretaries anymore."

"What do you mean? What do they call them?"

"Personal assistants."

"Since when?"

"I'm not sure since when. Since they just don't anymore. Also, you can't say 'girl' or at least you shouldn't call a young woman, or really any woman, a girl."

"Says who?"

"That's what I'm trying to explain. Did you see the way Ms. Templeton's personal assistant was looking at you two? It's not twenty years ago, or even ten years ago. You can't go around flirting that way. I don't want to see you get into any trouble because of a . . . misunderstanding."

"A *misunderstanding.*" He spoke the word contemptuously. "Okay, but allow me to explain what I believe is the misunderstanding. When I hired Susan Templeton over all of these college-educated"—and he almost said *girls* but stopped himself—"*women,* it was because I'd already seen her work. I'd had a motion to argue in the family courts, an estate issue, and hers was the case scheduled before mine on the judge's docket. Her husband was an abusive drunk and she couldn't afford counsel. She got up there, five months pregnant, and made her arguments for herself. I've never asked Suzie if her husband hit her, but watching him that day, the way he glowered at her in his crumpled suit, I could tell that he did. The judge must have seen what I saw. When both sides finished their arguments, he awarded Suzie sole custody of her unborn daughter. Her now ex-husband couldn't even be at the hospital the day of her delivery. I was the only person in the gallery when the judge made his ruling. I handed Suzie my card on her way out and hired her right after. She and I worked together on advancing the Equal Rights Amendment, we knocked out two challenges to *Roe v. Wade* in the state's lower courts and contributed pro bono hours to *United States v. Virginia*, that's when VMI refused to admit women. I even tried to help Suzie get her personal life back on track, having fixed her up with a number of very bright and honest young men along the way. So let's spare ourselves the lecture. I'll call a secretary a secretary, and I'll call a woman who never had her own chance to be a girl, a girl."

The silence was deep enough to drown in. I turned on the radio, to a pop station playing "Hey Ya!," which was a little much, and so switched to the local NPR affiliate. It was broadcasting a White House press briefing, in which President Gore had made an unscheduled appearance. We tuned in midway through his opening remarks, in which he was saying ". . . this scientific breakthrough, a discovery without precedent in the history of mankind, promises to reframe the trajectory of human life. Imagine a future that will benefit not only from the great minds of its time, but from the great minds of the past as well. Imagine Einstein or Newton training their genius on the problems of today. Think what they could do for renewable energy, for global hunger. From this moment forward, death, at least as we've always understood it, is no longer a constraint of life. I'm pleased to announce of the one hundred thirty-four cases who've been reborn"—Ableson cocked his head at the word "reborn," a turn of phrase neither of us had yet heard—"that all are recovering well." Gore went on with his remarks, praising certain geneticists by name, lauding the "close government cooperation" that had enabled this advance. If at times his fluency in the scientific vernacular of *rebirth* faltered, his fluency in the creation of government infrastructure to regulate this breakthrough was without parallel. Before death, a family would soon be able to apply to the Department of Health and Human Services for a "rebirth grant." Based on suitability—a vague criterion he did not fully define—the government would defray a portion, if not all, of the medical costs, making rebirth a possibility for "most any American," as he concluded. What was implied in his remarks—for it was woven into the very fabric of the society that birthed "most any American"—was that those wealthy citizens who could afford to pay full-freight need not concern themselves with rebirth grants and Gore's government administered meritocracy. They could have the same procedure performed on the private market for an exorbitant sum. The president then concluded his remarks, telling the assembled journalists that he'd be "pleased to take questions."

A veil of hypocrisy shrouded Gore's proposal: life everlasting for some but not for all. Perhaps this was why the first question offered by the White House press pool wasn't about "rebirth," as the president termed it, but about the coming election and Gore's steadily declining approval rating. He replied to the question with a blend of his characteristic stiffness—an attribute often parodied on late-night sketch comedy shows—as well as barely concealed contempt. "What we're talking about today," he answered, "transcends politics." The next question was asked along similar lines but was framed more pointedly. "Did the president believe that his recent pardon of Bill Clinton was responsible for his low approval rating?" This time, Gore didn't attempt to answer the question; instead, he sternly replied that he'd come out here today to discuss the most significant scientific breakthrough ever. What he didn't say, but what I was sure he must have been thinking, was that perhaps the American people were unworthy of this breakthrough. Science had conquered death but all anyone cared about was his predecessor's indiscretions. However, the reason the president was falling in the polls was because he'd yet to acknowledge that to some these weren't *indiscretions* but crimes. Before he could shift to another question, the offending journalist followed up: "Mr. President, if you're unable to win reelection are you concerned that a Republican administration might cut funding for your scientific initiatives?"

Ableson didn't listen to the answer. He'd had enough of Gore, the press conference, and the negative turn it had taken, which I now realized, ashamedly, mimicked my own sanctimonious questioning about Ms. Templeton. He tuned the radio to a classical music station. Mozart was playing.

Upon our return to Halcyon, Ableson invited me inside. "I'd like you to meet the rest of my family," he'd said. By the time I'd parked the Volvo in the large circular driveway it was a little after lunch. The house no longer possessed the whispering, empty feeling from that morning. To the contrary, it was festooned with little streamers hanging from the stairway and confetti swirls sprinkled on the console tables as if for a party. A clamor of voices came from the spacious eat-in kitchen in the back, each one shushing the other with a "He's here . . . he's here . . ." as Mary, Boose, and the two boys shut off the houselights through some hidden master switch. Then from the kitchen came singing, the Happy Birthday song. The swing door opened and in cadence with the song the four of them approached in a tight column. They hovered over a large white-frosted cake picketed with candles and carried by Boose. The candles flickered with her every step, threatening to blow out.

I wondered if he knew they would be waiting for him with this surprise. Had he intuited it? Did he want me to see how his family loved him? And, if so, why did Ableson need me to know that? The four of them held the cake, encouraging him to make a wish and blow out his candles. Ableson protested, explaining that it wasn't his birthday. "But it is," his wife explained. "It's official now. You're back."

Ableson shut his eyes to conjure his wish. He then opened them and inhaled deeply, as if placing all his hopes into his breath and its fierce exhalation. He craned his neck forward and blew. Every last candle went out. His family applauded and he regarded them one by one and through his gaze it was obvious that they would be the beneficiaries of whatever wish he'd made. But before he could cut a first slice of cake, the candles, which were still smoking, began to flicker again. One by one they relit themselves and as they did his family began to laugh.

Trick candles.

The joke was on Ableson.

He was a good sport about it, but as they migrated to the kitchen—a kitchen ablaze with sunshine that fell on the polished copperware and gleamed against freshly laid white tiles—I couldn't help but think that this trick had cancelled out whatever wish Ableson had made. They had gathered around the countertop, a fantastic and heavily striated marble slab added in the renovation, and Ableson cut the first slice of cake. He served it to Mary and gave a little speech about her patience, her strength, and how without her he wouldn't be standing here to celebrate another birthday with his family. This led to a discussion of Ableson's true age, a figure his children—as is often the case with children—struggled to recall precisely. "Dad was born in 1913," said Doug. "No, 1914," Bobby interjected, the two of them falling into a kneejerk contrarianism common to brothers. Before their disagreement could escalate, their mother interrupted. "*Today* is your father's birthday," she said, and with an emphasis appealing to her authority as matriarch, she added: "We'll start counting from today."

After taking a first bite of her cake, Boose asked how it had gone at the records office. Her question silenced the quibbling brothers, who were equally curious.

Ableson explained that it had gone well, that he'd successfully annulled the death certificate. "Susan Templeton is running the records office," he said to his wife, as if to give her an added measure of confidence about the finality of the annulment.

"Who is that?" the two brothers asked in near unison.

"Your father's personal assistant, from years ago," said Mary.

Boose remembered her vaguely as the young woman who would bring documents to their house at all hours of the night for her father to review. She remembered because Ms. Templeton's daughter was roughly her age. Without a babysitter, or any relative to help her, Ms. Templeton often had to strap her daughter into the car with her when Ableson needed some administrative task completed after working hours. The two girls never played together, or really got to know one another, but seeing this girl whose life was so very different from her own stayed with Boose. She never quite forgot Susan Templeton, and when she recalled this memory over the slices of birthday cake, her father responded: "I don't recall forcing Ms. Templeton to bring me documents at odd hours."

Boose didn't have to defend her memory because her mother swiftly did. "When you were on a case, you had that poor woman at our house any time of the night. If you were working late, so was she."

"If she did work that hard, I don't think she ever complained," answered Ableson. "Susan has done very well for herself, considering."

"Considering what?"

"Where she started from."

Mary didn't have a chance to answer Ableson before his stepson Bobby interjected, "So no issues at the records office?"

"Issues?" asked Ableson.

"Like the possibilities we discussed . . . ," added Doug.

"No," said Ableson. "No issues."

The brothers exchanged a glance, as if to gauge whether each was satisfied with Ableson's answer. The silence that followed was tense and awkward. Everyone in the family understood these *issues*, but not me. Had I not been there perhaps they could've spoken more forthrightly; however, I suspected that neither Doug nor Bobby—nor anyone else in the family for that matter—wanted to discuss this subject directly, and so my presence became a convenient excuse for obfuscation. And what the subject was became obvious through the family's anxious reaction to it: the division of Ableson's estate.

Eventually, I would learn the particulars. In his will Ableson had divided his financial assets between his two stepsons and Boose, leaving the lion's share to her but meaningful trusts to the boys. He'd appointed Mary as a co-trustee until her death, so that the children (particularly the boys) would always behave responsibly toward their mother. Halcyon had been placed in Mary's name and, aside from a few additional items of minor consequence, his will contained no other major provisions. The *issues* so obliquely brought up by Doug and Bobby were whether his will and the distribution of his estate remained valid.

No law existed on the matter. Ableson's return to life was unprecedented so by definition there was no legal precedent for the question. No jurisprudence existed to assure the continued validity of the will. During the annulment of his death certificate no official had raised the issue, calling for a renewed audit of Ableson's estate or the levying of additional inheritance or gift taxes; this was the best outcome his family could hope for. Bobby and Doug, through their respective expertise in law and finance, seemed satisfied with this state of affairs, insomuch as they changed the subject and began to inquire about my work and how I had come to rent their parents' guest cottage.

They listened patiently as I explained my research, in the way practical men accustomed to earning large sums of money weigh the exploits of those who through either their professions or their passions are consigned to never earning a dime. I couldn't help but feel that the brothers' curiosity wasn't rooted in my subject—the Civil War, Shelby Foote, the nature of American compromise— but rather in me, in my strange devotion to an academic quest that in their estimation was of so little consequence. By the time they'd finished eating their cake I could tell they'd grown bored.

Both Doug and Bobby excused themselves. Doug had a car picking him up in the morning for the drive back to his Tribeca apartment and Bobby had a flight to Boston at around the same ungodly hour. It was, by now, late in the afternoon and both wanted to pack before dinner. As for Ableson, he was tired. Our trip into Richmond had worn him out and he announced that he'd head upstairs for a nap. Wordlessly, Boose followed. She had moved out of the guest cottage and had installed herself one door down from her parents in the main house. Unlike her brothers, her obligations existed here, with her parents, and she had taken it upon herself to look after them, at least for a while. Everywhere Ableson went, she hovered over him.

This left Mary alone in the kitchen with the half-eaten birthday cake and the dishes. I helped her tidy up, wiping smears of frosting from the plates and rinsing the silver forks and serving knives. Above us came the sound of a first, then a second, and finally a third and fourth door shutting. She waited until everyone had returned to their rooms before she apologized for her sons' behavior, the way they "ogle over their inheritance." The situation was complicated, I said, and couldn't blame them for wanting to understand the implications of Ableson's return. "You're right," she said. "The situation *is* complicated. It has always been complicated. Do you know how Robert first came into my life? It's a funny story . . . depending, that is, on your sense of humor." I encouraged her to tell me, and so she continued: "Robert had, at one time, represented a group of creditors who sued my first husband, Doug and Bobby's father. By that time in our marriage my ex-husband had failed at every business he'd put his hands to. He had plenty of big ideas, from real estate deals, to pyramid schemes—once there was even a plan to short-sell shares of a Betamax home-video company. He was, admittedly, quite the salesman. Which was how he always managed to raise money from investors. Which was also why he wound up with so much debt. It's the debt that crushed him, crippling him with anxiety. The anxiety led him to pills. And the pills led to the drugs that turned him into an addict . . . so eventually I left. He knew he couldn't handle the boys so there was no custody to negotiate. Outside of that, I wanted our house. Surprisingly enough, he handed it over. Well, joke was on me. A few months later, a lawyer showed up on my front porch. According to him, the house wasn't mine anymore. Before our divorce, my husband had used it as collateral against a loan; his creditors had a lien. The lawyer sent to collect was Robert Ableson."

"Did he help you keep the house?"

"Of course not," she answered, insulted, it seemed, by the sentimentality of the question. "He asked me to dinner instead. What did I have to lose? So I said yes. As our relationship progressed, you can imagine how difficult it was to explain. Here was this man, more than twenty years my senior, who was in the process of repossessing my house, and I'm out to dinner with him a couple of nights a week and, later on, sneaking him into that very same house to spend the night with me while my boys are sleeping down the hall. To an outsider, it didn't make sense. Judgment came from everywhere. The arguments against us were many: our age difference; my being a single mother; him being a consummate bachelor; the power dynamic between us, in which outsiders always presumed he held the power in our relationship and that I was the vulnerable one."

Mary glanced up toward a corner of the ceiling, which was the floor of their shared room, where her daughter had helped her husband to bed. She placed her fingertips onto the pendant strung beneath her collarbone, the old dime set in platinum. "He's always been the vulnerable one," said Mary. "When Robert was a boy, twice a year his mother would send him west to visit his father, who worked in oil and spent long stretches away. The great technological advance in that era was commercial air travel. If the train took a couple of days, the airlines had whittled the journey down to a handful of hours. One year his mother booked him on a flight. When they arrived at the airfield, Robert panicked. He refused to board the plane. 'What if it crashes?' he pleaded. His mother assured him that it wouldn't, dragging him by the hand. 'How would you know if it did?' His mother again assured him, 'It won't.' But he was insistent and afraid. He imagined himself stranded in the middle of nowhere. His mother stopped. She crouched down next to him and reached into her purse. She took out this dime. 'If you crash, you use this for the pay phone to call me.' He was a boy and in the logic of his boyish mind it wasn't the crash that terrified him, but the idea of being lost and alone, unable to find a way home. With the coin in his hand, Robert boarded the plane. Afterward, he carried that dime with him everywhere he went. To college. To the war. To our first date even. At the restaurant he had pulled it from his wallet and placed it on the table between us when he first told me the story. He gave it to me on this pendant a few months later, when he asked me to marry him. When I imagine telling him that I'm sick, I think about that boy . . . and every time I lose my nerve."

The two of us had long since finished washing the dishes and the house was darkening as the afternoon turned toward evening. She thanked me for helping clean up, and for listening, and for "everything else you've done for us."

In a voice hovering just above a whisper, I said: "You need to tell him."

"I know."

"He needs to hear it from you."

"I know," she said, and then grew quiet before adding, "You understand what he's going to want me to do? He's going to want me to do what he's done, to come back." I wondered aloud whether that was even possible. "I don't know," she answered, and I could hear a slight tremor in her voice, like fear, like she might be asked to undertake a journey to a place beyond her capacity. I simply stood there, unequal to the task of consoling her. My eyes again fell onto her pendant. The dime was unlike any I'd seen before. Its heads side contained a laureled profile of Mercury, god of travelers, with a tiny date stamped beneath it: *1914*, the year of Ableson's birth.

THREE

PETITION

Thereafter the weeks passed in an idyll. Each day I would typically see some combination of Boose, Mary, or Robert Ableson. I would either bump into one of them during my afternoon walks around the property, or, as was most often the case, Ableson would stop by in the evening as part of his constitutional. He had heard precious little from Doug and Bobby—"the boys" as he called them—but didn't appear unduly concerned. With the matter of his will seemingly settled, his stepsons had secured their interests; also, displays of affection never came naturally between any of them. Boose, however, had stayed on with her father, which gave him great pleasure. On a few occasions—for instance, if Mary felt tired after dinner, or was taking one of her increasingly frequent naps—Ableson would bring his daughter along to the guest cottage to join us for a drink.

Boose boasted an impeccable academic pedigree. Groton followed by Yale, dual degrees at Harvard Law and Business, summa cum laude, Phi Beta Kappa, she dripped these accolades the way certain women drip diamonds. Except she had become impractical. Since the job she'd almost started but never did at the World Trade Center three years before, she hadn't held down another, to say nothing of bringing in a paycheck. When she applied for a credit card, she had had scant credit to speak of and ultimately settled for an AmEx tied to her parents' checking account. This didn't prevent her from holding opinions, well-formed opinions, on every issue of the day. Although Boose's intelligence was obvious, I found her rarefied detachment from "the real world" a little hard to stomach. While I endured her theorizing and sanctimony, her father indulged it. To him, she was like a spring coiled tight: an object filled with potential energy. Ableson waited patiently for that energy to take renewed direction.

Gathered around the fire in the guest cottage, each of us with a martini in hand, I relished these debates between father and daughter. The most contentious subject was the upcoming presidential election and Boose's staunch support of Gore. "How could you consider voting for someone else?" Boose asked her father one evening after they'd come by. She had yet to take a single sip from her martini while Ableson, recumbent, had already drained his glass. "I didn't say I was voting for someone else, darling. I simply understand why those who supported Gore in the last election might reconsider given the Clinton pardon." A look of incomprehension, equal to a full-blown psychological affliction, had settled on Boose's face. Her slender eyebrows notched together. Her cheeks reddened, while her father continued, "Gore purports to be progressive, pro-woman, yet I can't think of anything that undermines a woman more than exonerating a man for rape."

"The Senate convicted him of perjury." Boose could barely unlock her jaw to speak. "Not rape."

Her father took another olive between his teeth and slid it off the toothpick, good-naturedly continuing the debate. "But the recording is what enabled enough Democrats to cross the aisle and vote to convict. What does she say over and over, 'Are you sure, Mr. President . . . ? Maybe we shouldn't, Mr. President . . . ? Please, Mr. President . . .' Christ, he hasn't even extended her the courtesy of calling him Bill. She's a twenty-two-year-old intern. He's twice her age and the leader of the free world. The power discrepancy alone makes her consent impossible. It's like getting

Capone on tax evasion; perjury is the technicality that convicts Clinton of his true crime, which is rape. At the end of the day, what it really comes down to for Gore is hypocrisy. Voters will tolerate a great deal in their political candidates. The one thing they can't abide—and understandably so—is this flagrant degree of hypocrisy."

Ableson set down his drink. He began to pace up and down the room, his eyes fixed no further than his steps. "Hy-poc-ri-sy," he said, dismantling the word into its component syllables, as if this exercise might allow him to better dismantle the very concept. "Does understanding both sides of an argument make me a hypocrite?" Boose tried to interrupt, but her father cut her off. "Please, let me finish. Gore *is* a hypocrite. It's not because he doesn't have conviction, or values. It's not because he isn't a moral person. This Clinton thing has simply painted him into a corner; imagine the position Gore was in. If he grants the pardon, he's a hypocrite because of what Clinton did to Ms. Lewinsky. If he doesn't pardon him, he's a hypocrite because he owes his presidency to Clinton's political machine. What Gore is really guilty of is having been around too long, of having seen too much and taken too many positions on too many issues. Time itself has made Gore a hypocrite, as it does to everyone."

The mood in the room had turned somber. Unlike the other debates I'd witnessed between father and daughter—everything from the implications of resurrection on global overpopulation (she was concerned, he wasn't), to the installation of solar panels as part of the Halcyon renovation (she thought it a good investment, he doubted it)—I could see that Boose had touched a nerve. The relatively narrow topic of debate—Gore's potential reelection—had taken on outsized proportions, so that Boose relented, saying, "You're not a hypocrite, Dad."

Ableson returned to his seat, where a last sip of his martini awaited him. "But I am one, darling. I'm painted into a corner, not unlike Gore. If I vote for him, despite disagreeing with his pardon of Clinton, then I am betraying my own values. If I don't vote for him, as you pointed out, I'm turning my back on someone who has given me nothing less than a second lease on life."

Not long after that evening's debate, as the height of spring was announcing itself from the magnolia branches, with their pink buds and oblong leaves posed like sails, the Ablesons set a date for me to come up to Halcyon's main house for dinner. More than a month had passed since we'd eaten birthday cake in their kitchen. Since then, an army of workers had made enormous headway on the renovation. Each day, I could hear them from my attic desk in the guest cottage. The clamor was unrelenting: the buzz of their table saws, the bronchial wheezing of a backhoe's engine. Under any other set of circumstances, it would've driven my sanity to the brink as I struggled to concentrate on my own work; however, in the case of the Ablesons, I didn't mind so much. I was fond of them and knew the constant noise signaled progress on their home.

I walked to dinner that evening along a road banked densely with trees. Freshly laid gravel replaced the muddy driveway where I'd once parked my Volvo. The neoclassical façade of the main house, with its succession of Ionic columns, had received a fresh coat of paint, and rocking chairs in a matching eggshell white lined the replanked antebellum porch. The freshly sanded and stained walnut front door boasted a gaudy new brass knocker that hung like the ring from a bull's nose. After I knocked, Boose stood in the open foyer beneath the crystal chandelier that I'd last seen sitting beneath a tarp in the corner. She kissed me on the cheek, which she'd never done before, and behind her I could hear the pleasant hum of conversation.

She wore a mid-knee-length skirt, also a first, and led me by the hand across a great expanse of deep, soundless carpets and into the dining room, which on my previous visits the workmen had been using as a storage area. Now the dining room was complete; though rolled up outside its door was an old olive-green carpet of a 1970s vintage. Its replacement, a new sisal rug, covered the four corners of the room and on it was a racetrack-shaped table polished to an immaculate sheen that reflected the crystal pendants from the two other chandeliers hung overhead. The cutlery was laid out in ranks like two opposing armies confronting one another across the table. There were five gold-rimmed place settings; one for me, Boose, Mr. and Mrs. Ableson, and, as I now saw, Dr. Shields.

Robert Ableson was keen for me to speak again with Dr. Shields, and the two of us chitchatted with a forced ease, well aware circumstances might reveal that our prior meeting had less to do with Ableson's condition than with Mary's disease. Ever since Ableson's return, Dr. Shields had monitored his general health in parallel to the government physicians assigned to his case. "If ever anything were wrong with me," Ableson lamented over our first course, "I don't know if I'd trust those government doctors. To them, I'm a guinea pig." As Ableson explained this, Dr. Shields's gaze shifted across the table, to Mary. He watched her intently. I understood then that Dr. Shields's visit had little to do with Ableson and everything to do with her.

Of all of us, Mary was dressed the most elegantly. She wore a set of diamond earrings and a thin strand of pearls around her neck, as well as the dime pendant she never took off. Her gray hair, which she typically pinned up in a chignon, had lost some volume and she wore it down around her shoulders, so it hugged her scalp and revealed a frizzled and widening part. Beneath her eyes was an extra layer of makeup, brushed there to mask the cloudy dark circles that lingered no matter how many hours she napped. Her features, which even on her best days weren't distinct, now appeared as though they might dissolve into the vagueness of her every expression. I hadn't seen Mary in weeks, so the deterioration proved striking. Was it less obvious to Ableson, who saw her each day? Or could he simply refuse to acknowledge the changes in front of him because his wife wasn't changing so much as vanishing?

The conversation at dinner didn't center on Mary, but rather on the renovation—which Ableson believed was coming along nicely, to which everyone readily agreed—as well as a story Ableson had read in the local paper that morning, one he thought I might have an interest in. "Over the past few days," Ableson explained, "groups of students have been busing into Richmond. They're planning a protest at the records office tomorrow. They're demanding the Virginia Monument be replaced at Gettysburg. Have you heard about this?" Reluctantly, I admitted that I had already heard about the controversy surrounding this particular monument and that an old colleague of mine, a history professor, was one of the leading advocates for its removal. "A history professor!" Ableson was incensed. "Why would a history professor want to destroy a piece of history?"

Boose, who up to this moment had allowed her father to dominate the dinner conversation, couldn't restrain herself any longer. "It's a statue," she said. "A bunch of Robert E. Lee–loving Virginians put it there fifty years after the battle." She then let out a great, annoyed sigh and slumped down in her chair, as if the burden of her father's version of everything—not simply his views on the monument—threatened to crush her. "Does this mean we have to live with it forever? If those students can organize on MySpace and convince enough people to get rid of it through a petition, shouldn't the state remove it?"

"You can't simply get rid of history," said Ableson, turning ever more incredulous. "It's not like your mother's old rug," and he pointed to outside the door, where the olive-green rug was rolled up, the one that had been replaced by the sisal beneath us. "You can't decide it's gone out of fashion and switch it with something else."

"I never picked that green rug," interjected Mary. "You're the one who picked it. I never even liked it all that much."

"The rug doesn't matter," answered Ableson. "What matters is—"

"It matters quite a bit," she interrupted. Her voice, never highly inflected, was ironed flat, unyielding and irate. Mary was sitting alert and straight-backed in her seat as though a single steel rod ran from the top of her head to the base of her spine. "You're the one arguing that history is based on facts, and the fact of the matter is you picked that rug. If an ugly rug stays in a room for thirty years, I'd like to know the truth about who picked it and why that person insisted it stay there. You might also want to know why whoever picked the rug in the first place claimed to no longer like it."

"This isn't about the rug, Mary. It's about the preservation of Gettysburg, one of the most significant historical sites in the—"

"Not about the rug?" Again, she cut him off. "For nearly thirty years I had to endure that rug in our dining room because you chose it. Now you're going to tell me that it was my choice all along. You think anyone around this table is going to believe that I picked a rug like that?" She was up from her seat now, exasperated. Crimson blotches spread from the center of her forehead, cheeks, and chin, as though she burned with a sudden fever. She stepped out of the dining room quite dramatically, only to step right back inside dragging the rolled-up olive-green rug locked beneath her arm. Mary managed to peel back a corner, revealing a swatch of the fabric. "This!" she said. "You're telling me that I was responsible for this?"

Ableson rocketed up from his seat. "Darling, please." He motioned to take the rug from her—glancing once at us, his guests, and laughing nervously—but she wasn't quite ready to hand it over. "This!" She kept showing him the swatch. "You're right," he said obsequiously, yielding the point, offering her total surrender. "Let me take that," he said, lifting the weight from her arms. "Please, just sit down." By now, Dr. Shields had come to his feet and I could see his concern. Unlike Ableson, who was dragging the ugly old rug out of the room, Dr. Shields understood the nature of Mary's outburst, which wasn't irrational, but rather easily explainable; it was further evidence of her degeneration and proof that soon she'd have no choice but to reveal her condition to her husband.

By the time Ableson returned to the dining room, Dr. Shields had helped Mary back to her seat. The blotches were vanishing from her cheeks, forehead, and chin. The fever—or whatever it was—was clearing. She apologized to her husband, but he refused to hear it. "You're right," Ableson said. "It was my mistake. I did pick that rug. I'm sorry that I forgot and I'm sorry we didn't get rid of it sooner." If I had ever wondered about the nature of Mary's devotion to Ableson—despite their difference in age, the complexity of their blended family, or the way he'd upended her life by resurrecting his own—I never again doubted why she loved him or how their relationship had endured: he was capable of genuine apology, something I'd too often struggled with. Such a fine and rare trait in a person.

After Mary's outburst, the conversation turned antiseptic. Dr. Shields inquired about the schedule of the renovation. Mary explained in a small, quiet voice that by summer's end most of the remaining work would be complete. They would still need to finish terracing the gardens, planting hundreds of lilies, azaleas, and her favorite peonies, but nothing more significant than that. She went on at length about the garden, all the while speaking through a smile. Clearly, it gave her great pleasure to imagine it. I remarked that I hoped to see the finished product before I had to return to teaching in the autumn. When I mentioned teaching, Ableson explained to Dr. Shields my work as a Civil War scholar and the nature of my writing, specifically regarding Shelby Foote. By this point we'd made it through the soup, but at the mention of Shelby Foote and the sight of the main course—salmon beurre blanc with asparagus, brought out from the kitchen by Boose— Mary's smile from before faded and then altogether vanished. She excused herself. "I'm going to have a rest," she said, pushing her chair from the table. "I feel as though I might be coming down with something." Ableson stood, as if to help his wife to bed but Mary refused his arm. "You stay down here. I'm quite all right." As she stepped toward the stairs, she wove a bit like maybe she'd had too much to drink, except I had watched her all evening and knew she hadn't touched her wine. Dr. Shields, clearly concerned, followed her toward the stairs. Unlike with her husband, Mary didn't wave the doctor away and he helped her up to bed.

This left only the three of us.

We ate in silence until, eventually, Ableson asked me if I had any plans the next day. I explained that I didn't, except for my own work. "Well," he said, "I thought I might drive into Richmond, see about that protest the paper mentioned, find out what all the fuss is about. Why don't you tag along?" Resistant as I felt to throwing myself into the midst of a college protest, particularly one involving Lucas Harlow, the idea of accompanying Ableson intrigued me. My writing, which had begun as a historical analysis touching on the idea of compromise as an essential American virtue, had morphed into a current events project as momentum grew behind efforts to topple these monuments. Tomorrow in Richmond the ideas in my writing would play out in the streets.

Ableson and I agreed that we'd meet the next morning, early, to drive into Richmond. "I'd like to come, too," Boose said. Her father seemed surprised. "You would?" Upstairs came the sound of her mother coughing. "Yeah, just to get a break." And so it was arranged.

The next day, before the sun had even risen, I parked in the

Ablesons' driveway and walked up the steps to their front door. The workmen were just arriving too, parking their Dodge Rams and Ford F-150s beside the house next to a pair of large, industrial-sized dumpsters. Peeking out from the corner of one of the dumpsters, where Ableson must have tossed it the night before, was the olive-green carpet.

We arrived before eight a.m. and downtown was already abuzz. Colleges that spanned the I-95 corridor had their names written on placards slotted into the windshields of the tour buses they'd chartered. Drivers had tucked those buses on the main thoroughfares and side streets. Packs of students, unaccustomed to rising so early, wandered bleary-eyed along the sidewalks and filtered into the cafés and diners. The protest wouldn't begin for another hour. This was the breakfast crowd and, having not had breakfast myself, I went to join them.

Ableson and Boose had no appetite and so after we eventually found a place to park, they peeled off toward the records office, where I'd meet them in an hour. The protesters planned to congregate on its steps when it opened at nine thirty. They would then deliver a purported two million signatures from across the nation demanding the removal of the Virginia Monument at Gettysburg and its replacement with "an appropriate commemoration." I wandered to a coffee shop, then a diner, and then another coffee shop, and was in every case met with a line that snaked out the door. If I thought this protest might have drawn students in the hundreds, I was wrong: it had drawn them in the thousands.

Slowly, I worked my way forward through the line of a crowded café. A copy of that day's *Times-Dispatch* sat on a newspaper rack by the register. A headline on its front page was about the protest, but before I could read more the cashier badgered me for my order. The only breakfast food left was a batch of day-old blueberry muffins. I ordered one and a coffee and searched for a place to sit.

Of the half-dozen or so tables, all were occupied. Then I recognized the young woman who worked in Ms. Templeton's office, the assistant who had helped us annul Ableson's death certificate. She was crammed next to the window and joined by a friend. I might not have said anything, but as I left the café I recognized her recognizing me and in an awkward approximation of good manners decided to reintroduce myself, lest she think I'd chosen to ignore her. "Nice to see you again," I said, stepping toward her table, and in that instant, with her eyebrows peaked in curious expectation, it was obvious she couldn't quite recall where she'd seen me before. "We met in Susan Templeton's office a couple of months ago," I added, but to little effect. "I'm Martin Neumann, Robert Ableson's friend."

Her expression clamped down, as if stomping out the idea of any further conversation. I was about to excuse myself, to slink out the door and eat my breakfast alone on the sidewalk, when her friend, who up to this point had been silently sitting beside her, drawing no more attention than a shadow, offered me the third chair at their table. So I sat, and introduced myself to this other woman, who replied, "I know who you are." She was a senior at Virginia College and had, two years before, taken one of my courses on nineteenth-century American history. She introduced herself as Janet Templeton.

Janet Templeton and Claire—who finally offered her name—had until the year before lived as roommates at Virginia College. Claire was a newly minted graduate and had gone on to a job working for Janet's mother, Susan Templeton. Personal assistant to the registrar of the Commonwealth of Virginia was plum pre-law-school employment, or at least this was how Claire explained the arrangement before excusing herself with a wan little smile, leaving an almost visible trail of unfriendliness. Nine thirty was approaching, and she needed to get to her desk at the records office. Janet, who seemed in no rush, took up their story, explaining how the two of them had lived together for three out of their four years in college.

Observing Janet, I thought she was every bit her mother. She, too, was graceful, of a pale complexion, with dark hair worn up to further articulate the line of her neck. She spoke with her hands, her wrists unfolding between sentences. If some children are a complete facsimile of one parent, with the resemblance so uncanny that it leaves no allowance for the traits of the other, this seemed the case with Janet. Except for her eyes; outwardly, she was the picture of warmth, but these were a cold, inward-facing shade of blue. She wore heavy glasses, thick as magnifiers, allowing me to see deep into these eyes which I imagined came from her father. "Remarkable isn't it," she said, "that I would've taken your class." Two hundred students a semester filtered through my course so it really wasn't that remarkable, but there was something endearing about Janet thinking it so. The coincidences of the world still seemed to mystify her, as though each had a meaning for her alone and weren't simply a random overlay of events. I asked if she was a history major, to which she laughed, as if the idea itself were ridiculous. She confessed that her major was astronomy, but added, "What's really remarkable is that you know Robert Ableson."

At the evocation of Ableson's name, I grew cautious. Janet's friend Claire was at odds with Ableson. But I couldn't say if Janet held similar views. And so I answered, "He is a remarkable man," hoping to elicit a bit more from Janet, which she was quick to offer. "I've never spent any real time with him," she said. "But growing up, Mr. Ableson was very present in our lives." Her eyes dipped into her coffee, as if revisiting her past in the half-empty cup. "My mother would pack me into the car at all hours of the night if some piece of work needed finishing and we'd either head into the office or to his house. Do you know his house? Halcyon?"

I told her that I knew it but didn't quite feel assured enough to reveal that I was staying in the guest cottage. I imagined Janet as a little girl, stranded in the backseat of the car while her mother worked late into the night with Ableson. Perhaps Janet's interest in the stars began here, parked outside Halcyon, head against the glass, a creature of fate, a Cassandra, staring up for hours into the night sky. Knowing Ableson as I did, he surely would've invited the little girl inside. Why didn't Ms. Templeton mention her daughter in the car? But also, why didn't Ableson know to ask? Could he really have been that oblivious? I tried to change the subject and asked Janet about her plans after graduation. She was, through her presence at this protest, obviously engaged in activism. Did she also have an interest in law like her mother?

"No," she answered. "Not law. I really loved my major and so am applying for an advanced degree. I'll leave the law to my mother. She's always believed that the way to further an issue is from within the system"—although I didn't mention it, I thought of a younger Susan Templeton successfully arguing the custody case of her daughter—"but I look at where my mother has wound up. She and other women would have done better to tear down the system itself."

"And what does that mean?" I asked.

In the street, protesters had begun to converge toward the records office in ever greater numbers. "It's not good-ol'-boy types who've hurt women like my mother the most. Guys like that, who wear their misogyny on their sleeves, are at least honest about it. The worst culprits have always been the well-meaning ones, a bunch of oblivious wolves who don't so much wear sheep's cloth-ing as convince themselves that they are sheep. They're the ones who persuaded my mother to waste a lifetime of energy working within a system that would never be hers, but always theirs. Men like Robert Ableson."

When she evoked Ableson's name, it was with a snarl that must have elicited an involuntary reaction in me because she then apol-ogized, saying, "I know he's your friend." Still, this didn't prevent her from wondering aloud how "a relic" like him had become a person our society thought to bring back from the dead, concluding that "the generational selfishness of resurrection is what most astounds me."

I asked her if this was the real reason the protesters wanted to tear down the Virginia Monument? Was this about a monument on a battlefield, or was this about one generation ceding its power to the next?

She didn't answer right away. Rather, she considered the question with academic distance, as if I had posed it to her in a lecture. "The petition delivered today has two million signatures on it," she observed. "That's months of effort by thousands of students across the country. It represents an entire network of activism. Bringing it to the state capital is a massive accomplishment, and yet it isn't going to change a thing. The petition could have two hundred million signatures on it and it wouldn't make a difference. You're a historian—think back through time. How do statues come down? It's not through petitions. Statues come down when people get out in the streets and tear them down." And as she said this, something lit up inside her. The resemblance to her mother, which before had seemed so strong, was now consumed by a wild energy in those blue eyes.

"If a petition is a waste of time, why'd you come today?"

"I came because my mother asked me to."

The past couple of years, Susan Templeton had become a quiet champion of this initiative to remove the Virginia Monument, the gift of a state whose psyche was so deeply rooted in its tarnished past that it could never progress on the issues she cared about most if these statues remained in place. Late in life, Susan Templeton had also come to understand, as her daughter put it, that "some statues are like walls. They keep new ideas out." Which is why the elder Ms. Templeton had taken up this cause as her own. The professors and students had done the organizing, but it was Susan Templeton who had guided their efforts. She'd helped them draw up the petition. She'd issued meticulous instructions for the submission of signatures. "A single flaw on any one page," Janet explained to me, "nullifies every other signature on that page. Precision is everything. This is a big day for my mother."

"Then how can you think this is all a waste of time?"

Janet shrugged. "Just a hunch." She took a last sip of coffee, emptying her cup. Outside came the squawk from a megaphone in the direction of the records office. It was the first of what would be many speeches given that day.

I lost Janet Templeton in the crowd outside the café. Jostled shoulder to shoulder with strangers, I struggled to inch closer to the steps of the records office. Here I hoped to find Ableson and Boose. If I had anticipated the immense size of this protest, not only would I have made more specific plans for meeting them, I likely wouldn't have come in the first place. Despite Janet Templeton's arguments against the monument, I continued to believe it should remain as it stood; however, I wasn't inclined to express my convictions with the fervency of these protesters. I've never harbored any desire to participate in historical events. I prefer my history in the past as opposed to the present.

I continued searching for Ableson and Boose in the crowd. Copies of today's newspaper, which I'd glimpsed in the coffee shop, littered the street. Several were open to a now-trampled page inset with a large photograph of Susan Templeton, who, according to the text, "had played an essential behind-the-scenes role in the petition's success." While I tried to read, an overly enthusiastic protester behind me kept knocking his picket sign against my head. I finally snapped at him, telling him to be more careful, and when I turned around again none other than Lucas Harlow had assumed his perch atop the steps of the records office. "Do you know what these are!" he shouted through a megaphone.

Lucas gestured toward a half-dozen undergraduates who frantically stacked cardboard file boxes one on another. Lucas began to climb up the boxes as though ascending the winner's podium at the Olympiad. "These," he said, taking a first step. "Are," he added, measuring out his words with each step. "Your," and then he hesitated another awkward moment, as the final box was installed beneath his foot. "Voices!"

The crowd cheered.

Lucas Harlow gave a Nixonian two-handed wave, with both arms fluttering high over his head. He then recycled some of his familiar tropes, the same ones he'd delivered when we'd last seen each other that winter: to matter, history had to remain forward looking; only through the consistent, harsh gaze of the present could we properly judge the past. He was really getting going when, up from the crowd, a deep, throaty chant emerged. "Burn, baby, burn! Burn, baby, burn!" Lucas tilted his head, not quite sure what to make of it. "Burn, baby, burn! Burn, baby, burn!"

What was it they wanted to burn?

Even though Lucas couldn't see me, I felt as though he and I were sharing this moment of confusion. Did they want to burn their two million signatures? Did they want to burn the monument they'd come to protest? Perhaps. But you don't really burn a monument. You tear it down.

"Burn, baby, burn! Burn, baby, burn!" The chant kept up and whatever else Lucas had planned to say was consumed by it. Then someone chucked something from the crowd. Lucas flinched as it sailed over his shoulder. (I couldn't say for certain, but it looked like one of those day-old muffins I'd had for breakfast.) More people threw things: an apple core, an empty soda can, other bits of trash. This didn't go on for long, a minute, maybe more. But the crowd had worked itself into a frenzy. They weren't hurling these things at Lucas, but at the records office behind him. However, this didn't stop some of the trash pelting Lucas as he descended his perch.

This might have gone on for longer and the crowd might have even rushed the records office if its front door hadn't suddenly opened a crack. Susan Templeton, the registrar of the Commonwealth of Virginia, crept outside.

A cheer erupted.

From the top of the steps she offered a slight deferential wave. Lucas Harlow made some inaudible comment to her; she quickly shook her head, no. His posture was insistent. He said something else; again, she seemed to decline. Nevertheless, he placed the megaphone in her hands. The crowd shushed itself. The only sound was a ripple of whispers speculating what Susan Templeton might say. When she spoke through the megaphone, a high-pitched squawk drowned out her words. She turned red-faced and embarrassed. Lucas reached over, touched some button on the side of the megaphone, and then handed it back to Susan.

"Is that better?" She flinched as her voice became enormous. "Good morning."

The crowd, in its own voice, the one which a few moments ago had chanted "Burn, baby, burn!" returned her "Good morning."

"So nice to see you all," she added tentatively.

To this, the crowd erupted in cheers.

"Wow," she said, "these are quite a lot of signatures." She took a step backward, gesturing theatrically toward the many file boxes. The crowd grew louder and louder, egging her on. "I suppose these are for me?" They loved her and she was probing the character and extent of that adoration, quickly learning how to play it up. "Looks like things are changing around here." How quickly her reserve from moments before melted away when she realized she was in possession of the crowd. Not Lucas Harlow. Not the student organizers who'd brought up the file boxes filled with signatures.

But her, a bureaucrat, a woman who'd placed herself behind the scenes all her life. The crowd was hers. At least for this moment.

When Lucas Harlow took back the megaphone, they booed him. They didn't want to hear his formal announcement of the delivery of signatures. They didn't want to hear him tick off the alphabet soup of student organizations that had contributed to this effort. They didn't want his explanations of what this moment meant and where it might go if given full sail. The crowd wanted her. They knew without anyone telling them—least of all Lucas Harlow—that this was *her* moment. They knew, intuitively, that Susan Templeton wasn't accepting these signatures on behalf of them, the students; no, it was the reverse. They, the students, were submitting the signatures on behalf of Susan Templeton.

It was, finally, her time.

I searched the crowd for Janet Templeton, hoping I could find her, wondering if she was seeing what I saw, and also wondering whether this might cause her to revise her hunch that her mother's energies from "within the system" were a waste. I couldn't help but root for Ms. Templeton, despite wanting to preserve the monument she and the others so ardently sought to tear down. Watching her on the steps was like watching a sports team come from behind. When the crowd finally settled, when she'd finished playing them (and when they'd finished playing her), she produced a document. It was a receipt for the two million signatures. She brandished it in the air as though it were a rabbit she had pulled from a hat. Her signature would serve as the Commonwealth of Virginia's acknowledgment of the petition.

But she didn't have anywhere to sign the receipt.

In a last bit of theatrics—of which she was now proving herself adept—she tapped Lucas Harlow on the shoulder. She gestured for him to turn around. This he did, much to the delight of the crowd, which gave Ms. Templeton its greatest cheer of all as she used his back for a desk.

Then it was done. The petition submitted.

Like when the lights come up at the end of a show, the crowd's attention diverted from the steps of the records office back onto itself. The picket signs which they'd carried high now came low to the ground. Individuals turned one to another for a word of congratulations or an embrace. They had done what they had traveled all this way to do. Their celebratory mood from before turned slightly pensive. The question *What now?* seemed to linger in their every gesture.

The crowd filtered back into the cafés and diners, back toward the tour buses that would return them to that constellation of campuses from which they'd descended. However, the stacks of file boxes containing the signatures still remained in front of the records office. Susan Templeton needed to get them inside, but they were too heavy for her to manage on her own. Within minutes, the crowd had dispersed. No one had thought to remain behind and help her. Which is why no one was there to see that when the door to the records office did finally open, it was Robert Ableson who stood inside, ready to lend a hand.

I was slow to recognize the voice that called out my name. I turned in its direction, toward a woman behind me on the vacant sidewalk. She stood among the tossed cups and pitched signs from the morning's demonstration. "What are you doing here?" she asked as though I were a social inferior who'd snuck unwanted into a party; it was her characteristic superiority that placed her so firmly in my mind despite the several years since I had last seen Annette Harlow.

She and I had both lost the people we'd come here with. In my case, that was Boose and Ableson, though I understood he was somewhere inside the records office. For Annette, that was her husband and Ginny.

"You came with Ginny?" I asked.

"Lucas invited her. He thought it might take her mind off things." Annette walked beside me wearing flats and a skirt. She swished its hem back and forth across her shins in a playful, schoolgirlish way between steps, and like a schoolgirl she began to gossip. "Or did you not hear?"

"I'm sorry, hear what?"

"Oh, well, I just assumed you knew. She and Daryl split up a few weeks ago."

Annette arched a finely plucked eyebrow as I succumbed to a grin; this, my reaction, she would surely report to Ginny, and she would surely misinterpret it too. Perhaps they would decide I was pleased Ginny was again available because I still harbored a hope, no matter how remote, that we might reconcile; or perhaps she and Ginny would decide that I was still bitter, and my little grin revealed how I relished Ginny's failed romance. Neither of these interpretations would be correct. The source of my amusement was far simpler; it was a single memory, that of poor hapless Daryl turning pirouettes at the Four Seasons bar while he searched the crowd for Ginny.

I didn't need Annette to explain the reason for their breakup. Daryl hadn't stood a chance with Ginny—just as I hadn't stood a chance with her. If I recalled Daryl being a bit of a dope, what did that say about me? He hadn't married Ginny. I had. Beautiful, intelligent, driven, Ginny could only respect a man who was at least her equal. Except give-and-take wasn't in her nature. She also needed to dominate a relationship. The type of man she needed— meaning the type of accomplished man she could respect—wasn't one who would be so dominated. She could only dominate her inferiors: men like Daryl; men like me. When we could no longer hide our weaknesses from her, she came to resent us for them. Hers was a paradox. Annette was familiar with it, as was I. When we were newlyweds in Philadelphia, Annette and Lucas were fre- quent houseguests, visiting the city to escape provincial life at Gettysburg College. Over the course of those years—when Lucas's first book had become a sensation and his associate professorship had become a chaired professorship—I had failed to even finish my dissertation. I wasn't bringing in an income, so Ginny eventually quit her work at the public defender's office, signing on to a firm that specialized in forensic accounting applied to matrimonial law. Her higher hourly rate eased the strain on our finances but the diminished meaning she found in her career only heightened the strain on our marriage. When I finally did finish my dissertation, the plan had been to settle where I could find an academic job. Rural Virginia wasn't what Ginny had in mind. Which led to my lashing out with a single yet clichéd indiscretion with my undergraduate research assistant. It wasn't so much an affair as a cry for help. I threw myself on the floor to see whether Ginny would pick me up. When she found the hotel room receipts and text messages, she'd called me a loser instead.

I told Annette that I was sorry to hear about Daryl and Ginny going their separate ways. She nodded, as if only to acknowledge that she'd heard my answer and would take it under advisement. "And who did you come down here with?" she asked, changing the subject.

Before I could answer, we turned the sidewalk's corner and bumped into Ginny. She was delighted to find Annette, but equally perplexed to discover the two of us walking together. After a quick hello, Ginny repeated Annette's question, wondering who I'd traveled here with. When I explained that I'd come along with Robert Ableson and his daughter, Ginny was incredulous. "He's here?"

"Yes, but I can't seem to find—"

When Annette interjected "Isn't that your landlord?" Ginny launched into an aria of Ableson's professional accomplishments. Some of which—like his work on the Equal Rights Amendment and his successful defense of *Roe v. Wade* in the lower courts—

were familiar to me. Others—like his work in *Roe v. Roe* representing a gay father who because of his sexual orientation was denied custody of his son, and his work in *Bottoms v. Bottoms*, representing a gay mother who was similarly denied child custody—I had never heard of before. His opinions were taught widely, Ginny explained. He could formidably argue any side of a case. He was one of the only jurists ever vetted by presidents of both parties for a nomination to the D.C. Court of Appeals (although he had mysteriously removed his name from consideration on each occasion). Eventually, he cashed out for the private sector, working for defense and healthcare companies by the end of his career. Still, Ginny's admiration knew no bounds. It occurred to me as I listened to her that this was the level of respect she would need to have for any man she could possibly hope to love—clearly, I had never stood a chance.

Ginny's summary of Ableson's achievements ran out of steam, and so I observed, "Aren't you leaving something out?" She glanced back at me, momentarily forgetful, before adding, "Oh yes, and he's recently participated in that project with the Lazarus mice. He's one of the people they brought back."

I laughed.

"What's so funny?" Ginny asked.

I said, "He's risen from the dead but in your mind this is the least of his achievements." She shrugged, and then explained to Annette how she and Lucas had arranged to meet at the same café where I'd eaten breakfast. Believing that Ableson and Boose might search for me there, I decided to tag along.

When we arrived at the café, it was mostly empty. Lucas was waiting for us inside, brooding alone at a table in the back. With a wooden stirrer he poked at the dregs in his cup. Unlike Annette and Ginny, he seemed content to keep to himself. He simply nodded and then said my name not so much as a greeting but as an acknowledgment of my presence. The three of us joined Lucas and we fell into a long silence. As if to escape it, Annette offered to buy another round of coffee. Ginny waited until she left to mention "Martin is here with Robert Ableson."

"I'd heard," said Lucas. He turned to me, adding, "And I suppose it's only a coincidence that he's come today?" Lucas tilted his chair onto its back two legs. "I suppose you're going to try to convince me that you didn't bring him here to sabotage our petition . . . to undermine my work?" He dropped his chair down loudly onto four legs, and if on occasion I ever forgot that Lucas, erudite professor that he was, had once played nose tackle for Ole Miss, the smacking force with which his chair hit the ground served as a reminder. Leaning forward, with his ample chest hovering halfway across the table, he said, "I know you don't support what I'm doing. But I have always been supportive of you. Even when I had no reason to be. Even now, with your inherently problematic Shelby Foote project. And how do you thank me? You bring Robert Ableson here."

Before I could answer, Annette returned with our coffees. She placed one in front of each of us along with a pile of creamers and sweeteners in the center of the table. "What are you all talking about?" she asked, while Lucas extended our standoff with an icy stare, refusing to look anywhere but at me.

"Robert Ableson," said Ginny.

Annette, recognizing her husband's frustration, muttered, "Seems he's on everyone's mind."

Then the door to the café opened. It was Boose. She made a quick inspection and, upon finding me, leaned back outside. "He's in here!" she shouted down the sidewalk. Ableson jogged up behind her. The two of them approached our table.

At the sight of Ableson, I instinctively stood.

So did Ginny. Followed by Annette. And, reluctantly, Lucas.

"We checked almost every café and diner," said an exasperated Boose. I proceeded to make a round of introductions, starting with Annette followed by Ginny. But before I could go further, Ableson said, "You're Lucas Harlow. It's a real pleasure to meet you." Ableson's hand was extended. Lucas took it, and as he did Ableson added, "Congratulations on the petition." The two shook but on instinct Lucas angled his body awkwardly to the side, so he faced Ableson in profile, in much the same way a duelist turns himself in profile to offer less of a target to his opponent. Ableson added, "Your remarks today were very"—and there was a pause, a beat passed, as Ableson uncharacteristically struggled for a word, settling on "effective."

Lucas glanced at me, and then back at Ableson. "Thank you."

Annette offered to grab two more cups of coffee, while Ginny pulled out her chair, making room for us to combine our table with an empty one, so we six might sit together. Ableson declined, noting the length of the drive back to Halcyon and his desire to return home in time for dinner with his wife. Although relieved to avoid an awkward confrontation between Lucas and Ableson, I knew Ginny was disappointed. In consolation to her, I mentioned that she'd studied some of Ableson's cases in law school.

"Is that so?" he answered. "Which ones?"

Ginny recited a few of the cases she'd already mentioned as well as a few others I'd never heard of before. Ableson nodded appreciatively in much the same way a musician might to a fan who can tick off a list of his B-side tracks. "I'd offer you my business card," said Ableson, "but I'm afraid I no longer carry one." His smile was decorous and it sufficiently disarmed Ginny so that she was soon rifling through her handbag for a business card of her own, which she handed to Ableson. He read it carefully and took the opportunity to remark how impressive it was that someone as young as her was already a partner at so prestigious a law firm.

We were by the door as Ginny and Ableson finished their goodbyes. I had thought for a moment she might never let us leave and would follow us all the way out to the car and said as much to Ableson as we searched for where we'd parked.

"Oh, don't be a bad sport," Ableson said, still turning Ginny's business card over in his fingers. "Your ex-wife is lovely. It's to your credit that you were once married to her." I chose not to acknowledge the remark, or its obverse, which was that it was to my discredit we'd divorced. We piled into my Volvo. Ableson sat in the passenger seat and Boose in the backseat. Inch by inch the sun descended across the windshield as we navigated out of Richmond, toward the interstate. The city's tallest buildings fragmented our view, their windows winking back at us through the hazed light. We crossed the inky James River and beneath us a barge ambled sleepily along on its current. Not much was said, until Ableson observed, "That Lucas Harlow, he doesn't much like me, does he?"

It was odd to hear Ableson speak in terms of who "liked" or "disliked" him. Had such considerations ever bothered him when as a much younger man he'd argued the controversial cases that had made his name? I couldn't say, so only offered him what I knew about Lucas Harlow, which included my history with him and Lucas's unsubstantiated belief that Ableson planned to undermine his petition.

"What exactly do you mean?" Ableson asked.

I was staring straight ahead, into the torrent of oncoming traffic, as I explained the accusation Lucas had leveled against me that afternoon in the café. "He thinks I brought you to the demonstration to sabotage his petition." Ableson grew silent. The only sound was the swoosh of cars passing in the opposite direction. I glanced into the rearview mirror. Boose was asleep.

"That's ridiculous," he said.

"I know."

"You didn't bring me. I'm the one who brought you."

"Right . . . ," I said, feeling as if Ableson and I might be speaking past one another. "What upset him was not who brought who, but that you would try to sabotage his efforts . . . It's absurd."

"What's so absurd about it?" he asked. "Of course I'm not in favor of that misguided petition. Those kids don't understand what they're protesting. They want to rewrite history, but they couldn't tell you what side Longstreet, Meade, Pickett, or Armistead fought for. They want to tear up that battlefield. They want to trash the old monuments and replace them with something new despite having no knowledge of what happened on that ground. Their certainty about the present infects their understanding of the past. From the records office, I could hear them outside chanting 'Burn, baby, burn' . . . A bunch of ridiculous pyromaniacs; tell me, what is it that they want to burn?"

"What were you doing in the records office?"

"Helping Susan."

"Helping her with what?"

"Helping her avoid embarrassment. She's a public official. What do you think would happen if she certified those signatures? We're in Virginia. The validity of the petition would immediately come under scrutiny. *Public scrutiny*. Do you think she'd survive as state registrar? It'd cost Susan her job."

"But the petition? What happens to all those signatures?"

Overwhelmed by his own cleverness, Ableson's eyes slitted and his lips drew back from his teeth. He explained how the petition form contained a variety of contradictory instructions. The signature line, for instance, read "Sign here in block letters." Did this require a signature, or your name written in print? The instruction could be interpreted in either way. Also, the address provided by each signatory needed to match the address on file at the Department of Elections, which only updated their voter rolls annually. This meant that if a single person on the petition had moved in the past year state authorities could elect to classify the entire sheet of signatures as fraudulent. Ableson went on at length about the ins and outs of this single form, diagramming it as though he were a professor and it were a page torn from a great work of literature. "How do you know so much about this?" I asked rather naively. "Well...I designed the form." We were now far from the city. He stared out his window into the impenetrable darkness. It seemed that from memory he was reconstructing the countryside as it passed by. Absently, he continued, "Someone else had designed the version before mine, and someone else the version before that. Interpretation is everything, it's not the instructions on the form that count but how you interpret them, so that nothing changes around here unless the powers that be want it changed—that's the point. Susan needed a little reminder of that; otherwise, she was liable to get herself in a heap of trouble."

"Lucas was right then?"

"No," said Ableson, turning away from his window. "Nobody sabotaged your friend's petition. He accomplished that on his own. He's a history teacher. Why doesn't he focus on teaching history instead of trying to destroy it?" Ableson pointed out that I seemed bothered, which perhaps I did. This was hardly fair, and I found myself increasingly unsettled as he regurgitated many of my own arguments back to me, arguments about the compromises hardwired into American life, whether they be the division between church and state; or the essential tension between federalism and republicanism; or even the format of a petition drawn up by a records office in Virginia. The more he spoke, the more eloquent he became, expounding at length about the dangers of absolutism. He even went so far as to quote back to me Shelby Foote, who said that the Civil War was *a failure on our part to find a way not to fight that war. It was because we failed to do the thing we really have a genius for, which is compromise . . .* But was Ableson's genius and the genius of this country really compromise? Compromise wasn't what would preserve the Virginia Monument at Gettysburg. Compromise wasn't what had undermined Lucas

Harlow and the petitioners with their chants of "burn, baby, burn."
No, I had to give it another word. I had to call it something else . . .
I had to call it cheating.

Ableson had cheated them. This was the conclusion I arrived
at, shaken as we turned off the interstate and onto the unmarked,
weed-fringed roads that ran the last few miles toward Halcyon.
Boose was awake now in the backseat and she was the first to
comment on the presence of Dr. Shields's car in the driveway. He
should have left early that morning, but he remained there. Boose,
growing concerned, wondered why. Recalling our dinner from the
night before and how Mary had excused herself early, I suspected
that I knew why. I also felt certain of the news that awaited Boose
and Ableson when they entered the house. Something had happened. Some lapse in her health. Mary could no longer keep her
secret.

I parked the car. Boose and Ableson stepped onto the driveway. They invited me inside. None of us had eaten dinner and I
had every reason to join them. But I didn't. Boose said goodnight
and walked up to the front door, but Ableson lingered. He leaned
forward and spoke to me through the car's open window, now
holding the rim of it in both hands as though he thought to hold
the car motionless before it could begin to move, saying what it
seemed he'd been thinking off and on for the entirety of our drive:
"I'm sorry if you're upset with me."

"I'm not," I said. "Just tired."

"You sure?"

I nodded.

"Okay," he said. "Because I wouldn't want you ever to feel as
though I'd been dishonest with you." From over his shoulder, I
could see Boose standing on the porch fumbling for her key. A
silhouette appeared through the vestibule window. It must've been
Dr. Shields. "So we understand each other?" Ableson asked me.

"Yeah. We understand each other."

FOUR

DIAGNOSIS

The phone rang itself out. When it started to ring a second time, I rolled over to answer. It was Ginny on the caller ID. The sun was right at the trees, falling onto my bed in dusty strips. It was too early.

"Sorry to wake you," she said.

"You knew you'd wake me."

"I know, but I couldn't wait anymore. Did you hear the news?"

"What news?" I was sitting up now, wiping the sleep from my eyes as my legs caught in a complicated knot of sheets that tangled around my waist.

"Lucas's petition," she said. "The state invalidated the entire thing. Two million signatures, *poof*, gone."

I didn't feel like lying, or playing stupid, so simply answered, "Oh, that. Yeah, I'd heard." The line fell silent, as if Ginny expected me to say more, to admit that I'd received the news through Robert Ableson.

"Susan Templeton's assistant found us in the café after you left," she said. "She told Lucas that he needed to review the petition, that they'd discovered some irregularities. We nearly ran back to the records office. When we stepped out of the elevator, we could hear Ms. Templeton and her daughter arguing down the hall. Open boxes were stacked around the office. Rubber-banded batches of one thousand signatures covered every table and chair. Someone had scrawled a red X across the top of most of the coversheets. Ms. Templeton's daughter kept asking her, 'How could you have let him in here?' Meanwhile, Ms. Templeton started explaining to us how the petitioners had incorrectly filled out the forms. The errors were all ridiculous procedural stuff, but each invalidated the entire page, or so Ms. Templeton said. To his credit Lucas stayed pretty calm at first. He simply crawled over the boxes checking cover sheet after cover sheet, finding the red Xs."

"How long did you all stay?"

"Hours," said Ginny. "Where could I go? Lucas was my ride home and he wasn't leaving. He inspected every box. Ableson's hand in all of this was so obvious. He probably red-Xed the signature sheets himself. But I still can't understand his interest in preserving the monument, particularly given his history as a champion of other social issues. And what could Ms. Templeton do? If Ableson was right, and the petition was filled out incorrectly, did Lucas really expect her to risk her job over this?"

"Probably," I said.

Ginny laughed. "You're probably right. I don't feel bad for Lucas—what does he really care about that monument? This whole thing has been a performance for him, a gimmick to gain attention for his work, which he's always been good at, all the way back to his first book. And I don't feel bad for Susan Templeton, either—she should've known better before she got involved. No, the person I feel bad for is Ms. Templeton's daughter, Janet. The whole time while Susan and Lucas rifled through the boxes and argued about the signature sheets, Janet sat behind her mother's desk, glasses off, rubbing her exhausted eyes and going on and on about how 'You always do this . . .'"

I didn't have to ask: *do what?* The nature of Janet's disappointment was obvious. Her mother had come so close to an extraordinary achievement by shepherding the petition to completion. But she typified a certain type of person who possessed intelligence and competence, but who struggled to employ those talents on their own behalf. I'd come across people like this before, who are disempowered, who don't believe they have permission to succeed; or, worse, who wait for someone else to grant them that permission. When a person can't help themselves, they aren't the one who suffers the most; it's those closest to them. Particularly their children. Even grown children, like Janet.

"Janet's why I'm calling you," said Ginny. "She's got it in for Mr. Ableson."

"What do you mean?"

"She kept saying this was it, the last straw. That Mr. Ableson needed to watch out. She didn't care what her mother said. She was done keeping her mouth shut."

"Keeping her mouth shut about what?"

Ginny didn't know.

I worked the rest of the day and took a walk in the afternoon. When I passed by the main house at Halcyon, Dr. Shields's car remained parked out front. I returned to the guest cottage and wondered if Ableson would be paying me a visit that evening. I suspected he would. Wasn't this why Mary had taken me into her confidence in the first place, so that I might be there to support him when he learned of her illness? I wanted to be prepared for his visit and mentally rehearsed the many directions our conversation might take. Intuitively, I knew that Mary's condition would come as a shock to Ableson. Their age difference had always implied that his death would precede hers. The choices he'd made had obviously upended that. Was he capable of recognizing this and supporting her choices, no matter what they might be? I doubted it. Which is why, like Mary, I suspected that his reaction to her diagnosis would be to suggest she embark on the same journey he had undergone. They would cheat death together.

What would Mary say to that? Of course, I couldn't know for certain. However, I had a strong suspicion that she wouldn't be so cavalier as her husband when it came to upending the natural order. Life and death—the time for each and the choice between the two—this wasn't a question she would answer with his certainty. She wouldn't be like Ableson. Or like his hero, the philosopher Pascal. Those two shared a logic that now seemed impossibly naïve: *Wager, then, without hesitation that He is. There is here an infinity of an infinitely happy life to gain . . .*

That evening, I mixed the martinis. I sat in my chair. And I waited. But Ableson never came.

Three days passed into four, five days passed into six. I took my walks, I did my work, and I waited for Ableson. I was tempted to call at the main house but felt certain it would prove an intrusion. He knew where to find me. And he would come when he was ready. Still, I worried about him; and it wasn't only the news about Mary. What Ginny had told me about Janet Templeton also concerned me. Once or twice, I almost convinced myself to knock on Ableson's door to pass along this bit of information. If someone had an accusation to make, wouldn't Ableson want to hear it? But in deference to his privacy, I remained in the guest cottage.

I continued this way, seeing no one, not Ableson, Boose, Dr. Shields, or even Ableson's two stepsons, Doug and Bobby, who had in all likelihood arrived at this moment of maximum crisis to attend to their mother. Then, on the afternoon of the sixth day, a suspicious white panel van pulled up to the main house. I was sitting in my attic study, struggling to work, when I glimpsed the van through a partition of trees. Unable to contain my curiosity, concern, and general state of suspicion, I abandoned my work and stepped outside for a walk. I made a wide loop of the property, not wanting to draw attention to myself. Before long, I was passing by the main house on my return to the guest cottage. This got me close enough to observe the van's license plate; it was government issued.

This fact had hardly registered when a man and a woman whom I'd never seen before stepped out the front door of the house. They noticed me immediately. "Hi there," said the woman, in a neighborly way.

"Hi."

"Out for a walk?" asked the man, whose tone was equally congenial.

"Seems so."

Neither of them took another step forward as though I were a small animal they didn't wish to spook. The woman was middle-aged, dressed in a purple Patagonia pullover fleece and khakis. The man was around the same age and equally unthreatening, also dressed in a fleece and khakis. Both wore running sneakers and prescription glasses and they appeared like any other unremarkable couple, minus the government van.

"You live around here?" the man inquired.

I nodded.

"Where's that?" asked the woman, as she took a first step toward me.

"I rent the guest cottage."

The two shared a glance, as if each were asking the other how it was they'd missed the presence of a renter on the estate. "How long you been there?" asked the woman. Her colleague was unlocking the driver's-side door of the van.

"Are you both friends of the Ablesons?"

The woman said, "We'd like to think so," and then introduced herself as Dr. Jones and her colleague introduced himself also as Dr. Jones, while assiduously pointing out that the two were not related. "We're the physicians assigned to Mr. Ableson's case," said the woman. "You want to come in the house?"

"Are you sure that's all right?"

"It's probably best," she said. "No one told us about a renter and we need to keep everyone on the same sheet of music."

I followed Dr. Jones to the porch while her colleague took a cellphone from the glove compartment of the van. He wandered off a safe distance to make a call in private. Inside, all of the Ableson children plus Dr. Shields were gathered in the kitchen. They were neither pleased nor displeased at my arrival. In general, they seemed stunned, as if pummeled by recent events. Half-finished cups of coffee and empty containers of food were scattered on the counter. Dishes filled the sink. On seeing Dr. Jones, Doug and Bobby Ableson both asked if her colleague was placing his call. She assured them that he was, and that he would return in a moment.

Boose, who was sitting at one of the counter stools, volunteered in a defeated voice that her father had gone missing.

"Missing?" I asked. "For how long?"

The kitchen had an open floor plan and Dr. Shields sat slumped in a sofa on its far side. "For the last two days," he said. His eyes were red-rimmed and his face swollen from lack of sleep. He explained that this had all begun on the evening before we'd left for Richmond, when Mary had stepped away from dinner. A case of mild dehydration had sapped her energy, but she had slept through that night and seemed fine the following morning. She had even insisted on making Dr. Shields breakfast before he returned to Philadelphia. She had then collapsed at the stove. "The cancer's accelerated," he said. "It's metastasized into her bones." That night, when we had returned from the protest, she was already in the hospital and Dr. Shields was waiting to take Ableson to her. "It's not the diagnosis that has been hardest for Robert," Dr. Shields explained. "It's that Mary has chosen to accept it."

At which point, Dr. Jones commented, "There were other options. Immediate cryopreservation . . . advanced stem cell therapies . . . Mr. Ableson was hoping his wife might elect such a procedure."

"Do we have to go over this again?" said Boose. She sat at the kitchen counter with her forehead cradled in her palm. "She doesn't want to do it."

"I know," said Dr. Shields. "We're simply explaining to Martin."

To which Dr. Jones reiterated, "It's important everyone remain on the same sheet of music."

"You keep saying that," I replied.

"Because this is bigger than Robert Ableson," said Dr. Jones. "Keep in mind the profound experiment he's participating in."

"Where have you looked for him?" I asked.

Collectively, they ticked off a list of significant places in Ableson's life, places where he might have gone or been seen. His boyhood home an hour away. His old office. His favorite restaurant where he'd given Mary the Mercury dime. They'd had to remain discreet in their search. If news of Ableson's disappearance leaked out, it would surely reach the papers and could, potentially, undermine the slim majority of public support that existed for resurrection. "Federal funding for this program is anything but assured," said Dr. Jones, "particularly in an election year." It had taken the past two days, but they had exhausted everywhere they could think to look. This was the growing consensus among the family as the other Dr. Jones returned from placing his call. "They say it's time to notify the local authorities," he announced to the group. "They don't want us to wait anymore."

Who the "they" was in this equation remained vague, and I could only surmise it was the conglomeration of government agencies responsible for overseeing Ableson's case—NIH, HHS, DOE. A missing person's report with Ableson's name on it would lead to a minor media frenzy, and, quite possibly, a major one. This was what the doctors and administrators at their attendant agencies so diligently wished to avoid. Nevertheless, it seemed inevitable that news of Ableson's disappearance would get out. That is, until Mary appeared in the kitchen.

To stand she relied on a chair, whose seatback she grasped like the rails of a walker. Her face was a shocked and wild-eyed ruin. Gaunt, sunken-cheeked, with her ghost already contained in her body, she had shed at least fifteen pounds since I'd last seen her; fifteen pounds that she could ill afford to lose. Her attempts at hiding the disease—which before had proven rudimentary at best—had diminished to nothing. Her relationship to life was like that of a sinking ship to the sea; she no longer existed for it and it would shortly consume her. But not yet.

"His plot at the cemetery," she said. "We haven't tried there."

Oak Ridge Cemetery was as its name described. The headstones were interspersed among the ancient trees and the ridge was one of many that bracketed the northeast-by-southwest-running Shenandoah Valley. It lacked the grandeur of Arlington National Cemetery, where his military service had entitled him to a plot; instead, he had opted for this quieter and less trafficked place. Before Mary mentioned his grave, it had never occurred to me that Ableson had one. But without a grave you can't really have a funeral and his had been a well-attended affair. Mourners had crowded the cemetery from all four corners of the country, but few of those who would mourn him in death had been confidants in life and the only one among them who'd known that the casket was empty and that Ableson had made other arrangements was Dr. Shields. Even so, at Ableson's funeral it continued to seem an improbability that those arrangements would yield a result.

It was Mary who'd asked me to search the cemetery. Of those of us gathered in the kitchen, she recognized that I had the least to do. It was a modest drive from Halcyon, twenty minutes. Scribbled on a scrap of paper in my pocket was a section, row, and grave number. Having parked my Volvo, I was referencing this scrap as I ascended a gravel path that wound through the terraced rows of headstones, family plots, and marble angels with their lichened wings.

When I crested the ridge, I found him on its far side. He sat with his back leaning against one of the ubiquitous oaks. He was facing away from me, down into the valley. The view was sprawling. It was one of those spring afternoons where slanted light catches every mote of pollen, making the invisible air visible. A few clouds lumbered overhead. The Shenandoah River meandered in the distance and when the sun fell on the water it glistened like foundry iron and when the clouds obscured the sun it appeared as water again. I watched Ableson watching the elemental interplay between sun and clouds and water. Then he turned over his shoulder, saw me, and stood.

"I'm glad it's you who came," he said, brushing dirt from the seat of his pants.

"Is that your plot?"

He glanced down at the simple white marble headstone behind him. "It is."

The marker was the same as those modest ones used for graves at Arlington. Etched into the white stone were the dates *1914–1999* and I ran my hand over the numerals. Other facts were etched into the headstone as well. His name, his branch of service and rank during the war. However, none of those held my fascination like those two dates. The year of your birth. The year of your death. They're supposed to be immutable brackets. But he'd proven otherwise. This made him a time traveler of sorts.

"Right after they brought me back," he said, "when I was in social quarantine, I'd sneak out here." He wasn't looking at me as he spoke, but down into the valley.

"I can see why."

"No, it wasn't the view I came for." He again turned toward me. "I wanted to know if anyone had visited." Pebbles rested on top of many of the headstones around us and I could see how Ableson jealously counted them. "Sometimes I'd come and a person would've placed one on my headstone. More often there'd be nothing. It's terrible to feel as though you've been forgotten." He squatted to the ground and picked up a small stone. He weighed it in his hand. He then slung it out a great distance so that it sailed down the ridge, disappearing in the late-day sun. "Amazing to think that now, if you want, your life can just keep going on and on."

"Except Mary doesn't want hers to," I said.

"No," he answered somberly. "She doesn't."

"Everyone is pretty worried about you."

"I know," he said, dropping his shoulders with a little sigh, as if the burden of other people's worries had exhausted him. "What do they think I'll do? . . . Kill myself?"

I measured his words carefully, weighing the seriousness with which he'd uttered them. Ableson had stopped aging (or so it seemed) and so had escaped death entirely, and to hear his flirtation with suicide shocked me, though given his position I recognized its logic. If Mary wouldn't choose life, Ableson had one last recourse, which was to choose death. Would it even be a suicide then? Or would it be a resumption of the natural order? A return to life as it should be lived. He must've read concern across my face because he was quick to say, "How could I do that? Think of what I've put myself through to live."

"Why don't you come home?" I asked.

Ableson didn't answer, but instead placed his palm on the smooth reverse side of his headstone. "Right here," he said. "This is where they'll etch Mary's name. We've already arranged to share this plot. I'm on the front of the headstone, she's on the back." He gazed down the ridge, to the backs of the other headstones, where here and there a married couple had been lain together to rest. "What do we do now? Should they stack her coffin on top of my empty one? Am I supposed to visit her like that?"

I told him that I wasn't sure.

"I didn't think coming back would be like this," he said. "I thought the world would have changed more, that it'd be different."

"Different how? Like science fiction different?"

He laughed. "Maybe. The thing of it is you can have more than one life, but there's only this one world to live it in."

I thought to mention that this was perhaps why Mary had chosen to make a separate set of choices than his, but the observation felt obvious. Ableson knew his wife. He knew her reasons for allowing the disease to overtake her. Had he known at the outset what it would be like to return to a time that was no longer his own, he would have anticipated that Mary wouldn't follow him. He had believed the world would either be the same or radically different. He wasn't prepared for this tyranny of incremental differences.

He asked if I'd heard any more news about the Virginia Monument.

"Only that the records office has invalidated most of the signatures," I answered. "Looks like they'll annul the entire petition."

He seemed pleased by the news. "Who'd you hear that from?"

"My ex-wife, who you met."

"Ginny," he said, as if proud that he could recall her name. "And how is she?"

"Fine," I said. "A big admirer of yours. She was asking me something about you, something I didn't quite know how to answer."

"Which is?"

"She didn't understand your interest in preserving the monument. According to her, it seems"—and I chose my words carefully—"well, counter to so much of your other work."

Ableson crossed his arms and pressed his index finger to his temple as he considered the point. He was gazing northeast, up the Shenandoah Valley, along the path that Lee and his men had marched toward Gettysburg. If he was gazing in the direction of their great battle, his mind seemed to travel backward, over the battles of his own legal career. He must have recognized Ginny's point. By any objective measure, Ableson had been a champion of liberalism, or at least what had passed for liberalism in another era. Time—it now seemed—had conspired to leave him ideologically disenfranchised. His values had not evolved at a rapid enough pace and so he found himself stranded on the shoals of conservatism—or at least this was what Ginny had implied.

"I could have had a grave at Arlington," he commented, continuing to stare off into the valley. "My service in the war qualified me for one. The plot they offered was ideal, in a prominent part of the cemetery, not too far from Section 16." He glanced back at me as if to gauge whether I knew the special significance of this section—which I did not—and he disappointedly turned away. "That's the section for Confederate war dead. There's 482 of them buried there. You know the story of Arlington, of course." I did but this didn't stop Ableson from recounting it, how the land was originally owned by the grandson of George Washington, who was in turn the grandfather of Robert E. Lee's wife, Mary Custis. The white porticoed house that still stands at Arlington, and which bore a striking resemblance to Halcyon, is named the Custis-Lee Mansion. If you look out from its front porch across the Potomac River you can see the Capitol dome, which remained under construction in 1864, the war's third year. By then, the cemeteries in Washington overflowed with dead. The government needed more space and they charged the quartermaster general of the Union army, General Montgomery C. Meigs, with finding it. Meigs, who was mourning the battlefield death of his own son, twenty-two-year-old John, appropriated the land around the Custis-Lee Mansion for the new cemetery. Specifically, he chose Mary Custis Lee's rose garden as the site to bury the first bodies, so she could never return home. "A hundred and fifty years later," said Ableson, "and you can still feel the perfect enmity of that gesture. How do we then go from burying our dead children in each other's gardens to honoring Confederate soldiers with an internment at Arlington?"

This part of the story I also knew and taught in my course at

Virginia College. Thirty-seven years would pass until, in 1901, the U.S. government would exhume the graves of Confederate war dead and inter them at Arlington. The reason was national reconciliation in the wake of the Spanish-American War. Only blood can wash away blood and the United States, North and South, inspired by a new grievance, had come together to form a fist. When the dead returned from that war many also found their resting place at Arlington. Among those dead were African American soldiers and they too had a place at Arlington, though not in Mary Custis Lee's rose garden, nor in the centrally located environs of the newly dedicated Section 16. Their segregated acreage was in an isolated corner, less visited, and on low ground that in heavy rains collected runoff and remained sodden for weeks. All it took was a minor skirmish like the Spanish-American War to create the political impetus for Confederate and Union soldiers to reconcile within Arlington, while for African American soldiers it would take another fifty years and something far larger than a Caribbean quarrel; it would take a world war for the dead—of all races—to finally mingle within Arlington's sacred soil.

"Do you know what pattern the graves of the Confederate dead are arrayed in at Arlington?" Ableson asked.

I had to confess, I did not.

"The other graves in the cemetery are laid out in rows, easy to elongate," he said. "The Confederate dead are arranged in concentric circles. They're set up that way so you can't add any more graves. Someone like Ginny looks at me—at the cases I've tried, at the causes I've championed—and she can't understand why I would want to preserve the Virginia Monument. She probably believes that I should be leading the protest myself, shouting 'Burn, baby, burn' with the rest of them. But tearing down monuments isn't too many steps removed from digging up graves. I know better than most what happens when you bring up the dead—they find their place again among the living."

It was Ableson's place among the living that had come to concern me. He couldn't stay here, loitering in Oak Ridge Cemetery. He would need to return to Halcyon. What awaited him there wasn't only Mary's disease; there was also the threat made by Janet Templeton, that she was done "keeping her mouth shut," whatever that meant. This was hardly an opportune time to raise the issue, but I didn't know when I'd have another moment alone with Ableson.

"There's something else," I said. "The annulment of the petition has made you some new enemies. One of them is Susan Templeton's daughter, Janet." I paused a beat. What did that name mean to him? I hoped he might say but didn't. So I added, "She's making threats."

"What kind of threats?"

"She said she's done keeping her mouth shut."

"About what?"

"I thought you might know."

"I have no idea," said Ableson.

His disavowal did nothing to ease my anxiety; actually, it had quite the opposite effect. Ableson was likely unaware of his transgression, which would make it all the more difficult for him to mount a defense. Janet Templeton was coming for him, of this I felt certain. Right now, I needed to get Ableson home and said as much.

"You're right," he answered. "Let's go. No doubt Mary's worried."

But before leaving, Ableson bent over. He fussed about in the grass near his and Mary's shared plot. He was stamping around, searching for something. Then he stopped. Whatever it was that he'd found, he was clutching it in his hand as he stood. As we left the cemetery, I saw what it was. He had placed a single dark pebble on top of his headstone.

FIVE

ACCUSATION

Here is the story Janet Templeton told:

Her mother, a single woman with no support, worked tirelessly on Robert Ableson's behalf. Why? Because she had no other options. Susan Templeton's first husband (a man Janet never referred to as her father because he had not once fulfilled that role) proved a physically abusive drunk who gave Susan little choice but to leave before her daughter was born. Yes, it was true that Ableson had first seen Susan in a courtroom arguing her own child custody case before a judge; and it was equally true that based on her performance and despite her lack of experience, Ableson had offered Susan a job. What wasn't true—and had never been true, at least according to Janet—was that Ableson had offered his mother this job with wholly altruistic motives. According to Janet, Ableson's motive that day adhered to what his motive was in every aspect of his life, from his law practice, to his friendships, to his family: flagrant self-interest.

Hiring Susan Templeton over any number of college-educated pre-law applicants proved a shrewd choice because unlike these upwardly mobile young people, Susan had nowhere else to go. Her resume wasn't just thin; it was nonexistent. As such, Ableson could exert more control over her. He would have both a reliable and a reliant assistant. Susan would need him for everything. And so, Janet's mother became indentured to her boss. Regular hours soon turned to overtime hours. Overtime then became double time. And this became normal. What could Susan do? She had no degree, no other options. Many of their cases were for upstanding causes, important causes. Ableson consistently argued in front of the Supreme Court of Virginia, and for the decade she worked for him, Susan Templeton sat in the first row, ever at the ready.

It was easy for Ableson to justify the relentless pace of their work. The cases they'd taken on demanded no less of a commitment from their champions. As he racked up victories in the major courts, rumors swirled that one day he might contend for a position sitting on the bench at the state supreme court, the D.C. Court of Appeals, or even the Supreme Court itself. And as Ableson's stature grew, so too did Susan Templeton's. Among his colleagues and those who argued cases against him, Susan's contribution to Ableson's victories could hardly be ignored. Some murmured that she was his secret weapon. A certain type of prominent individual might feel threatened by having their successes attributed—even in part—to a subordinate. Not Ableson. Janet Templeton did concede that Ableson had always amply credited her mother. Sharing credit wasn't Ableson's weakness. His great, even tragic weakness was that he wanted too much, not only for himself but for those closest to him. Which included Susan Templeton.

On those many nights when he'd ask Susan Templeton to drop off a critical document at Halcyon or help him develop a possible line of argument for trial the next day, he had no idea that her daughter waited in the parked car out front. Gradually, however, Ableson began to detect a certain sloppiness in Susan's work. She seemed increasingly distracted, scatterbrained. Although Susan insisted she was fine, Ableson suspected a latent discontent. Of course, Ableson never thought to solve this problem by reducing her hours. He assumed her dedication to their work was tantamount to his and that she might even be offended by such a suggestion. No, when conducting his own cursory audit of Susan

Templeton's life, Ableson determined that loneliness was her problem. She didn't need less hours, or fewer personal commitments. What she needed was more. What she needed was companionship, a husband. Assiduously, Ableson set himself to the task. As a partner in one of the most distinguished law firms in Richmond, he was well positioned to find Susan a match who was her equal. Countless young men of promise and ambition cycled in and out of Ableson's office each day. Ableson had only to pick the best of the lot.

His name was Patrick O'Toole. Raven-haired with high cheekbones and stark blue eyes, he spoke in rapid-fire cadence and his mind seemed to work twice as fast. He was rail thin, even though his appetite was enormous. At the first of his working lunches with Ableson he had ordered three full courses plus coffee, stretching their meeting into a second hour. He wore baggy designer suits, the cut and quality of which Ableson admired, even if he didn't admire the fit. Which was how he generally felt about O'Toole. He was a corporate client, an executive at a pharmaceutical company that the state government had allegedly shorted millions of dollars on an unfulfilled contract. O'Toole had hired Ableson to recoup the losses. These lucrative cases funded the pro bono crusades that took Ableson in front of the higher courts, where he burnished his name and legal reputation, while increasingly he resented his mercenary corporate work.

O'Toole's case and the promised settlement would net Ableson's law firm hundreds of thousands and perhaps millions of dollars in fees. After Ableson's first interminable lunch with O'Toole, he pawned the second off on Susan. The two of them met downtown at the Roosevelt and in characteristic fashion O'Toole ordered amply for them both. Susan had been warned about his manners but, despite Ableson's warning, she found O'Toole charming. He was smart, quick-witted, and fearlessly funny. Susan had a series of complex documents they needed to review, a paper trail that showed fraudulent intent on the part of the state and included whole binders filled with runic bank statements. She thought it'd take the entirety of their lunch for O'Toole to grasp the matter; not so, they were done by the time the waiter had cleared their salads. This left the two of them to their meal. The more they spoke the more Susan felt at ease with O'Toole, even drawn to him. He came from nothing, less than nothing really. Raised by an aunt, he had put himself through school with odd jobs and later scholarships and had, relatively recently, found his way into the lucrative field of pharmaceuticals. He called it the "pill industry" after a second glass of lunchtime wine and explained that it was enjoying a boon of deregulation under the current president, who then was Reagan. By the end of lunch, O'Toole had asked Susan Templeton to dinner the following night. She said she'd think about it.

His stark, even cold blue eyes reminded Susan of Janet's father. Years later, she would admit this to her daughter when trying to describe the nature of her initial attraction to O'Toole, how she'd felt both drawn toward him and repulsed by him. She was thinking of O'Toole and her contradictory feelings as she returned to the office that same afternoon. As soon as she stepped through the door, Ableson had asked her over to his desk. A phone call from O'Toole had preceded her back to work. He had confessed to Ableson about having asked Susan to dinner. He'd apologized, recognizing the inappropriateness of the invitation given the professional nature of the relationship. The phone call had surprised Ableson, or so he had explained to Susan. His surprise wasn't that O'Toole had asked Susan to dinner, but rather that he'd called to apologize. Ableson said, "Perhaps I was wrong. Manners like that speak very well for a man of his upbringing." Susan didn't appreciate the backhanded compliment. She and O'Toole had similar upbringings, except Ableson had stopped seeing her as a product of her circumstances long ago. She might have readily accepted O'Toole's dinner invitation, but what held her back was how O'Toole felt sinisterly familiar. If she had had to pinpoint her reservation, she would have concluded it was something about those eyes of his.

Then Ableson had said, "Why not go out with him?"

To which Susan had replied, "Are you saying I should?"

Ableson's response, down to the specific words he used, would come under intense scrutiny in the years ahead and would form the crux of Janet Templeton's argument against him. After a long pause, he had said: "I would be disappointed if you didn't."

At this point could Susan Templeton really answer no? Given the power disparity between them, Ableson's disappointment might have come at great cost to Susan considering her reliance on him and what she perceived as his generosity. One might even say that the prospect of Ableson's disappointment was akin to a threat. This would be the argument Janet Templeton chose to make a decade and a half later on her mother's behalf. Susan's response to Ableson proved equally telling, as her choice of words revealed her lack of agency, and those words would prove crucial to the argument leveled against him. In response, Susan had said: "Then I guess I'll be seeing him for dinner."

With the above exchange, the decision was made. Susan accepted O'Toole's invitation and the two spent a pleasant evening together. They ate by candlelight on fresh white linens at a back-corner table of a restaurant where O'Toole knew the maître d' (or at least expressed a familiarity with him designed to impress his date). They hardly spoke about work, but rather shared abridged stories of their lives, which were equally characterized by adversity and their ability through good luck and hard work to overcome it. After the waiter cleared their entrees, Susan began to nervously twirl her dessert spoon in her fingers. O'Toole reached across the table and placed his hand gently on hers to steady it. When he walked her to the front door of her small, neat shoebox of a house built close enough to the other houses to hear their washing machines, flushing toilets, and conversations, he didn't ask to be let in, neither did he linger long enough for her to offer. He kissed her on the cheek and simply went on his way. The following day at the office, Ableson knew not to ask about the evening and for this Susan was grateful. She would see O'Toole that weekend and over the space of the three days until then she believed that perhaps for the second time in her life her fortunes were changing.

That weekend it was an afternoon movie and a stroll along the James River. The next week it was another lunch and then on Friday another dinner. They hardly spoke about work, or much about family either. They kept their conversation light, which is what they both needed; or, what Susan had told herself they both needed. Neither was old in terms of age, but experience beyond their years was part of their kinship, even if neither knew the gritty specifics of that experience. At the end of the afternoon or evening, when their time together had finished, O'Toole would walk her up to her front door, place his kiss on her cheek, and go on his way. His patience astounded her. A certain woman might have interpreted it as a lack of interest, or an emasculate timidity. However, Susan knew it was O'Toole's way of acknowledging her situation and respecting the child who lived on the other side of that door. Not surprisingly, his restraint served as an accelerant to her affections.

Susan now wanted to find a way for the two of them to be alone. He wouldn't be so forward as to invite her to his place, at least not yet, so the problem fell to her. Two weeks into their relationship she was making arrangements: a babysitter who would stay late and the excuse of an early morning meeting to get him out of the house before Janet woke up. On the planned night, she took his hand as he kissed her at the door and she didn't let it go. When he followed her inside, the house was dim lit and quiet. When Susan went to pay the babysitter, O'Toole interfered and paid cash from his pocket. She turned on a single lamp in her bedroom and in the shabby light she undressed him. Soon she lay naked beside him on the bed. He asked that they slip beneath the covers. Which they did, and—limb-tangled and awkward—locked their bodies together. When they'd finished they both lay apart, silent from their unconvincing sex. She reached to switch off the lamp, but he asked that she leave it on. "It helps me sleep," he said. Unquestioningly, she'd obliged him. She put her fingers through his black hair. His polite, lightly sweating face offered a despairing smile that she struggled to interpret. Then he turned on his side, so that his back faced her. He slept this way through the night.

They were scheduled for dinner two nights later, which he cancelled and rescheduled for lunch the day after. His corporate bank statements came to her as part of his case and she had noticed their meals together were charged to the account. When she raised this with him at lunch, he grew uncommonly defensive. He asked for their check as their entrees were served and didn't finish his food, sulking over his plate like a child. When Susan returned to the office, she reluctantly mentioned the statements to Ableson. He responded with a shrug and instructions for her to "Look into it," which she promptly did. What she found was a first account, tied to a second, a second tied to a third and then to a fourth. Each account was leveraged against another, forming a daisy chain of revolving credit that existed around a nonexistent asset pool. The next day she took this information to Ableson. As she walked him through it, he turned increasingly pale. Susan would learn that he had accepted equity in O'Toole's pharmaceutical company as remittance for legal fees. The optics on this weren't good. Susan stayed into the night peeling back each layer of O'Toole's finances until Ableson said he'd seen enough. The next day he didn't come into the office.

That following evening, after returning from work, there was a ring at Susan's door. She was inside with her daughter, and when she answered it was O'Toole. He stood on her stoop in jeans and a pullover. It was the first time she had seen him out of a suit. He seemed diminished. "Mind if I come in?" he asked. Before Susan could answer, he'd stepped over the threshold. His gaze roamed the walls as if viewing her modest bungalow for the first time, which in a way he was, having only snuck in and out once before on the night of their disappointing sex. "We need to talk," he said. The two of them sat on the sofa, but as they did Susan glanced toward the back of the house, where Janet watched cartoons in another room. "That your daughter back there?" asked O'Toole. Susan nodded. "Maybe you'll introduce me later?" An awkward silence descended but Susan knew it wasn't hers to fill. His blue eyes fell on her very intensely and with a determination that terrified her. "Could we talk in your room?" he asked.

Susan said she'd rather they stay in the living room, where she could hear her daughter. "All right," he said. "Wherever you like." Then he reached for her, thrusting one hand between her legs and the other to the back of her neck.

"What are you doing!"

When she'd seen him at her front door, she thought he would give her some excuse about his troubled expenses, some muddled explanation of how it all added up, was legitimate, or at least not his fault; she thought he might be angry that she'd gone directly to Ableson; she had expected an argument, not this. But, of course, this was what she should have expected. O'Toole and Ableson had already had whatever conversation they were going to have, the resolution of which she didn't know as she desperately pulled away on the couch. What he wanted and why he'd come here was to take something from her before he disappeared.

"You wanted it here, in the living room, right . . . ?" he said through his breaths. "So let's do it here." She had by now crawled to the far corner of the sofa. He was still pushing against her, so much so that her shoulders brushed up against a lamp balanced on the end table. It tottered and then crashed to the floor. He glanced up at the noise, exposing his chin. Which she took the opportunity to smack. She struck him close-fisted and hard, hard enough to elicit his involuntary whimper. He looked back at her with eyes as wide as portals. "Cunt!" and he struck her back.

"Mom?"

The little girl with glasses stood behind the sofa, the sound of cartoons coming from the open door, a daze in her soft voice.

A reflexive sob escaped Susan, one that she quickly stifled. "Go back to your room," she said. But her daughter stood there, glowering at O'Toole. He gathered himself up, hunched over as if gut-shot, clasping his open waistband and the end of his belt. He shambled toward the front door, the cuffs of his jeans tangling on the heels of his shoes. He left as abruptly as he'd arrived. Whatever he'd come to take from Susan, he would leave without it (or without all of it). When Susan glanced once more at her daughter, she could see that it was her gaze that was driving O'Toole away, a gaze that in its blue-eyed coldness exceeded his own.

This was Janet Templeton's story. It arrived via process server in the form of a workplace sexual harassment complaint against Ableson. I didn't learn about this complaint from him, or from Boose. I learned about it from his stepsons, Doug and Bobby, who arrived on my front porch to discuss the matter. I promptly invited the two of them inside and, for a moment, a sense of foreboding overcame me. The only reason I could imagine for their visit was that Mary's health had taken another sharp decline. This was why I couldn't help but feel relieved when they explained their visit had to do with this complaint and not their mother.

Bobby noticed my relief. "You don't seem particularly concerned."

Before I could answer, his brother Doug added: "This complaint could have major implications for our family." I was now presented with a potentially disastrous chain of events. In submitting her lawsuit, Janet Templeton had also filed a claim against Ableson's assets. This begged the question of what composed those assets. On his death, Ableson had through his will transferred sums in various bank accounts to his heirs and had transferred the deed for Halcyon to his wife. However, if he was no longer dead (he had, after all, had his death certificate annulled) ownership of those assets would forcibly revert back to him. As such, Janet could lay a claim against those inherited funds that currently sat in his children's bank accounts when filing for damages.

"He's retained a lawyer," Bobby explained.

"Who is it?" I asked.

Doug reached into his pocket and removed a business card. "He told us that you knew her. He said that you put the two of them in touch." Of course, it was Ginny. "We're trying to convince him to settle," Doug continued. "What does he gain from fighting this thing out?"

"And he's got plenty to lose," interjected Bobby. "We all do," and I could only surmise he was referring to his own assets as well.

"What do you want me to do?" I asked.

"We need this lawyer on our side," said Doug.

To which his brother added, "See if you can talk some sense into her."

If they had known what a poor record I had when it came to talking sense into Ginny, they likely wouldn't have entrusted me with the task. Still, I assured them that I would try.

I could have picked up the phone to call her, but I thought that was doomed to failure. This was a conversation best had in person. I reached her assistant, who put me on her schedule for the next afternoon. That morning I drove north to Philadelphia. Unlike my last trip, when we'd had drinks at the Four Seasons, this would be a more formal meeting in her office. In the years since our divorce, her firm had moved into a new building off

Rittenhouse Square, bigger and taller than the one it had occupied before, all made of glass and as bright and greedy-looking as the people who spun through its revolving doors. Four security guards sat at a raised desk inside the multistoried vestibule. They took my picture, handed me a temporary badge, and directed me to an elevator that ran silently up to the twenty-seventh floor, the majority of which was now occupied by Ginny and her partners.

We didn't meet in her office, as I expected we might, but rather in an anodyne conference room. I was standing by a picture window, admiring the view of both the Schuylkill River and a ribbon of haze that suggested the Atlantic beyond, when she stepped inside, cradling a notepad and clutching a cup of coffee. Knowing her, this was likely her fifth or sixth of the day. I was wearing a wool sweater beneath a corduroy sports coat and chinos, and I felt sloppy next tò Ginny, who was in a sharp gray skirt, white blouse, and matching jacket with heels that seemed as if they'd been designed to step on your throat. She looked the part of a high-powered attorney, and I looked my part: that of a disheveled professor.

"Seems your friend Robert Ableson is in a bit of trouble," she said. Tucked under one arm was a sheaf of documents. I could only assume these were the particulars of the case against him.

"Seems he's asked for your help," I answered.

She took a seat at the head of the conference table and gestured for me to sit beside her. One by one she placed the documents in front of us, stopping to explain each like a fortune-teller dealing a deck of Tarot cards. First was the complaint, which outlined Janet Templeton's story, the one that included O'Toole's assault against her mother and Ableson's role in introducing them and, according to Janet, the inappropriate way Ableson had pressured her mother into a romantic relationship with a client. However, it wasn't this incident alone in the complaint. The charge against Ableson was "ongoing harassment" to include his interference with

Susan Templeton's petition. When I raised the issue of statute of limitations, Ginny was ready. She removed a copy of Title VII of the Civil Rights Act of 1964. Several pages into the document, she came to the Enforcement Provisions section, with the following highlighted: "liability may accrue and an aggrieved person may obtain relief as provided." Accrued liability. In what amount I wondered? Ginny placed on the table the deed to Halcyon, which was in Mary's name. Then came the statements of several since-liquidated bank accounts with amounts transferred to Doug and Bobby, but with the most significant balances having been trans-ferred to Boose. My stomach sank when I read the figures. These weren't modest sums but vast ones. Millions of dollars. Susan Templeton's claim was to a portion of that wealth.

"Where did he get all this money?" I asked.

"Corporate clients. Large settlements. Prudent investing. It's not uncommon for certain types of lawyers to earn like this." She spoke to me gently, as if I were a child who needed to give up an imaginary friend. "He was twice under consideration for an appointment to the D.C. Court of Appeals, under both Republi-can and Democratic administrations. He didn't make it through their vetting either time, withdrawing his own name instead. What does that tell you? This issue with O'Toole isn't the only issue. Your friend Ableson has got a past."

"We've all got a past."

"Some of us more than others," she said without elaboration, and so I thought she might be referring to a fault of mine from our marriage. If I needed any reminder that she was my ex-wife, she delivered it through this remark and the ensuing silence. For a moment the old bitterness returned. But I swallowed it, refocusing on the task at hand, which was Ableson. When I asked how much Janet Templeton was demanding on her mother's behalf, Ginny placed a terms sheet in front of me. She had received it the day before from opposing counsel. The amount on the sheet exceeded the amount in the accounts. "This is ridiculous," I said. "How did she come to that number?"

What followed was a laborious cataloguing of setbacks and difficulties endured by Janet Templeton and her mother. If theirs was a universe of grievance, its point of inception was the moment Ableson had introduced O'Toole into their lives. In the years since, Janet had suffered crippling anxiety associated with the day she'd discovered her mother struggling against O'Toole on the couch. This had led to years of therapy, in which she had to deconstruct and reconstruct that moment ad nauseam in an effort to purge it from her consciousness; a task she had never entirely succeeded at according to the affidavit of a therapist included in the complaint. The episode with O'Toole had also degraded her relationship with her mother, eroding the trust between parent and child, which led her into an adolescence in which she trusted many of the wrong people, who led her to the wrong parties, into the wrong beds, and onto the wrong drugs. In short, Ableson and O'Toole had robbed her of a fully realized self. That self, whoever it might have been, lurked between the lines of text in the complaint.

I told Ginny that I still didn't understand how Janet Templeton could credibly claim such stratospheric damages on her mother's behalf. If awarded all she asked for, she'd bankrupt Ableson, repossess his house, and strip his children of their inheritance. Ginny agreed. The amount was ridiculous and the case overreaching, but she feared that Janet Templeton had other aims. "Her strategy isn't necessarily to win all she's asking for," said Ginny. "It's to get a judge to acknowledge that Ableson's will is no longer valid. If she does that, his assets revert back to him. And by reverting back to him, they're transferred away from his children."

"For how long?"

"Until he dies, I guess."

Therein lay both the cruelty and the genius of Janet Templeton's plan. So long as Ableson walked the earth, she would rob his children of the inheritance all three had built lives upon. He had wanted to live as an emissary of the past, inserting himself into a present that was not his own. He could still do this, but only at an enormous cost, one that would cripple his children financially if they had to pay back money already spent. Wasn't there a way for Ableson to better protect these assets? Perhaps instead of classifying this wealth as *inheritance* he could transfer it as a *gift* to his children? Ginny had already done the back-of-the-envelope math. Federal and state gift taxes whittled the sum into near extinction. Inheritance was the key. And there could be no inheritance without death. So just as Ableson had robbed Janet of her life, she would either rob him of this new one or force him to live it on her terms, with his heirs indebted and his assets tangled up by his own stubborn existence.

"And why?" I asked. "Why is she doing this now?" Emotion constricted my voice, surprising me. The source of that emotion wasn't love of Ableson, though I admired him and considered him a friend, but that this all seemed so impossibly unfair.

"Do you remember how they cheered Susan at the records office?" said Ginny. "You were in that crowd. That was *her* day. She had waited so long—a lifetime, really—and at last they were recognizing *her*. When Ableson swept in and invalidated that petition, he robbed Susan of her moment. This isn't about a monument, or the Civil War, or Lee, or Longstreet. This is about time and who owns it."

The door to the conference room swung open, interrupting us. It was Daryl. He apologized but had several urgent documents that the other partners needed Ginny to sign. He removed them from an overstuffed folder clutched awkwardly to his chest, placing them in front of her. Silently, she reviewed them. Big, dumb Daryl as I couldn't help but think of him stood vigilantly beside her. When our gazes met, he wore a fixed and vulnerable smile. He rocked back and forth on his heels good-naturedly. When Ginny finished signing the documents, she handed them back to Daryl followed by a curt set of instructions as to where they needed to be routed. He had a look of high moral injury as he scribbled those instructions into a notepad so as not to forget them. He again apologized for interrupting us and went on his way.

Daryl's interruption allowed me to ask Ginny what up to this point hadn't made sense. She had said the complaint against Ableson was really about time and who owns it. If so, then why was she defending him against Janet Templeton. "Doesn't he represent everything you're against?"

"C'mon," said Ginny. "You know me better than that." She leaned back in her chair, clasping her hands behind her head like a boss. "You really think I want to live like Janet Templeton, parsing who did what to me and when, and how come that means I can never achieve x or become y, trapped in an endless feedback loop of my own trauma? That's not progress." She came out of her seat, stepping toward the window. She glanced below her to the grid of traffic and then outward to the river, toward the Atlantic, and into a mirage of haze on the horizon. She stood transfixed, as if the view existed for her alone. "Still, Robert should've known better than to insist Susan go out with that creep."

"His stepsons want to settle."

"You think I don't know that?" she said. "And I'd settle this if I could, but this case isn't only about money. What O'Toole did was criminal. That Janet had to witness it as a little girl makes it doubly so. But what Janet wants isn't justice; it's revenge. She wants to destroy Robert Ableson, to wipe him from the earth. She's not going to settle, no matter what we offer. So it's best not to offer anything."

"What happens now?" I eventually asked.

Slowly, she paced back to the desk. She consulted her calendar. "A preliminary hearing with the court is scheduled for the end of next month. We need the judge to acknowledge our motion on the validity of Ableson's will. If the judge does that, Janet Templeton won't have any claim on the assets that have already transferred to his heirs. Then we could likely register a motion to dismiss the case."

"And if the judge rules against us and invalidates Ableson's will?"

"Then all bets are off," said Ginny. "We'll be slogging it out about who said what to Susan Templeton almost twenty years ago, parsing every word."

"What do you think our odds are?"

"Examining only the facts, I'd say fifty-fifty. But it's really a bit higher."

"How come?"

"Because I'm a damn good lawyer," she said. "That's how come." When I offered her a sidelong glance, she added, "You should know that from personal experience." She then checked her watch. One by one she gathered up the papers. I shuddered to think of her billable hourly rate and asked if someone in her office could validate my parking. She gestured vaguely toward a pool of cubicles where Daryl and the other associates kept their desks.

I pulled out of the subterranean lot beneath Ginny's building and into a thick wall of traffic. Rush hour had begun and my progress through the city was maddeningly slow. I was reaching the conclusion that it might make more sense to park and get an early dinner when I realized that I was only a couple of blocks from Dr. Shields's office. I had no idea if he was in, or if he had time to see me, but I decided to stop by on the off chance. When I phoned from the lobby, he said he'd come right down. The idea of an early dinner also appealed to him and he suggested a greasy spoon diner around the corner. We took up our positions in a two-person booth and ordered.

"What brought you up here?" he asked as the waiter gathered our menus.

I explained the nature of the complaint against Ableson, which he was already familiar with. I also explained how Doug and Bobby had approached me, hoping I might convince his lawyer to settle the case. "What'd she say?" he asked, and I explained Ginny's theory about how Janet Templeton really didn't care about the money so much as destroying Ableson's legacy. She wouldn't settle and so it was best not to offer. This logic made sense to Dr. Shields, who added, "Even if this Templeton woman wanted to settle, I doubt Robert would go for it. On principle alone, he'd fight out the case. Not that it would be the smartest thing. But in his eyes, it would be the right thing, seeing as he's done nothing wrong."

"Do you believe that?" I asked. "That he's done nothing wrong."

We'd each ordered cups of vegetable soup, which our waiter now placed in front of us. "This isn't the first time something like this has come up," Dr. Shields said after blowing ripples across the surface of his soup. "Robert's got a history of getting in over his head with clients. I'm not just talking about O'Toole. Robert has never been very good when it comes to boundaries. Clients would pay him in preferred stock, in real estate; he knew better but couldn't resist. His pro bono work always meant his other work had to pay, to say nothing of the cost of Halcyon's upkeep. But this mess doesn't invalidate everything he's built over a lifetime. It doesn't mean you should target his children's inheritance." Dr. Shields took a sip of his soup. He grimaced; it was still too hot.

He asked why Doug and Bobby had wanted me to talk to the lawyer.

"She's my ex-wife," I said.

Dr. Shields laughed into his cup, apologizing as he wiped a few drops of spilt soup off the table with a napkin.

"It's all right," I said. "I'd laugh too." I mentioned Ginny's admiration of Ableson and described their meeting in Richmond when she'd given him her business card. Her admiration was probably why Ableson retained her. He needed someone who revered his history because it was his history that would be on trial. I told Dr. Shields about the upcoming preliminary hearing and the better-than-even odds that Ginny had placed on the case.

As I spoke, Dr. Shields drew his mouth to one side and began to slowly shake his head. "Is Robert perfect?" he asked. "No. But he's lived a life worth defending. If only he hadn't come back. I should've figured a way to talk him out of it."

"This isn't your fault," I said.

"No," he answered. "It isn't entirely. But it is partially; and that's enough. Let's say Robert loses this case. Let's say this Janet Templeton woman succeeds in robbing the Ableson children of their inheritance—and for what? Because Robert outsmarted her mother when she wanted to help tear down a monument? If that happens, then bringing him back will mean that he's had to witness his legacy stolen and also his wife's death. Is watching everything you care about destroyed really a life?"

In the time it took me to swallow my mouthful of briny soup I had concluded that, yes, watching everything you care about destroyed is in fact the very definition of a life—at least any long one. Tempted though I was to register this point, silence seemed better. The waiter cleared our cups and brought out our dinners. The more Dr. Shields spoke the more distraught he became. His gnawing guilt about Ableson was like that felt by a parent—any parent, really—who by granting life is to a degree forever culpable for whatever pain their child endures.

"When Mary's gone, who's going to look after him?" asked Dr. Shields. "Doug and Bobby have their own families. Boose might do it for a while, but she's a young woman. How long can her father expect her to remain at Halcyon?" Caring for an elderly parent was hardly a unique challenge. Surely Ableson's children could figure this out. When I gave voice to that view, Dr. Shields explained that it wasn't so simple. Time affected Ableson differently. "Cryoregeneration dramatically slows the aging process," said Dr. Shields. "Robert will likely outlive us all."

We finished the rest of our meal. If Ableson's future possessed a terrifying lack of definition, Mary's could be plotted nearly to the day. Dr. Shields gave her six to eight weeks and could describe with morbid precision the glide slope of her deterioration. He measured out enough detail to reinforce his broader point, which was "it's good you'll be around to help."

"It would seem I've wandered into the deep end with the Ablesons," and as I said this, I wasn't entirely sure how I'd got there, to say nothing of how I'd get back.

Outside, the traffic had thinned. With summer's onset, the days were stretching. Long shadows toppled from the buildings into the street, mingling with golden evening light. I still had a long distance to drive and neither of us had an appetite for dessert. The waiter tore our check from his pad. When I reached into my pocket to pay, I realized that I'd forgotten my wallet in the car. Dr. Shields insisted that I not worry about it and that he would cover the bill.

The return drive extended deep into the hours of darkness. The radio kept me company. The election was on the news again. Gore's poll numbers had continued to slip through the end of spring. Speculation had begun about a contested Democratic convention later that summer. The stakes in the fall were too high to run a weak candidate. Certain pundits evoked the Carter versus Kennedy primary of 1980 and its calamitous result, concluding that this was the time for party unity. While others opined that too much talent existed within the party for Gore to run a weak second-term campaign. The program then mentioned a senatorial candidate in Illinois who was surging, breaking fundraising records. His potential was national and so too were his ambitions. The Democrats had already invited him to speak at their convention. To shore up Gore's candidacy, former president Clinton had taken it upon himself to grant a series of media interviews. He defended his successor's decision to pardon him. He played down his own perjury conviction. When Ms. Lewinsky's name came up, he evaded, and when cornered he went so far as to insinuate that their relationship had been consensual. The result of Clinton's ad-libbed interviews proved predictably disastrous, leading to Gore's single largest drop in the polls. All the while the Republicans, it seemed, were coalescing around a second candidacy for George W. Bush. After all, he had come so close before.

It was a little after midnight as I crossed the state line into Virginia. My fuel gauge hovered near empty as I exited into a service center off the interstate. When I pulled up to the pump, I left the passenger-side window down so I could keep listening to the radio. Standing beneath the umbrellaed glare of the arc lights, I heard how Bush was gaining ground. As the program segued to commercial, the teaser for the next segment promised to outline what his presidency might entail, to include a first hundred days agenda with expansions in defense spending and cuts in everything from taxes to scientific research. When the program returned, I wondered whether it would mention cryoregeneration. Maybe the pundits could shed some light on what the future held for Ableson.

A black pickup truck on lifts with tires the size of hay bales parked beside me at the pump, bass woofing from its sound system. I noticed a Virginia College parking sticker on the windshield. When its door swung open, a carpet of cannabinoid smoke tumbled to the ground. A redheaded boy, lank and twentyish, slid out of the driver's seat. He planted his foot on the running boards and two-stepped onto the asphalt. In the passenger seat sat a blond girl, her cheeks dusted with freckles and her head slung backward, passed out. The boy ambled around the tailgate, bobbing his head to his migraine-inducing techno music. He took the gas pump off its handle and stuck it in his truck. He left it fueling as he shuffled into the adjacent mini-mart. He also left the door to his truck open, and with his music pouring out of it I could no longer hear my radio program. I needed a coffee if I was going to finish my drive, so I followed him.

The mini-mart attendant, an elderly, moon-faced man with a bulbous, age-ravaged nose, sat behind the counter, paging through a gossip magazine he'd taken from the rack beside his register. I wove through the parallel rows of candy, chips, and beef snacks, to a set of twin coffeepots. The redheaded boy was back here too, at the soda fountain. He carried an empty cup from somewhere else. He acknowledged me with an upward tilt of his chin, and then began to fill that cup with Cheerwine, holding his gaze over his shoulder to make sure the attendant didn't glance up from his magazine. He grabbed a 99-cent bag of Fritos and headed for the register. I poured my coffee and waited behind the boy while the attendant rang him up.

"Two twenty-nine," said the attendant with a vowelly accent.

The boy slapped a dollar on the counter.

The attendant repeated the price.

"This says 99 cents." The boy pointed to the bag of chips.

"Soda is one-dollar-twenty-five, plus tax."

The boy shook his cup in the attendant's face. "This soda ain't from here." He pointed at the crumpled dollar on the counter and turned on his heels out the door. "And neither is you," he called from over his shoulder.

The attendant reached for something under the counter— maybe a security alarm? or a lock to the door? or a weapon of some kind? Whatever it was, it didn't matter. The ensuing confrontation wasn't worth one-dollar-twenty-five, plus tax. "I've got it," I said, rifling through my pockets for a fistful of bills and change that I dumped on the counter. The mini-mart door shut with a jangle.

The attendant tracked the boy as he walked across the asphalt toward the gas pumps and his truck. When he turned back to me, his jaw was set and his gaze was wide and consuming. He rang up the price of my coffee and the boy's soda and announced the sum in a depleted whisper. I picked through the loose bills and coins on the counter. "He a friend of yours?" asked the attendant.

I shook my head, no.

"Then why do you pay for him?"

I didn't have an answer, or at least not a good one. I added up what was owed and gathered the rest of my money. By paying I had inadvertently taken something away from the attendant, something he valued far more than the price of a soda: he had wanted to teach the boy a lesson. Perhaps the attendant had planned to lock the boy in the store and call the cops; or, maybe, he had a gun under the counter that he would've held on the boy until he came up with the money. Unwittingly, I had allied myself with the boy and this made me an enemy of the attendant. I hurried out the door.

The boy was holstering the nozzle of the gas pump as I returned to my car. He threw me a long, arching look and I could see as I drew closer that he had something he wanted to say. I half expected he might stop, thank me, and apologize for the minor scene he'd made (of course, this isn't what he did but what did it say about me that despite all evidence to the contrary I would continue to grant him the benefit of the doubt); instead, over his music he said, "You teach at VC, right?" He gestured to the Virginia College parking sticker in the corner of his windshield. Glancing in that direction I couldn't help but notice the girl who remained passed out in the passenger seat. She had begun to stir. "I go there," said the boy. "You do that class on the Civil War."

"That's right. Have you taken my course?"

"Naw, but I hear it's good; that it gets it right if you know what I mean."

I didn't quite know what to say to this.

He continued, "I was at the protest a few weeks back, in Richmond at the records office. You too, right? You're friends with that lawyer guy, ain't you? The one they brought back to life. I read about him in the paper . . . crazy. I hear he's the one who jammed up that petition. He's a good man, that Mr.—" and the boy hesitated for a moment, screwing his eyes up toward the arc lights as if searching there for the name that eluded him.

"Ableson," I said.

"Yeah, Ableson." Increasingly, the boy's voice escaped him in dreamy purrs. He was standing right next to me at the pump and had opened his bag of chips, which he was munching on laconically between sips of Cheerwine. Starbursts of red clouded the otherwise whites of his eyes. The boy muttered to himself, and he touched his mouth with his fingertips. Then, as if still contained within a dream, he began to speak about the protest in Richmond, the monument, and even his own father: ". . . he used to take me out to the Gettysburg battlefield. He'd run me up Little Round Top like it was just him and me coming for Chamberlain and we'd stand on Culp's Hill and he'd tell me about what might have happened if Jackson had been there to take it. He'd go through all the *could'ves* and *would'ves* and *should'ves* . . . You been there, so you know. Memories in that place hang in the air so thick it's like battlefield smoke and you have to breathe different. Story goes an ancestor of mine took a bullet through the chest fighting under Hood's command in the Devil's Den. We'd always finish the day at the Virginia Monument. Dad would take out a fifth of whiskey, have himself a sip, and leave the rest. My tenth birthday he let me join. First time I ever got a little drunk."

The memories of his father and the battlefield had their own narcotic effect, as if he were still getting drunk off them as he spoke. The boy then thanked me for the work I'd done along with Ableson to "preserve our heritage," and as uncomfortable and perplexed as it made me to think that he and I shared a heritage—my people are, after all, Ukrainian Jews who fled Russian pogroms and then a holocaust to come to this country—I nevertheless found myself shaking his hand. I suggested that perhaps I could offer him a ride someplace, that maybe it'd be best if he didn't drive in his condition. The boy glanced at my Volvo and laughed at the prospect of going anywhere in such a car. "Don't worry," he said. "I'm good."

I pointed up to the young woman in the passenger seat. "Is she good?"

The boy grew sober and defensive. "Yeah, she's fine."

He opened the door to his truck. When he climbed inside, the young woman awoke. She blinked like a newborn and gazed vaguely in my direction. Her face was shaped like a cut diamond, wide with high cheekbones at the top and narrowly tapered to her chin. She yawned showing the pink curve of her tongue. When she saw me watching her, she covered her mouth. When she removed her hand, it revealed her smile. She ran her fingers through her hair which fell onto her supple, pale shoulders, each one bare except for the two spaghetti straps of her halter top. The truck's engine turned over and still she kept looking at me in that vague way. Unlike the boy, I didn't consider her an accomplice to her drunkenness but rather a victim of it. Where was he taking her? I imagined a beer-sodden dorm room, a futon pocked with cigarette burns, her pleas for him to stop, and her shame when it was over. By the mini-mart there was a bank of pay phones. I glanced at the truck's license plate, committing it to memory. I imagined myself calling the police, the boy hauled in for DUI, the girl safely returned ...

Her attention shifted away from me and toward the redheaded

boy in the driver's seat. He was explaining something to her. She glanced back in my direction. She raised her hand. I thought for an instant she might be waving me down, pleading for my help. But that wasn't it. Instead, she mouthed the word "creep" and gave me the finger. Then she and the boy sped back onto the interstate.

SIX

INQUIRY

I delivered the news to Doug and Bobby: there would be no settlement. Even if I had convinced Ginny to the contrary, she would have had to convince Ableson. This, I felt certain, was an impossibility. "They're going to fight this thing out," I told the brothers, who arrived on the front porch of the guest cottage the morning after I returned. I had invited them inside but instead they chose to stand on the stoop, again reciting their arguments. That they carried on in this impotent way demonstrated how little influence they had over Ableson. Litigation was inevitable. I didn't know how the brothers would take that news but wasn't surprised the next day when I heard from Boose that they'd chosen to return home to their own families, at least for the time being.

I was now free to focus on my work. When I returned to the attic desk, I struggled to concentrate. It wasn't the Ablesons who preoccupied me, but the incident at the rest stop. I kept thinking of that redheaded boy. Central to the argument in my writing was a conviction that compromise underwrote our society. Without it, we were nothing more than a constellation of warring factions defined by shifting allegiances and ever narrowing self-interests as opposed to any broader, shared set of beliefs and ideals. I thought of the way the boy paid the attendant but not in full. I revisited my decision to pay on the boy's behalf, thus robbing the attendant of his opportunity to teach him a lesson. Did my writings on the virtue of compromise perform a similar function?

Each word I wrote had come to feel like a cent dropped on the attendant's counter to benefit the redheaded boy. He knew about my course on the Civil War, though he had never taken it and never would. His father had already taught him the history; he had taught it to him on the battlefield itself. What did the boy need my class for? History for him wasn't a subject in school but an inheritance. He wanted to see the Virginia Monument preserved not because it was part of history but because it was part of him. How often had I heard it said that America is not a blood-and-soil nation, but a nation founded on an ideal. Was this true for the redheaded boy? At Gettysburg his family's blood was, literally, in the soil.

I was at a loss for answers. Because something existed in the past, did that give it the right to exist in the present . . . ?

There was the girl, too. I had felt so certain about her. Did she wind up as I had imagined, drunk or stoned on a dorm room futon? Perhaps that's what she had wanted, and I was guilty of presumption. I had thought to tell her how to be.

How could I write about the centrality of compromise in American life if I didn't have sufficient answers to even these most basic questions in my own life? For nearly two weeks, I isolated myself in the guest cottage and dutifully tried to find answers through my work but made little headway. It proved a welcome relief when, unexpectedly, Boose arrived on my doorstep. It was midmorning and I'd already taken two breaks when I invited her inside to join me for a third. I poured us both some tea. When she asked about my work, I told her only that it was progressing. When I asked about her mother and the disease, she used that same word, "progressing," and explained the favor she'd come to ask. Mary had an appointment in Philadelphia at the hospital with Dr. Shields later that week. Boose and her father would take her. The appointment, however, conflicted with a pre-existing visit they'd scheduled with a house appraiser. When I asked the purpose of the appraisal ("Are your parents planning to sell?"), she explained that before the preliminary hearing with the judge, her father had to provide a net-worth statement, which needed to include Halcyon's value. "It's just that it's very difficult to book these appraisers ... and this appointment in Philadelphia was kind of last minute ... Doug and Bobby would help but they aren't sure when they can come down ..."

The strain in her voice was obvious. Her life had become a balancing act of commitments. "It's no problem," I said, and topped off her cup of tea.

She raised a smile, but it soon crumbled. "Do you think we'll lose the house?"

"Of course not." My answer was reflexive: I really didn't know.

She looked at me as if gauging the sincerity of my response. "My father used to say once you got in front of a judge that every case was a coin toss. Imagine that, an entire system of justice based on coin tosses. What if we lose? I can't imagine my family without Halcyon. My father bought this house before he'd even met my mother. They've never lived anywhere else. For years, I tried to escape this place. I never wanted to come back, and when I did come to visit I never wanted to stay in the main house. I would insist on having my space in this guest cottage. That used to upset my mother. Looking back that seems very childish of me. The adult decision would've been to sleep in my old room. Odd, isn't it, when the most adult thing a person can do is sleep in the room where they were a child."

Two days later I found myself standing outside the door of Boose's childhood room. I had let the appraiser in that morning and was offering him a cursory tour. The house was a mess. Unlike some appraisals, in which a family typically wants a high value assessed to their home, it was obvious that the Ablesons wanted the value depressed. As such, a pile of muddy boots were scattered in the entry, the kitchen sink was half-filled with dishes, where someone had taken a nap a blanket was bunched in the corner of the living room sofa, and as I entered Boose's room it came as no surprise to find her suitcase in its center with an explosion of her dirty clothes strewn in a radius that covered the desk, its chair, and even the headboard above the bed.

The appraiser, with clipboard in hand and tape measure holstered on his belt, maintained the strictest of poker faces as we progressed room to room. His controlled demeanor reminded me of a mortician; he was also similarly grim and dressed mostly in black as if to vanish his presence, and as he opened and closed doors, checked the functionality of everything from the HVAC system to faucets to electric outlets, his long tapered fingers moved with a spidery precision. I tried to grant him his space as he worked, at first installing myself downstairs in the kitchen, but each time he discovered some deficiency, say, an improperly metered light fixture or a closet not quite built to code, he would summon me as he logged it in his notes. Perhaps he did this so I might show the Ablesons; still, I mildly resented each shortcoming he assessed within Halcyon. Eventually, to avoid the trips across the house, I chose to wait in the hallway outside whatever room he'd entered.

"Who did you say lives in this room?" asked the appraiser, stepping into the second-story hallway where I was waiting.

"Their daughter," I answered.

"And how old is she?"

"Late twenties."

Through the break in the door, I again glimpsed the familiar explosion of clothes. "Late twenties?" he repeated and then took up his pen, clicked its end, jotted something on his clipboard, and returned to Boose's room. In fastidiousness she was not so much a woman as a girl, and I wondered how the appraiser might factor this observation into the value of the house. He had made a note of it, after all.

He was making many notes as I continued to escort him from one room to the next. Despite the extraneous mess, the house was in remarkably good shape. The renovation was nearing completion and the appraiser inspected aspects of that work with slight, nodding gestures of approval. We traveled the rooms in no specific order but when it came time to enter the master suite, I found myself unexpectedly hesitant. I didn't want to see how Mary was living with her disease. Nevertheless, I led the appraiser inside.

The double doors opened up into a sitting area, sun-bright and upholstered in plush white, bracketed by a three-sided westward-facing bay window. Old magazines and books formed little towers on the end tables. Assemblages of family photos cheered the room. In them I recognized less outwardly distressed versions of the people I had come to know. On a tiered writer's desk beneath the window sat a cluster of silver-framed ancestral photos, including that of a sepia-toned couple on their wedding day. There was also a desk set, of the traditional sort, with an ivory-handled letter opener, a clock, and a silver tray. The beams of light that poured through the window seemed to accentuate these but not other objects.

When the appraiser tried to open a set of pocket doors that connected the sitting area to the master bedroom itself, they were locked. I didn't have the key and had no idea where it might be. I excused myself to the hallway and tried Boose on her cellphone. No luck. I then tried Ableson. Still, no luck. The appraiser was completing his notes about the sitting area when I returned. His assessment of the room hadn't taken him long to complete, and he explained that it was essential he also examine the master bedroom. He asked if perhaps the key was in the desk by the window.

I opened a first drawer and then a second. Old papers, receipts, legal documents, loose photographs, and business cards filled them. Typically, I wasn't one to rifle through another person's things, but I felt this was justified. The Ablesons needed this appraisal finished, particularly before the judge's initial inquiry. When I came to a third drawer, it was mostly empty. It contained only a single large folder and, luckily enough, a key on a green ribbon. "Try this," I said, handing it to the appraiser.

He fondled the key as he crossed the room, slotting it into the lock and sliding the doors open. Inside was dusky. Light angled through the shut blinds of another bay window. Partially filled cups of water and plastic pill bottles littered a side table next to an adjustable hospital bed. A canvas cot made up with military precision sat on the bed's other side. At its head rested a white pillow, at its foot a folded quilt. I imagined the nights spent here, with Ableson an arm's length from Mary as she tried to sleep through her pain. On the room's opposite end was a king-sized bed. Papers and clothes and books cluttered its surface. No one slept there anymore.

While the appraiser got to work, I excused myself to the sitting room. When I returned the key to the desk drawer, I again noticed the large folder. It was stuffed with yellowed newspaper clippings, the most recent of which was the story of the Lazarus mice from several months before. One by one, I worked my way backward: Ableson's obituary; his court cases; his name listed among a dozen others in an article about judicial nominees for the Reagan administration; a legal prize named in his honor; more of his court cases; another article with his name listed among judicial nominees for the Carter administration; legal prizes he won early in his career, both as a litigator and as a student.

I came to the last and oldest story in the folder. I carefully held the brittle edges of the newspaper sheet between pinched fingers. It was an article from *Stars and Stripes*, which recounted in some detail the exploits of the 27th Infantry Division during the month-long battle on Saipan. Scanning the columns of text,

I read place-names like "Hells Pocket," "Purple Heart Ridge," and "Death Valley" as well as the names of commanders like General Holland "Howlin' Mad" Smith and the Japanese commander, General Yoshitsugu Saitō. What I couldn't find was any mention of Ableson. The article was three pages and when I finished reading, I glanced over the inset photographs. All were taken after the battle. One was of the funeral Smith had granted his vanquished adversary Saitō, who had taken his own life; another was of the airfield, a smoldering hellscape where the Japanese had launched the largest banzai charge of the war; and then I came to a photograph of a half-dozen hollow-eyed, underfed infantrymen, their uniforms in tatters and their faces unshaven, who were listed as the surviving members of "Echo Company" which had absorbed the brunt of that suicidal charge. As individuals, these men were indistinguishable. They all possessed the same, anonymous look of stupefaction. Below the group photograph, their names were captioned. Among them, I found Captain Robert J. Ableson. But, strangely, I also found Medic James R. Shields included with these survivors.

The appraiser stepped out from the bedroom. "Ready to head downstairs?"

Catching me at the desk, with the many newspaper clippings scattered across its surface, he offered me an inquisitive little glance. I tidied up and returned the folder to its drawer. Before we left, the appraiser suggested that perhaps we should again lock the pocket doors. "Probably best to leave things as we found them."

I told him there was no need for that.

Ten days later came the preliminary inquiry. The assigned judge had determined for the sake of expediency that a conference call would be sufficient. The parties to the case had assembled on a shared line. Their arguments centered on two distinct issues: first, did the workplace harassment complaint Susan Templeton had brought against Ableson fall outside the statute of limitations; second, did Ableson's will remain a valid document despite the annulment of his death certificate and would the assets transferred to his heirs under that will remain in a protected status. Boose had been on the call along with her parents and Ginny. It was, she told me the next day, one of the most anxiety-producing experiences of her life. "The silences were terrible." We were sitting in the kitchen of the guest cottage while I fixed her a drink. "You can't see the opposing side, or the judge, so you have no idea what they're thinking. All the meaning is in those silences." She had begun to pick at the cuticles of one finger as she spoke, and I noticed her other fingers were equally raw.

Boose explained the argument opposing counsel had made to the judge, which she insisted was "the most ridiculous thing I'd ever heard." According to their logic, no statute of limitations should exist on the harassment claim because of the ongoing trauma suffered by both Susan and Janet Templeton. When the judge asked Janet if this theory of "ongoing trauma" accurately represented her experience, she responded by launching into an aria of her troubles. From her academic struggles to her personal struggles, every setback and defeat germinated in the moment she had witnessed O'Toole hit her mother. However, the judge had pointed out to an exercised Janet Templeton that it was her mother who was filing the complaint, not her. The judge asked Susan Templeton the same question. She at first faltered. Reflexively, she mentioned how Ableson had hired her when no one else would have. His heart was, she said, "in the right place." The judge grew impatient and again asked about the enduring impact of Ableson's actions. Janet interjected. She rattled off the many ways Ableson continued to interfere in her mother's life. "What do you mean by interfere?" the judge wanted to know. Janet Templeton explained Ableson's meddling with the Virginia Monument petition, how he'd seen to its invalidation. The judge seemed surprised, asking Susan Templeton whether this was true. "It is," she said. This was met with another ambiguous silence.

"After that," said Boose, "the judge determined the complaint fell within the statute of limitations due to an enduring pattern of harassment."

"What about your father's will?" I asked. "Can you and your brothers keep your inheritance?"

Boose rubbed the side of her head. "It's still under review. We should find out next month."

"And Halcyon?"

"The appraisal came back high," she said. "Too high. Seems my parents made a mistake by renovating the place. It's now worth more than ever. The Templetons will also come after that. The house is in my mother's name. What type of people would run a dying woman out of her home?"

I didn't have an answer, so instead asked after her mother's health.

"Stop by tomorrow morning if you can. My father's going to be on legal calls. You'll have her all to yourself. It's important you see her."

Shortly thereafter Boose left. That evening and all through the night, I wondered why it was "important" that I see her mother. Boose could have said it'd be "nice for you to see her" or that "she'd like to see you" but instead she had used that specific word, "important," and it left me feeling certain that—whether I liked it or not—I continued to have a role to play for the Ableson family.

The low sun was still filtering its light through the branches of the trees and onto the path of dirt and brittle asphalt as I walked up to the main house the following morning. Earlier, I had prepared myself breakfast but only had a bite, pitching a plate's worth of scrambled eggs into the trash. I increasingly felt a sense of foreboding about whatever it was Mary had to tell me. When

Halcyon's white portico came into view Boose stood there beneath
it. She was leaning her shoulder against one of the freshly painted
columns. Cupped in her hand was a steaming mug of tea. I wondered whether she had come out here to enjoy it, or whether she'd
come out to intercept me; either way, she ushered us into the foyer,
where I noticed several suitcases.

"My brothers are back," she said. Then, as if on cue, I heard
Doug's and Bobby's voices blending with Ableson's from down a
long corridor. Each was talking over the other and it sounded as if
the three of them were on a conference call. I imagined they were
strategizing with Ginny about their next move. Boose escorted me
upstairs, to the master suite. When we stepped inside, I noticed
that the room was cleaner than it'd been several days before when
I'd walked through with the appraiser. The books and magazines
on the side tables had been put away. The desk beneath the bay
window didn't have a single object on its surface. The pocket doors
leading to the master bedroom remained shut and inserted in the
lock was the key with the green ribbon.

Boose slid open the doors and announced me in an amplified
voice. She then gave me an encouraging nod before stepping backward out of the room. Mary sat reclined in the hospital bed by
the window. A blanket covered her legs, but from the waist up
she'd dressed in a white blouse that must have once fit but now
swallowed her emaciated body. Someone had neatly arranged her
medications in rows on the side table and tidied up the many
half-filled cups of water and replaced them with a drinking bottle
she could sip from. The only other item on the side table was a
compact. Mary was impeccably made up and I suspected this was
done for my benefit. Still, she hardly acknowledged me. Her eyes
tracked absently out the window, to her garden below, the only
portion of the renovation that remained incomplete.

I announced myself with a "Good morning."

She turned toward me, saying my name in a voice that sounded as though it needed a drink of water. "Come closer," she added. Tentatively, I approached her bed, and when I got to an arm's length she tugged my shirt with some effort so that I was bent over her, craning my neck upward, but looking out the window from the same vantage she did. "You see that row of flower beds?" Our heads were side by side. Her breath smelled faintly sour like dead flowers and it was the flowers that interested her. "Those buds there, can you see them?"

I gazed out the window. "Third row of flower beds?" I asked.

She nodded, adjusting herself upward. "That's where my peonies are planted. They're late. They should've bloomed back in May, or even early this month."

All I could see was green bushes.

"No," she answered. "Look closer. I'm certain I saw some yellow buds."

Little droplets of sweat gathered on her forehead and her top lip. Her gaze had an unsteady quality to it. "Wait," I said. "Maybe there is a little bit of yellow."

"See, I told you." Her chest was heaving up and down as though she'd finished a race.

I offered to go outside, to check their progress, thinking this might calm her.

She thanked me and relaxed into the bed. "The buds come in yellow," she said. "Then they bloom white and yellow-rimmed. Robert and I had them planted all over this garden when we were first married. At the end of every May, they would arrive like clockwork. Friends would visit us simply to see them. Gradually, we let the garden lapse. I can't even say why. It was a lot of upkeep, but that wasn't the reason. For the life of me, I can't remember why we stopped planting peonies . . ."

Her speech had begun to tangle and slur. She had grown delirious and offered me a weak, bewildered look, as though recognizing me one moment only to lose the thread and forget who I was the next. I offered her a sip from her water bottle. She swallowed with great effort, shutting her eyes. I continued to watch the ragged rise and fall of the pendant on her chest. Its cadence evened, then she began to speak more steadily:

"We hired a new gardener as part of the renovation, and he promised me the peonies he planted would be just like the ones before." Her head was against her pillow and she had again opened her eyes to look outside. "What a mistake. We never should have tried to renovate this house. You can't imagine how much it's cost us. And now Janet Templeton wants to take it away. She won't, of course; or rather I won't let her . . . Even so, she's not *wrong* in her anger. No child should have to see what she saw. She's simply *wrong* in the object of her anger. That man—O'Toole, or whatever his name was—he's the one Janet should have her sights set on, not my husband. If anything, Janet and Robert are alike, though neither would ever admit it. This horrible thing Janet saw as a child, it defines her. The horrible things Robert saw on that island in the war, they've defined him. Both their lives shaped in the same way. Their lives . . . and now this house. Still, for all the expense, I'd at least like to see the peonies."

I wondered what news Dr. Shields had delivered on their last visit.

Mary reached for her compact, opened it, and applied another layer of foundation. When she turned back, her face seemed to be made of putty and her eyes were like dusty marbles. "I can feel the disease inside me," she said. "It's like balancing on the edge of a pit. If I lean in one direction, I can fall right in. I'm the one holding on, Martin. You understand? I can let go whenever I like. It's just—" and she turned out toward her disappointing garden. "When you leave, be a dear and take a closer look at the peonies; tell me if they're coming in."

I promised her that I would.

"Good," she said. Once more, her breath became increasingly labored. "It'd be nice to see them around this house again."

A week later, the peonies bloomed everywhere. They came in all colors, not just white and yellow but in bright reds and oranges and mixes of both. They appeared in my garden at the guest cottage and along the road that connected it to the main house at Halcyon. I cut them with short stems and placed them in mugs in almost every room, which greatly cheered the place. Their fragrance permeated the grounds, and the day after they reached their fullest bloom I sat out on my front stoop enjoying the air until dusk. Which is when I saw Ableson slowly walking toward the guest cottage.

The evening sun was at the treetops and in front of him his shadow ran very long on the path. Immediately, I knew what this was about. Like a coward, I stepped inside. A moment later, he was knocking on my door. Mary's death was written on his face.

"When?" I asked.

"Late yesterday morning," he said, slumping into his usual seat by the empty fireplace. "I was up about an hour before her and when I saw the peonies in full bloom out our window, I knew this was the day. I didn't let her know that I knew ... but I knew. I had watched her sleep a while but eventually decided to wake her up as it made me feel like I was giving this last gift to her. God, she was excited when she saw how brightly they'd bloomed. She was worried, you know, she thought maybe they would never bloom that way again. But when they did, she said it seemed like they'd returned only for her. She said she couldn't remember ever seeing them so beautiful. I offered to go pick a few stems. I was outside for maybe twenty minutes. When I got back, her head was turned to the window and she was gone. She had been watching me in the garden."

Again, I told him how sorry I was and, mechanically, he thanked me. He said that he knew I was sorry and that he appreciated the sentiment. He made me feel as though my grief was persuasive and sufficient. "Do you think she held on for the peonies?" I asked. Ableson glanced around my guest cottage, taking particular notice of the blossoms I had picked and placed on nearly every surface. "No," he said, "she wanted to see the peonies but that's not the reason she let go."

I glanced back at him, confused.

"Isn't it obvious?" he said. "She let go for Halcyon. In her will, the property passes down to Boose. That added degree of inheritance—from me to Mary, from Mary to Boose—makes it so the Templetons can't touch Halcyon now. Dr. Shields could have given her more time if she'd wanted it. Six months, maybe a year. Instead, after her last appointment with him, she'd stopped all of her treatments. He upped her pain meds but took her off everything else. We knew this was coming."

Ableson's expression contained no anguish or outward signs of heartache. His pain was beyond that. He was numb and sat in his chair staring at the empty fireplace with the same dazed transfixion as if a blaze roared inside it. His look reminded me of the photograph I'd seen in his desk drawer, the one of him and Dr. Shields's father on Saipan. I now mentioned to him that I'd seen it.

"I figured you had," he said. "You returned the clippings in the wrong order."

"I thought Charles Shields's father died on Saipan?"

Ableson shrugged. "He did and he didn't." Ableson explained that Doc Shields hadn't died that night on the airfield. There'd been no grenade pitched into their shared foxhole, no opportunity for him to dive on it and sacrifice himself. After the battle, Doc Shields's behavior had turned erratic. He couldn't sleep. He stopped eating. Like anyone else who suffered symptoms of combat stress, he was shipped to a rear area rest camp. When this didn't help, he was shipped to a hospital in Hawaii. Whenever they talked about sending him the remainder of the way home, his symptoms grew worse. Ableson believed that in Doc Shields's own mind he had died that night at the airfield. Each step closer to home was a step closer to a life he was no longer capable of living. "He didn't want to come back, but they were forcing him to," Ableson explained. "Eventually, in that last hospital, he ended it himself."

"But why lie about it?"

"'Lie' is a pretty strong word," he said. "No one lied. Jimmy Shields did sacrifice himself at the airfield on Saipan. Whether he took his life jumping on a grenade that night, or whether he took his life in a psych ward four months later because of what he'd seen, what's the difference? Both are suicidal acts."

"Depends on your definition of suicide."

Ableson's jaw tightened and he sat up straight. "No," he said. "It depends on your definition of sacrifice. Whether it's by a little or by a lot, at a certain point we all let go. The real question is what are you letting go for?"

Ableson allowed the question to hang in the air. Would the son of Doc Shields have become the successful and widely renowned oncologist Dr. Shields if he'd been raised by a traumatized father? Likely not, and Ableson had too much respect for his long-dead comrade to speak this ugly truth. But an ugly truth existed in Mary's sacrifice, too. She could have lived on for Ableson. And she'd chosen not to. By letting go she had instead made certain Halcyon would pass to her daughter. When I eventually got around to offering Ableson a drink, he declined. He explained that he'd already stayed too long. All three of his children were waiting for him at the main house. They had preparations to make.

He had only come down here to pass along the details of Mary's funeral service. It would be held the following Thursday, nine a.m., at Oak Ridge Cemetery.

Thursday came with a fog so thick it wetted your skin. The treetops vanished and their trunks appeared like an anchorage of pylons on a gray sea. A twenty-minute drive separated Halcyon from Oak Ridge Cemetery. In the fog I missed my turnoff, making me late. If I had any inclination to believe that the funeral of Mary Ableson would be an understated, intimate affair, the parking lot disabused me of this notion. The mourners had wedged their cars bumper-to-bumper on the asphalt, spilling onto the surrounding grass. The license plates hailed from up and down the Eastern Seaboard, from states as far north as New Hampshire and as far south as Florida. As I hurried along the unfamiliar paths, a murmur of voices laced through the headstones and oriented me toward the ceremony. Soon, the darkly attired crowd appeared through the fog and I assumed my place at its back.

With its sweeping views of the Shenandoah obscured, the cemetery seemed a run-down and unremarkable resting place. Tomorrow, or the day after, the sky would clear, but I wondered how many of those gathered graveside would ever return and have a chance to behold the vast expanse of valley below. Surely, Mary had wanted to share the beauty of this place with those who had traveled from so far away to mourn her, yet this unfortunate weather seemed to reach beyond her death, to rob her even of that. Although Mary had never struck me as particularly religious, a young pastor of an indeterminate denomination presided over the ceremony. He read passages of scripture with too much enthusiasm, like an actor who's overprepared for an audition. I couldn't help but wonder if he had chosen the familiar passages, ones that seemed to be read at every funeral (Isaiah 41:10: *"So do not fear . . ."*; John 3:16:

". . . *whoever believes in him* . . ."; Proverbs 12:28: ". . . *there is no death.*") or whether Mary had chosen them.

The pastor's liturgy assumed a droning cadence. Growing restless, I studied the unfamiliar crowd. I had—at least in my own consciousness—assumed a central place in the life of the Ablesons over the past several months; however, I knew none of these other mourners. The life of any person consists of many chapters. I happened to attend the last chapter of Mary's life. But these strangers had attended many of the others. I felt small and inconsequential standing among them, like a guest in a room where no one has yet asked me to sit down. For a moment, I even thought to leave. If I hurried to my car, I could avoid getting stuck in the parking lot at the end of the service. I might have done so if I hadn't suddenly noticed Susan Templeton beside me.

She was meticulously dressed in black. Black skirt, blouse, jacket, and shoes. She'd brought an umbrella, which was also black. Reports of continued bad weather had appeared in the news. I caught her glancing furtively in my direction and she caught me doing the same, so that by the time the pastor finished his readings and the mourners began filtering one by one up to the grave, it was inevitable that we would exchange a few words. She went first: "I'm sorry for your loss," and I thought it a remarkable concession. Compared to her, who was I to mourn Mary Ableson? When I asked whether her daughter had come, she shook her head, no. "That's probably for the best," I answered, to which she agreed.

A line was forming to express condolences to the family, who stood graveside. I suggested we join it. "Do you think that's a good idea?" she asked. I didn't answer because whether it was or was not a good idea hardly mattered. Despite her reticence, I could see that she needed to say something to the Ablesons. She had spent much of her life within the security of their orbit, even if that security had at times betrayed her. What would it say about her if she didn't face Robert Ableson on the day that he buried his wife, if only to express sympathy? That imperative existed within her and she didn't need to explain it as we waited together in line.

What I did ask her about was the complaint she'd brought against Ableson. How could she justify taking so much from his children? I framed the question as a statement, saying, "I'm sure this court case has been painful for everyone." To which she answered, "It's the last thing I ever wanted." I believed her, too. Left to her own devices, Susan Templeton never would have revived this old complaint against Ableson. Her daughter had taken up the grievance; unlike the Ableson children, it was the only inheritance Janet Templeton possessed. The line was moving more quickly. We'd soon be graveside, standing in front of the family.

"Why not drop the whole thing?" I asked. "What can you really hope to gain? It happened twenty years ago, in a different time."

"You can correct the past," said Susan. "That's what my daughter believes. You're a historian; that should make sense to you." And it made perfect sense, except I wasn't the type of historian who believed the past could or should be corrected. It had happened and by definition *was*. A hush fell over us as we approached within earshot of the Ablesons. One by one they accepted the whispered condolences of the other mourners. Then Mary's grave came into view. A bundle of green-stemmed peonies rested on the coffin lid. Moisture beaded on their many-colored petals and also on the well-polished mahogany. Susan was a step ahead. With a quickly averted glance, she offered her condolences to Boose and her two brothers, moving rapidly past them so that I doubt they even recognized her. When she got to Robert, Susan Templeton's eyes met his squarely. "I thought I should be here today."

He took her hand in both of his. "Thank you for coming."

Susan then stepped out of the line.

Unlike Susan, I offered a more elaborate and awkward set of condolences, in which I tossed out inadequate little phrases like

"I'm so sorry for your loss" and "she meant a great deal to us all" and used words like "honor" and "gratitude" when it came to how I felt about having known Mary Ableson; this is to say my many words paled in comparison with Susan's simple dignity. After availing myself of Robert Ableson for a drink whenever he "felt up to it," I began to search for Susan Templeton among the thinning crowd.

The fog was beginning to lift when I heard my name called in the loudest possible voice a person could use in a cemetery. It was Ginny. She walked in a straight line toward me with no regard to stepping on the many graves. "I've been looking for you," she said, kissing my cheek. "Can you believe this weather?" and she made a sour face; then, holding that face, she nodded over my right shoulder and added, "Can you believe she came?" Susan Templeton was walking away from us, slowly and meticulously threading her steps between the headstones. The pathway back to the parking lot was clogged with mourners. It snaked through the cemetery like the line to an amusement park ride. "It takes a lot of nerve for her to show up here. You haven't seen her daughter, have you?" I shook my head, no. "Good," said Ginny. "If Janet Templeton came, that would be beyond." When I asked her how the case was shaping up, she conspiratorially checked behind her, to make certain there was no one who might eavesdrop. "*This* has been helpful," she said. When I asked, "This what?" her expression collapsed in that exasperated way that had become so familiar to me over the course of our marriage, a look that said *Do I really need to spell everything out for you?* Which she now did: "*Mary*, her passing, *this*," and she made a gesture with her hand as if tossing away a palmful of sand. "Halcyon is now off the table. The property transfers from Mary directly to her daughter. That woman"—Ginny nodded disgustedly up the path toward Susan Templeton—"can't touch it."

I said that I understood, but what I meant wasn't only that I understood how Mary dying allowed Boose to inherit Halcyon—

this was obvious—but that I also sympathized with Ginny's logic of Mary's death as "helpful," even if her use of that word seemed in poor taste. Had Mary survived for six months or a year more, the Ablesons might have lost Halcyon to Susan Templeton's claim. This gave Mary's death a saintly veneer. But it also juxtaposed her acquiescence to death with Ableson's tenacious claim on life and all that it might cost his children in the end. "We've got three weeks until our next conference with the court," Ginny explained. "That's when the judge will rule on the validity of Robert's will." When I asked her the odds of a ruling in Ableson's favor, one in which the will would remain valid and Susan Templeton would have no claim on the already inherited assets, Ginny replied with her typical nonchalance: "No better than even; that's assuming no one makes a rash choice." She glanced back at the gravesite from where we'd just come, the one with the headstone that already had Robert Ableson's name etched into its face.

She changed the subject and asked whether I'd heard the latest news about the Virginia Monument, which I hadn't. Earlier in the week, without any fanfare, Lucas Harlow had filed a fresh petition at the records office. Already, it was circulating for signatures and gathering strong support among campus groups, despite many students having returned home for the summer break. I imagined Ginny had received this news through her careful monitoring of byzantine legal developments across the state. "Oh no," she said. "You're giving me too much credit. Annette's the one who told me. That woman even gossips about her own husband." While on the topic of gossip, I worked up the nerve to ask her how she'd been doing since her breakup, whether she'd started seeing anyone after Daryl. "No," she said. "No one at the moment. This case has eaten up all of my time."

We were nearly to our cars now, each of us digging about for our keys before going our separate ways. Behind us, a few beams of sun slanted through the overcast and touched their light on the valley floor, which, slowly, had begun to reveal itself. An eastward wind was picking up, hurrying off one set of clouds but bringing another set in.

"Do you ever wonder about us, Ginny?"

"What about us?" she asked distractedly, still rifling through her purse.

"If the timing had been different, if we'd been further along in our lives, whether things might have worked out?"

She stopped searching for her keys and tilted her head to the side. She touched my arm, piteously. She reminded me of what I always said, which was that the past should remain in the past. Then she added, "It's better that way. Don't you think?"

Eventually, Ginny found her keys; but not before emptying the contents of her purse across the hood of my Volvo. We each pulled out of the parking lot. The beams of sun that had momentarily pierced the clouds yielded to a steady rain. It pelted my windshield as I traveled the highway that would return me to Halcyon. I drove with the radio off. The nonsense I'd spoken to Ginny gnawed at me; sure, had we met at this moment, as strangers, we might have stood a chance—I was further along in my career, she was older and not looking for as much in a partner—but to make a second go of it, we would've had to unsay and undo so much. Our history condemned us. I, of all people, should have understood that. She was right to remind me of it and I was wrong to have brought it up, embarrassing us both.

I drove distractedly in the left lane, my mind turning over our exchange as though it were a precious stone that required examination from varied angles and in varied light. Soon I had approached too close to the tractor-trailer in front, so that its back tires sprayed rooster tails of water and bits of debris up my hood. I sped my windshield wipers, which stuttered across the glass, and then I signaled a lane change to the right. As I eased in that direction, a furious and baritone horn blew, and I jerked the wheel back to the left. Another tractor-trailer lingered in my blind spot. When I tried to decelerate, the car behind me had crowded up to my fender. I was boxed in. A blue tarp, with its loose hem flapping violently, covered the load lashed to the tractor-trailer. Fragments of something kept pummeling my car. They glanced off the hood and rattled beneath the undercarriage. I leaned on my horn. Its thin sound hardly rose above the throttling rain. My steering wheel spasmed sharply left then sharply right, snatching itself from my grip, and another sound came from beneath my seat like a fistful of silverware chucked down a garbage disposal. I was no longer driving so much as skating across the highway. I regripped the steering wheel. The car swerved toward the shoulder of the road. All I could do was pump the brakes. I imagined flipping over . . . I imagined being crushed in the oncoming traffic . . . I imagined death on this ridiculous stretch of highway . . . Instead, I lurched into the grass.

The only sound was the sizzle of rain and the traffic that rushed past in a scream of wind. I rested my forehead between my hands, which remained white-knuckled on the steering wheel at ten and two o'clock. I was stranded on the side of the road, but I knew that I'd avoided something far worse. This was, in fact, the nearest I'd ever come to death, and the rush of emotions surprised me. I recalled how I'd once asked Ableson what it was like to die. He'd told me that it was different for each person. Gradually, from the center of my chest, a warm, glowing euphoria spread. Trapped as I'd felt only moments before—boxed in by traffic and brooding about Ginny—I now felt as though anything was possible. History had no hold on the present, not with Ginny, not with Ableson, and not with me. My view turned expansive as I sat, stranded by the side of the road.

I stepped into the rain to inspect the damage to my car. Whatever had fallen off the back of that truck had punctured both of my front tires, shredding the right one. I had only a single spare in the trunk and wondered how far I could drive on a flat. The gas station where I'd stopped a couple of weeks before wasn't too far off. I imagined the Volvo could limp there. If I came across the same attendant, I hoped that he wouldn't remind me about the redheaded boy and how I'd paid for his Cheerwine. The more I thought about it, the less the gas station appealed to me.

I got to work, placing a couple of signal flares on the shoulder of the road. I then lifted the car on its jack. One by one, I unloosened the circle of lug nuts on the wheel rim. In no time the rain had soaked through my shirt, my trousers, and even down to my socks. Traffic slowed as it passed. People gawked from their rolled-up windows that anyone would prove so unfortunate as to endure a double flat in this weather. Their stares hardly bothered me, nor did the storm. The good fortune of being alive consumed my thoughts; then, the last of the six lug nuts refused to budge. I wrestled against it, twice slipping into the mud. Behind me, a car eased onto the shoulder of the road with its hazards flashing. I stood, gripping one end of my heavy X-shaped wrench while I made a visor with my other hand and peered into the rain. A man sat in the driver's seat with a woman beside him. She fumbled around at her feet and then handed him something. He unlatched the car door, popped open the umbrella, and stepped tentatively outside. The wind was blowing hard down the road, right at him, so that he walked with the umbrella tilted forward. He only lifted it, revealing his face, when he was a few steps away.

"Looks like you could use some help," said Lucas Harlow.

He simply stood there, dry and self-satisfied beneath his umbrella. With his free hand, he clamped the top of his jacket collar shut. He kept tabs on the oncoming traffic from the corner of his eye.

"That's all right. You didn't need to stop."

"It wasn't my idea," he said. "After we passed by, it was Susan who insisted we turn around for you." I glanced back toward the silhouette in the passenger seat; she was watching us intently. Lucas crouched onto his haunches, examining the two flat tires and the stuck lug nut. "You'll be out here all night trying to get that wheel off." He gestured toward me with his open palm and I passed him the wrench. He slid its socket over the lug nut. With us both gripping the handle we strained to lever it loose. Eventually, we dropped the wrench on the wet grass, our palms smarting with the effort. "That won't budge," he said through a heavy breath.

I nodded, catching my own breath. Neither of us was yet ready to make another attempt, so I mentioned how I hadn't seen him at the funeral. With his umbrella set aside, he was now as soaked as I was. "I didn't think it was my place to come," he said, and then glanced again in Susan Templeton's direction. "But she needed a ride, so I brought her and waited in the parking lot." He wiped his hands on the seat of his pants and wandered around to the trunk of his car. When he marched back up the shoulder of the road, he carried a black Pelican case by its handle in one hand and in the other was his own spare tire. "You can replace your second flat with this," he said, leaning the spare against my car door. Then he opened up the case and removed a pneumatic wrench. While he fussed around, searching for the right-sized socket for the lug nut, I watched him and resented his preparedness. Lucas Harlow: always one step ahead of you—always so eager to help.

"I hear you got the petition going again."

He slid the mouth of one socket onto the lug nut for a perfect fit. Satisfied, he smiled to himself, saying, "Yeah, that's right."

"You think it'll work this time?"

"The support is there so I don't see why not. The country is ready for this." He was locking the socket into the mouth of the wrench and the rain was falling on his hunched shoulders as he kneeled in the grass by the wheel. "Did you hear about that senator, the one who just spoke at the Democratic convention? He gave a pretty amazing speech, historic really. Bush is up in the polls and if he beats Gore this time around, that'd clear the slate for a new Democrat to run in '08. Maybe it'd be this guy? They're already saying he could be president. Imagine that? An African American president, in this country. It's possible. But what I can't imagine is an African American president in this country with those goddamn monuments still littered everywhere. Now, I understand where you're coming from," he said this expansively and with all of the arrogance of someone who felt assured he could understand the mind of anyone and everyone. "Those old Confederate monuments hold a certain"—and he paused, as if browsing his own vocabulary so he might pluck the ripest word—"*significance*. But they don't belong on public land." He squeezed the trigger on the pneumatic wrench and it made a wheezing sound.

"Then where do they belong?"

"In a museum," he answered with total certainty. "There's one in South Carolina. They're already gathering up a lot of this stuff. The war began down there. It might as well end there, too. Don't you think?" Before I could answer, Lucas Harlow had gotten to work. As much as we'd struggled before with my old manual wrench, this pneumatic one popped the stuck lug nut off the wheel like a cork out of a champagne bottle. With a similar ease, he replaced the first and then the second tire. As I watched him work, I wondered why he hadn't simply brought out the pneumatic wrench in the first place. It was as if he had wanted us to struggle with the manual wrench, to prove that I needed his help.

"Finished," he said, kicking loose the jack.

The Volvo dropped to the ground.

"These two spares will get you home," he said and carefully replaced his wrench in its case. When he asked how my work was coming along, I told him "really well" with an optimism I didn't feel. He nodded courteously, said, "Glad to hear it," and wiped his hands clean on his trousers. "You know I've still got those three volumes of Shelby Foote you had signed for me." I could tell he was trying to be conciliatory; but then, as if he couldn't quite help himself, he crossed his arms and leaned back. He made a face as he took a long appraising look at my Volvo. "Jesus, Martin . . ." Slowly, he'd started shaking his head. "What you really need is a whole new set of tires; you've run this old car ragged."

The week that followed, I took to my desk. To an outsider, it wouldn't have appeared as if I was working so much as holding a vigil in the attic. I sat each day in my appointed place, surrounded by my books, only breaking for meals and hoping for the arrival of any idea that might disprove what to me had become excruciatingly clear: that is, if an ability to compromise underwrote American life, I could no longer see that same spirit of compromise anywhere in my own life, which had become a tapestry of absolutes: the Virginia Monument would be torn down; Susan and Janet Templeton would strip the Ableson children of their inheritance; and Mary's death would leave Robert Ableson to live out the rest of his life alone. Yes, absolutes abounded.

If the struggles in my writing weren't pressure enough, I was scheduled to teach the fall term at Virginia College. A reminder arrived via mail that course descriptions were due to departmental chairs by August 15th. I would offer my signature series of lectures on the origins and history of the Civil War, but I had also committed to an advanced-level seminar for seniors. Months before, I had provisionally titled it "Compromise and American Identity: Perspectives on the Civil War." That description now felt wholly inadequate. *Perspectives?* It seemed only one perspective could exist on any issue, and I now entertained overhauling the syllabus, though I hardly knew with what.

Before I slipped too far down this rabbit hole, a delegation of visitors appeared at my front door. When I peered out the attic window, I immediately recognized the white government van. However, joining the Drs. Jones that afternoon was Dr. Shields. I had no sooner invited them inside than the male Dr. Jones, who was dressed in his same fleece and khakis, began inquiring about my car. He had noticed the two spare tires.

By now the four of us—myself, the two Drs. Jones, and Dr. Shields—were settled on the twin sofas in my living room. I had chosen to serve tea, though I was tempted to pour something stronger. The full pot, the cups on their saucers, and a plate of cookies rested on the table between us. The female Dr. Jones chewed slowly, with a look of amazement, as I described to her my interaction with Susan Templeton and Lucas Harlow the day of the funeral. "Given the legal situation," she said, "I find it surprising that Ms. Templeton would've attended." It was difficult to take the Drs. Jones seriously as the crumbs accumulated down the fronts of their matching fleeces.

I glanced at Dr. Shields on the sofa next to me. He offered a noncommittal shrug and I wondered whether Susan Templeton's decision to attend Mary's funeral proved equally surprising to him. I, for one, had thought her presence was an appropriate and obvious gesture, both magnanimous and graceful. But the two doctors seemed like emissaries from a future that I didn't understand, one where the rules of decorum differed from those I'd always known. They continued to munch their cookies and slurp their tea, while the female Dr. Jones explained, "We've followed the developments of Ms. Templeton's complaint closely. As you can imagine, the success of our program depends on the success of those we've brought back. A high-profile harassment case—not that this is *that* high profile, at least not yet—could inflict irreparable harm."

I reached for one of the cookies with a nonchalance that I hoped matched that of the two doctors. I then crossed one leg over the other, extending my arms along the back of the sofa. "Define 'irreparable harm'?"

"The program's termination," answered the other Dr. Jones, the male one. He replaced his empty cup in its faintly chattering saucer. "This is an election year. Have you heard Bush's campaign rhetoric? What his surrogates are saying? What he's saying?" Although I consistently listened to the news, I clearly hadn't been watching the campaign as closely as the two doctors. "Simply put, Bush's election would cut all federal funding for the program. What's worse is that a significant failure within the program could swing votes away from Gore."

The female Dr. Jones reached into a briefcase at her side. From it she removed a folder, which she placed on the table between us. I finished my cookies and, wiping my hands, placed the folder on my lap. In it was a news story from a local paper in Boise, Idaho. I glanced at Dr. Shields as if he might also want to read. But he stayed in his corner of the sofa. He seemed already familiar with the story. It was about a woman named Julia Benson, wife of Lloyd Benson, mother of two, grandmother of four; no mention was made of her age but rather that she had also participated in the program. Not long after "resuming her life," as the article put it, Julia Benson's husband had died suddenly of a glioblastoma. Then, a month after his death, she had gone missing. Local authorities had initially begun their search in a park where several witnesses had last seen her walking. After a month, at the behest of her family, they had called off that search. Julia Benson was now presumed dead. A photograph of her inset within the columns of text showed a silver-haired, smiling, and seemingly vivacious woman, the type of person cast to appear in sunny television commercials advertising arthritis medications and blood thinners. She certainly didn't look like a suicide, which was the implication I assumed the two doctors were making by showing me this story.

Both doctors stared at me gravely, until the female Dr. Jones said, "We don't believe the body of Julia Benson will ever be recovered." To which the male Dr. Jones immediately added, "If it was found that she'd harmed herself in some way, that could endanger the survival of the program. Do you understand?"

I wasn't certain that I did.

Dr. Shields, who up to this point had maintained a noticeable silence, spoke in less oblique terms. "From what I know of it," he began, "this woman's situation wasn't too different from Robert's. Her husband's sudden death left her isolated and alone. Her longevity complicated matters of inheritance within her family and threatened to financially compromise her children. She seemed to reach the conclusion that everyone would be better off if she were no longer around. We're worried that Robert might reach a similar conclusion."

"Has he said anything?" I asked.

"No," said Dr. Shields, speaking not only to me but also to the other two doctors, who craved reassurance. "But it's important that we keep close tabs on him, especially now, when he's figuring out what comes next."

The female Dr. Jones interjected, "You often visit with one another, correct?"

"It's been a while," I said. "But we used to."

To which her colleague added, "Perhaps you could pick that up again."

Dr. Shields had already suggested to Ableson that he pay me a visit, "to let off a little steam," as he'd put it to him, and now added, "This case against Robert is going to get worse in the coming weeks. I'm concerned what he might do if the judge invalidates his will. If you keep talking to him, that might keep him steady."

I assured everyone that I would.

The doctors exchanged a batch of nods around the table, no different than if they had reached a consensus on a course of treatment for a patient. As they finished their tea and gathered their things, the female Dr. Jones glanced at the stairs that led to the attic. "What's up there?"

"Not much, just my study."

"You know that's why he confides in you," she said. "You're sympathetic to the time he comes from. Few people are these days." The remark left me feeling exposed, as if she'd revealed that Ableson and I harbored a shared affinity for the occult. As she headed toward the door, I noticed that she'd forgotten the news story about Julia Benson in the folder on the table. When I handed it back, she told me to keep it. "I printed it out for you."

"What'll happen to her?" I asked.

"Who? Julia Benson?" She spoke the name like an afterthought. It was only us standing at the door; the other two were already climbing into the white van. "She'll remain classified as a missing person until enough time passes. After that, the authorities will update her case file and reclassify her as deceased. It's only a matter of filling out a few new forms and listing a cause of death. In her case, I imagine they'd simply use what originally killed her."

"What was that?"

"As I recall, it was something to do with her heart."

I remained home that first evening, but Ableson didn't come. The next day, I had errands to run. I needed to replace the set of worn tires on my car. After a few phone calls, I found a service station off the interstate that sold the size of tire I needed; however, it was the same service station where I'd encountered the redheaded boy.

I left the guest cottage early that morning, hoping to have the matter settled before lunch, as any time after lunch I was anticipating a visit from Ableson. I crept northward on the interstate, driving carefully on my replacement tires with my hazard lights flashing as traffic shuttled past on either side. When the exit appeared, the service station seemed smaller than I remembered it from those many nights before, the arc lights towered less grandly and, without the darkness, the surrounding countryside seemed less vast and consuming. Previously, I hadn't noticed the mechanic's single-bay garage behind the mini-mart, which is where I now pulled up with the Volvo.

The mechanic, himself a gangly limbed grease aficionado with a potbelly and perpetual squint that seemed to disassemble people as well as machines into their component parts, met me outside. "You the fella I spoke with on the phone?" he asked, his lower lip shelving forward as he circled my car with a part from another car in his hand—a carburetor or air filter, or some other under-the-hood mechanism that he massaged with a filthy rag. He had a pale, pinched face, and lowered himself into a squat as he scuttled crab-like around the four corners of the Volvo. I gave him my name and told him that, yes, I was the one he'd spoken to on the phone. I needed him to replace my tires. "Yep, you do," he said. "And you also need me to fix your alignment." He came down into a modified push-up and glanced beneath the undercarriage, where he touched some mysterious nether region. When he removed his hand, a neon liquid slickened his two fingers, which he sniffed, and this resulted in him shaking his head despondently. "You also need me to rebalance your Freon levels and install a new reservoir." He gave me one final, disappointed look. "How long's it been leakin'?"

I told him that I didn't precisely know but I needed to be home by lunch.

"I'll get you sorted out by then," he said. When he smiled, filthy as he was, I expected stains on his teeth—or whatever teeth he had—so was surprised when he revealed a perfect smile, one which was immaculate and whose whiteness exceeded my own. He removed a pad from his coveralls and scribbled out an invoice. The amount was more than twice what I'd expected to pay and, seeing it, I might have insisted he only replace the tires, or I might have taken my business elsewhere; but the clarity of his perfect teeth left me feeling as though this was a man I could trust. I reached into my wallet and handed over my card almost gladly.

He explained that I could wait, if I wanted, in "the lounge," and he gestured to a room off the garage that contained a radio, a few magazines scattered across a low table, and an empty coffeepot. With a little imagination I could conjure the stale reek inside. Then he hopped into the driver's seat of my Volvo and slowly piloted it into the repair bay, shaking his head with disgust as he felt how poorly it handled.

Not wanting to wait in the lounge and having skipped breakfast, I wandered over to the mini-mart. Although I was hungry, it wasn't my appetite that drew me there but rather a sudden guilt. I felt an awkward obligation to reconcile with the attendant yet wondered if he would remember me; that is, if he was even working.

As I shouldered through the door, the bell overhead made a little chime. The attendant was working. He didn't glance up; instead, he sat barricaded behind the counter, in the exact same position as before, with one of the glossy gossip magazines from the checkout rack spread in front of him. I wandered down the aisles searching for anything that might qualify as a suitable breakfast, while taking furtive side glances at the attendant. He remained utterly absorbed in his reading, slowly turning the lavish pages, his expression set with ecclesiastical concentration as he continued to study the magazine.

I poured myself a coffee and picked up two granola bars. With my hands full, I slid a bottle of orange juice into my back pocket, but I didn't approach the counter. Not yet. I lingered in the aisle until the attendant finished his magazine. He gave a slight, self-satisfied nod as if approving of the premise of what he read as he shut the last page. He returned the magazine to its rack, strumming the tops of the other issues as he considered what to read next. Before he could make a choice, I stepped up to the counter, setting down the granola bars and coffee. Surveying the items, the attendant's eyes and hands worked together at the cash register like those of a maestro whose fingers instinctively dance over piano keys when reading sheet music. He announced the price, which was a little less than five dollars.

"I was here a few weeks ago," I said, fishing the wallet from my pants.

The attendant glanced up.

"I don't know if you remember," I added.

Our eyes met. Slowly, he shook his head, no.

"A young man came in here . . . was very rude. He had red hair and refused to pay."

"Many people come in here," said the attendant, who now bagged my items. "Often they are rude." He spoke the words in a monotone that consigned me to this cohort of rude people. He passed me the bag and blinked with irritation at the five-dollar bill I'd removed from my wallet. I didn't hand over the money, not yet. "Surely you remember," I said. "He stole some soda. When you confronted him about it, he refused to pay. On his way out the door he—" The words caught in my throat; I didn't want to repeat the ugliness spoken by the redheaded boy, though could still hear him sneering "And neither is you" as he sauntered into the night. Instead, I said, "He . . . made a nasty remark."

The attendant stared at me emptily; again, he dipped his eyes impatiently to my five-dollar bill. I palmed it onto the counter and took my bag. When he offered me change, I refused, "You keep it." But he was insistent that he didn't want it. When I became equally insistent that he keep it, he tried unsuccessfully to stuff the dollar and few coins into the bag. Clearly, he remembered the redheaded boy and didn't want to accept any gesture of reconciliation from me. Frustrated as I was, I went to leave. The attendant ducked beneath his counter and stepped toward the door as if he might block my way (in the manner he surely wished he'd blocked the redheaded boy those weeks before). But then he stopped himself. "That orange juice," he said, gesturing toward my back pocket. "You didn't pay for that."

I'd forgotten that I'd taken it.

"What you've left isn't enough." The attendant did some quick math as he returned to the counter, took a dime and two pennies from his own pocket, dropped them in his register and slammed its drawer shut. "Now you can go."

I walked firmly away from the mini-mart and back to the mechanic's garage. Against the outside wall was a bench. A persistent summer sun heated the asphalt and was only made endurable by a steady, light breeze. Disinterestedly, I nibbled at my granola bars, waiting for the mechanic to finish his work and finding that I'd lost much of my appetite. I didn't entirely understand what had happened with the attendant. I had only wanted to apologize. I had wanted to let him know that I acknowledged my mistake. But had the attendant wanted to forget? Had he wanted to forget the indignity that I'd unwittingly inflicted on him with the red-headed boy? If so, he surely wanted to forget the myriad other indignities he must've suffered over a lifetime. Still, I've never understood willful forgetfulness and this desire to obliterate certain, unpleasant memories.

I drank my coffee and my orange juice. I finished my two granola bars. And I sat on the bench for the remainder of the hour. Inside, I could hear the pneumatic shriek of the mechanic's tools as well as the breakneck rumble of his music (some type of heavy metal). Eventually, the music switched off and the tools grew silent. The mechanic threw open the garage door and ducked outside. He squinted into the sun and massaged his filthy hands with his familiar rag. "You're all set," he said, nodding toward my Volvo. The effect of the four gleaming new tires on the car was like fine tailoring on a once-impoverished but now suddenly wealthy man. Leaving the car door open, the mechanic slid behind the driver's seat. He pointed out a gauge on the dashboard that I'd never paid attention to and explained why I needed to start paying better attention to it (something about viscosity and oil levels). He opened the glove box and showed where he'd tucked away the warranty for the tires (three years plus a rebate for my next set). I had owned this car for decades, yet with an hour's work the mechanic had transformed it.

When he stepped out of the driver's seat, I asked him about the attendant at the mini-mart.

"Mr. Omid? Pain in the ass." The mechanic glanced across the few dozen yards of steaming asphalt. "Try being late on your rent with him."

"He owns this place?"

"Technically, his sons now own it. He passed it all down to them. One lives in Richmond, the other in New York . . . at least I think it's New York. Anyways, they own dozens of these service stations, all up and down the interstate, also apartments, commercial real estate, and land, plenty of it. This garage used to be my father's, but Mr. Omid bought him out. I guess it was . . . ," and he glanced upward as if counting the days as they shuttled past overhead, "twenty-two years ago. The money gave my father a nice retirement, but he passed awhile back." When I said I was sorry to hear that, the mechanic shrugged, as if no condolences were necessary; this was the way with things, and so he continued: "Mr. Omid, he refuses to retire. When his sons drop by, they make sure that I'm keeping an eye on him, that he isn't working too hard. That old man's a millionaire many times over. He doesn't need to work another day in his life, but he always takes his shifts out here. It'd probably kill Mr. Omid if he had to stay at home. People get set in their ways. Who are we to change them, right?"

SEVEN

ADJUDICATION

A handful of days passed before Ableson arrived. I had expected him sooner but knew the time he had taken before paying me this visit was time he'd allotted to his thoughts. So that when I opened my front door and saw the warm smile on his upturned face, he appeared much the same as when we'd first met. Or, put another way, he appeared like a man who had regained possession of himself, despite all that he had endured and would have to endure. A sense of ease and self-awareness exuded from him. I noticed that he wore new clothes—nothing fancy, simple khakis and a blue polo shirt—and he clasped a dark bottle by the neck, which he proudly presented. It was a bottle of Bowmore Scotch. "Bought twenty-seven years ago, a gift to myself when Boose was born," he explained as we sat across from one another companionably. I examined its unbroken red wax seal. "Grab a couple of glasses," he added.

I went to the kitchen and rifled through the cupboards, searching for a pair of tumblers. Our martini glasses, teacups, and a couple of ceramic mugs littered a high shelf. I took down the mugs, which would have to suffice. If Ableson felt any disappointment at having to drink so fine a Scotch in so unceremonious a manner, he didn't reveal it. Instead, he leaned against his seat and regarded the bottle in his hand with sentiment, staring into the ochre liquid as if memorizing the face of a loved one. I said that we could always mix our customary martinis and save the bottle for some other occasion.

"No, no," he insisted. "Let's open it now."

"What were you saving it for?"

He'd set the bottle on the table between us as I finished cleaning out the inside of our mugs with a square of paper towel. "The thing is, I've never really known. I had once thought that Mary and I might drink it on our fiftieth wedding anniversary. Or that I might drink it with Boose's future husband to celebrate their engagement; that is, if she ever got married. No matter—"

I unhinged my jaw to speak, to tell him that he should wait, that even if none of those things would ever happen, something else might happen, something worth saving the bottle for. Before I could put words to any of that, he had, in a single jerk of his wrist, yanked out the cork; it released with a hollow, sucking sound, that loosened like an expiring breath. Ableson's whole face came alight as if he'd discovered a renewed capacity to surprise himself. As he held the now open bottle in his hand, he placed its neck beneath his nose. He blinked and then moistened his lips. "Take a sniff," he offered, reaching across the table. Hesitantly, I craned my neck forward, inhaling. The fragrance of the Scotch existed in an accumulation of layers. The soil: the grain mash grown in that soil. The water: the rocks from the brook where that water was drawn. The wood of the cask: the iron that bound the cask. I could even smell the bottle itself: the fired sand that had made the glass. But it was a single ingredient that brought these others into harmony: time.

"You thirsty?" asked Ableson. But he didn't wait for my answer and splashed the Scotch in our mugs. He held his aloft.

"What should we drink to?" I asked.

"Nothing," he said. "Let's just drink."

"Here's to nothing," and as I tilted back my mug, I noticed him giving me a mildly reproachful look, as though by speaking I had spoiled the solemnity of his non-toast; still, we drank. Or, to be precise, we drank in silence. I nursed my Scotch and Ableson soon outpaced me, pouring himself a second. The silence was a way to savor the drink. Although I could appreciate a good Scotch, I struggled to decide whether the price and age of this bottle gave it any great advantage over the cheaper varieties I was accustomed to on the rare occasions that I drank Scotch at all.

Toward the end of his second drink, Ableson had had enough of the silence and he started talking about Halcyon. "Boose has taken over the garden's redesign," he announced. "She's even convinced the workmen to come in on weekends to finish." He took great pride in explaining how his daughter was not only completing Mary's plan but also expanding on it: digging out a pond and hemming in the back of the garden with a grove of pear trees that would blossom and bear fruit. "It's nice to see she's got her own vision of this place," he said, topping off what would be his third Scotch. I nodded, pleased that he was pleased, although I struggled to imagine Boose—who seemed unable to place her own life in order—neatly organizing a garden on grounds as expansive as Halcyon's. Perhaps Ableson sensed my skepticism because he added, "It's remarkable what children are capable of when their parents stand out of the way. I did have to put my foot down about one thing, though."

"What's that?"

"Her mother's peonies," said Ableson. "Boose wanted to dig them up." He swirled his mug, staring into the well-aged Scotch before taking another mouthful and continuing: "I guess I see her point. She says having the flowers bloom the same time each year is too painful a reminder of her mother. She insists that her mother would've wanted her to plant the garden her own way. Still, I said no . . . Well, that's not exactly what I said. What I said was that she couldn't dig them up so long as I was around."

"What's that supposed to mean?" I set down my mug.

He leaned against the sofa, expanding his arms across its back with a forced casualness. "Just what I said. I don't want Boose digging up her mother's flowers while I'm still around. After I'm gone, she can do what she likes." He knew, however, that he hadn't quite answered my question. I induced an uncomfortable silence between us. "Oh, c'mon," he said. "Who got to you? Was it Shields? The two Joneses? Or wait, let me guess: all three."

"They're worried about you." I shifted in my seat, concealing my mouth with another sip of the Scotch.

"Worried about what?"

I didn't want to answer him.

He asked again and still I didn't answer, so he answered the question himself. "When you think of everything I've put myself through to eke out more time on this earth, do you really think I would take my own life? Even if I wanted to, do you think I could do it?" The bottle sat between us. It was a third empty. He noticed me noticing it. He snatched it by the neck and replaced its cork. "Best to save the rest for later," he said, as if what we'd drunk proved the validity of the doctors' suspicions.

I wondered, though. When a person's life ceased having a logic to it, or when it began to inhibit the lives of those whom they loved, did a threshold exist beyond which any decent person would take their own life? From what I'd learned of Julia Benson's story, she seemed like a woman who had reached that threshold and had thus committed a sacrifice, not a suicide. It was the same for Ableson's old comrade Doc Shields. But what about Ableson himself? What was his threshold? Or, as he insinuated, was it possible that it didn't exist? For some, perhaps life was always worth living in whatever form it was lived. Of course, there was no way of knowing whether or not Ableson was one of these people. For now, I would simply have to take his word for it.

Our evening together had deteriorated into awkward tension. To salvage the rapport between us, Ableson invited me to Halcyon for the following morning. He thought Boose might enjoy showing off her progress on the garden. When I arrived at a little after ten a.m., the front door was ajar and led to the open bank of French doors on the far side of the foyer. A breeze that passed through gave the distinct effect that the entire house was breathing and thus alive.

The garden was an eruption of blooms, everything chirping and croaking, whistling and splashing, as though in conversation with itself. Boose had planted a border of purple aster around a modest fountain that gurgled in the center. The many-colored peonies sat crowded in their rows. Thick hydrangeas hung heavy as crowns. I'm not one of these people who has an exhaustive vocabulary of flowers, but dozens of varieties blended in with these few that I've mentioned. The effect was kaleidoscopic, mesmerizing, so that as I stood by the open French doors, looking out at this creation which I recognized as a combination of Boose's ingenuity and her mother's, I didn't notice that Boose herself was standing beside me.

She carried a tray with her elbows tightly bent. Balanced on it was a glass carafe of lemonade as well as three crystal tumblers, of the type that would've been more appropriate for the Scotch from the night before, the effects of which had left me with an obstinate headache. "Good morning," she said in an uncharacteristically sunny manner, and I noticed her white hostess dress. It was simple and linen and light seemed to pass through it. "My father's still upstairs, but let's go sit in the garden." I followed her out onto the terrace, to a shaded table beneath a portico that smelled like a fresh coat of paint. A used ashtray sat on the table, which she promptly removed, not wanting me to see it, and I could imagine her sitting out here at night, after her father had drifted to sleep, trying to calm her anxieties one cigarette at a time. This house was hers now. The lemonade, the hostess dress, such gestures of conventional hospitality came awkwardly as she assumed her role as family matriarch and mistress of Halcyon. She poured us a lemonade each and we settled into our seats in the shade.

"Those pear trees already blossomed," she said, gesturing across the garden with her glass so that the ice cubes clinked pleasantly against the crystal. "The fruit should be ripe by now." I half thought she might cross the garden and pluck us a few of the pears but she didn't, at least not yet. She spoke about the hydrangeas, which she'd need to clip soon. "If you don't, they rot on their stems." Then she talked about other perennials, like lilac and rhododendron, slipping into a horticultural lexicon I struggled to understand, except by understanding that it was a language of regeneration and growth. The constant upkeep, the needed attention—this, of course, was the allure.

She hoped to plant more fruit trees. When the pears ripened, she planned to package and mail them to friends. Her brothers were top of that list. When I asked if they were still staying in the house, she said, "Both went home," and I imagined Doug and Bobby re-ensconced in their lives, two grown men among their families while Boose took up her lonelier inheritance here, in Halcyon. I had a sense from Boose that she not only felt her half brothers withdrawing from her, but the rest of the world as well. Shipping fruit from her garden out into that world must have seemed like a way to remain connected to it, to fight off the burden of isolation she had assumed with Halcyon.

Although her mother's death had settled Halcyon's ownership, the rest of the Ableson estate remained an open question. A week from now, the entire family would gather on a conference call with the judge, who would finally rule on the validity of Ableson's will and the disposition of its several millions of dollars. "I'll be talking to my brothers then," she said. "The judge is simply going to read the ruling so there's no reason for them to travel back down here." Without Mary binding the Ableson children together, I suspected they might become the type of extended family that passed for little better than acquaintances. No matter what Boose sent Doug and Bobby from her garden, it seemed that eventually her father would be the only family she had left.

"And what are you two plotting?" asked Robert Ableson as he stepped through the French doors. He cleared away a mess of paint cans and thinner left out by the workmen and brought over another seat that he placed beside Boose, who poured him a lemonade, which he drank half of in a single, thirsty gulp.

"I was telling Martin about our upcoming phone call with the judge."

"Ah, that," said Ableson. He finished his glass, which his daughter promptly refreshed. Similar to our last visit, he wore a new set of clothes; this time, it was a billowy red linen shirt and tan linen pants. The breeze on the portico passed easily through the fabric and gave him the appearance of being a man at leisure, certainly not a man who might harm himself as his doctors feared. (Why would a person intent on suicide buy new clothes?) "The ruling will be what it will be," Ableson said, clinking the ice cubes in his glass. "Your friend Ginny has done an excellent job presenting our case. There's really nothing else to do . . . well, except maybe this . . ." Ableson unfastened the second button of his shirt and for the first time I noticed the pendant against his chest—the 1914 Mercury dime. Ableson unhooked the clasp from around his neck. He threaded the dime off its chain and pinched it between his thumb and index finger, holding it up to us both. "I used to rehearse my closing arguments in front of Mary. She had a great ear. We'd go over and over them together, until I was exhausted. Then, ultimately, we'd flip a coin to predict how the judge would rule the next day. You ready?" he asked, glancing first at Boose and then at me. "Call it."

He tossed the coin in the air, allowing it to tumble end over end before snatching it in one hand and slapping it down on the back of the other.

His eyes rested on Boose. She shook her head; no, she didn't want to call it.

He leveled his gaze on me. I didn't want to call it either.

"You two aren't any fun," he said playfully. He removed the dime from the back of his hand without seeing if it had come out heads or tails. "That's okay," said Ableson. "We don't need to see how it lands."

He refastened the pendant around his neck and rebuttoned his collar. Boose then excused herself. She walked down into the garden, leaving me with Ableson at the table. She was going to check on her pears, to see if they were ripe.

The story appeared a few days later in the metro section of the *Times-Dispatch*. A single column announced that the records office had certified Lucas Harlow's petition for the removal of the Virginia Monument from Gettysburg. When asked about the timeframe, the quote attributed to Susan Templeton was a single word: "Immediately." The article then specified the date—which was the day after tomorrow—when a work crew would demolish the pedestal and begin the process of transferring the bronze sculpture into storage until it could be housed in a museum or some other similarly suitable venue.

Evidently, Lucas Harlow and his associates had recognized their mistake from before, in which they'd organized a massive demonstration to coincide with their submittal of the petition signatures. This time they'd ensured the effort remained quiet, no crowds at the records office, no speeches. The monument's dismantling would elicit no more inches of newspaper print than the obscurest of obituaries. Perhaps it was this lack of fanfare that compelled me to drive north, into the Pennsylvania countryside, in the blue-black morning darkness of that appointed day to ensure the presence of at least one witness.

I suspected others might come. Lucas Harlow for one. When I

pulled into the visitor parking lot, it was beside several large dump trucks and a vehicle-mounted crane but also a white Prius with a Gettysburg College parking sticker adhered to the front left windshield. The same leafy grove of trees that had once obscured Pickett and his troops now obscured the demolition crew up ahead. Already, I could hear the cadence of their jackhammers, the shout of the foreman, the siren that bleated every time a truck reversed.

The monument was sealed off like a crime scene. Inside the yellow tape a dozen men worked. A dozen men to erase the history of the fifteen thousand who had crossed the field to our front. Of course, it wasn't the demolition crew who would alter that history, so much as the many who had lent their names to Lucas Harlow's petition. I remained outside the taped-off perimeter, watching from a distance. The crane arm hovered overhead, reaching higher than the treetops, while the workmen noosed steel cables around the necks of the bronze Confederate soldiers at the base of the monument's granite pedestal. After each of the workmen gave their foreman the thumbs-up, he shouted his okay into a handheld radio. The slack came out of the cables with a steel-on-bronze shriek as the crane arm lifted. The Confederate soldiers—those seven representative figures of a bygone and misbegotten cause—dangled by their necks, swaying gently among the trees, before the crane swooped round in an arc and dropped them unceremoniously in the bed of an awaiting truck. Immediately, one of the workmen flung a tarp over the load, shrouding their now skyward-looking faces.

With the figures removed from the base of the monument, I could see Lucas Harlow standing on its far side. He walked in my direction around the perimeter of yellow tape while the workmen prepared for the next phase of dismantling; this required them to remove the statue of General Lee himself, mounted on Traveller, which sat affixed to its twenty-seven-foot-tall granite pedestal. When Lucas Harlow came up beside me, my head was tilted backward. I was watching a single intrepid member of the demolition crew—a boy not older than eighteen—monkeying his way up the bronze work with a noosed pair of steel cables slung cross-body over his chest. He looped the first around Traveller's neck and the second around Lee's.

"Did you ever think you'd see this?" said Lucas Harlow as the nooses tightened. He was also staring upward, his head flung back.

I told him how clever I thought it was that he'd chosen not to publicize his petition this time around.

"I can't take credit for that," he said. "If I'd had my druthers, our supporters would have marched on the state capitol and sued the governor after what Ableson did. Susan convinced me otherwise. She said that if we handed in our petition quietly, we could get rid of the monument quietly. That's how real change comes about, I guess, when no one's looking." Then he asked about Ableson.

"He's doing all right," I said. "There's Susan's complaint, of course . . . ," and Lucas Harlow simply nodded, acknowledging its existence but refusing to comment. "The judge is supposed to rule on the will in the next few days so that might clear the matter up, depending on the decision."

"The decision about what?" he asked.

"Whether his children keep their inheritance."

The boy who'd set the steel cable around Lee's neck shimmied down the flank of Traveller in his climb to the ground. The other workers who stood at the base of the pedestal clapped him on the back for a job well done. Everyone backed away and the foreman once again spoke into his radio, signaling for the crane to hoist Lee from his pedestal. The steel noose cinched tight; and as it bit into the bronze the noise was terrific. Then Lee was up in the air, dangling. Before the crane swiveled toward the bed of the second truck—the one that would consign the old general to storage—an unexpected and eerie gust of wind blew up from between the ranks of trees. The gust mustered itself into a sustained wind. On and on the wind came. The foreman shouted panicky instructions into his radio. The crane arm struggled to steady itself. Despite the sheer weight of the statue, the violent wind that came out from the trees threatened to free the old general, to fling Lee back up onto his pedestal.

Then, as suddenly as the wind appeared, it vanished. The air around us grew still. The workmen, Lucas Harlow, and I, we all stood beneath the statue as it swung on the arm of the crane like the pendulum inside an obsolete clock. The foreman said something into his radio, though I couldn't hear the particulars as he spoke in little more than a whisper. Very slowly—even tentatively—the crane operator set the statue of Lee into the bed of the second truck. Only after the workmen had thrown a tarp over it did Lucas Harlow turn to me and say, "That was the damnedest thing I ever saw."

A furious jackhammering commenced on the granite pedestal. Neither Lucas Harlow nor I had earplugs and the head-splitting noise was unendurable. "You want to take a walk?" he shouted. He pointed to his watch. It was two o'clock, the same hour that Pickett's men had departed this row of trees, stepping out across a mile of open fields, toward the low stone wall that concealed a frontage of ten thousand Union soldiers.

I nodded and we left.

More so than other Civil War battlefields—the Wilderness, Chancellorsville, Shiloh—the topography of Gettysburg tells the story of the battle. Whether it's Culp's Hill or Little Round Top, the land itself with its dictates—with its immutable advantages and disadvantages—determined the outcome. It was the same with Pickett's Charge, which Lucas Harlow and I now walked. The grass stands ankle high across the mile-wide field. In the afternoon it is dry and makes a brushing sound as you pass through it, kicking up motes of dust in the summer, as it must have done in the stifling heat of that July day nearly one hundred and fifty years before. At first, the ground descends slightly. It is easy to imagine Pickett and his men taking these early, encouraging steps, in which the terrain conceals their advance. At the lowest point of the field, about a third of the way before the Union line, a deep quiet permeates. The soil is damp. You vanish into the landscape, concealed within its gentle folds. Gradually, the ground rises again. The first of several split rail fences appear. After climbing over each fence Pickett's advancing troops struggled to re-form their lines. Then up out of the rise they came.

Lee's trusted deputy Longstreet had never wanted them to make this charge, which at this point commenced less like a charge and more like a steady walk. The December before he had fought at Fredericksburg, where the positions had been switched and the Union troops had charged the Confederates who had assembled their thousands behind a low stone wall. That had been a winter battle, and one participant had observed how watching whole lines of advancing Union soldiers dissolve into musket fire was like watching snow fall and then melt against a pane of warm glass. The Southerners had harvested a crop of thousands of Union dead that day, delivering the rebellion one of its greatest victories. That winter night, when the sky turned dark, lashes of aurora borealis appeared overhead. Both the Southern troops tucked behind their fortifications and the Northern troops stranded on the field, barricaded behind corpses and the writhing bodies of their mortally wounded, stared upward. The northern lights never appeared this far south and they all struggled to interpret the occurrence. The Southerners declared it was God himself celebrating a Confederate victory. Gripped by defeat, the Northerners reacted more somberly, concluding that the swirl of brilliant colors were the souls of their recently departed comrades ascending heavenward. With Pickett's Charge, Longstreet knew this was all about to repeat but in reverse. He brimmed with impotent fury and refused to watch the battle alongside Lee at his headquarters.

When Pickett's troops marched up the gradual rise they could—for the first time—see the distant stone wall they knew as their objective. Multiple accounts from Union soldiers attested to an audible Confederate groan, the sound lifting from the throats of thousands of men as they despaired all at once when seeing how much farther they'd have to advance and the impossibility of their task. Here, again, topography plays its role. At that exact moment, the Union gunners could also see Pickett's men. A fusillade of shells tore into both flanks of the mile-wide line. Walking up the rise with Lucas Harlow, I could see what Pickett's men had seen: the low stone wall to my front; Cemetery Hill to my left, where clusters of Union guns gathered; the Devil's Den and Little Round Top to my right, where the day before the battle had almost been won; but right here, on this field, this was the place where it had all finally come apart. At the top of the rise, with the stone wall in view, Lucas Harlow and I began to walk faster. The reaction was instinctual. We weren't at a run, but the desire to run was in our legs, the urge like a ghost, or a message communicated by the land itself, from those who'd fallen right here. *Run*, it seemed to say. *Run for your life.*

Inside of two hundred yards, Pickett's men came within range of the Union rifles. His mile-long line had contracted to a half mile after the Union artillery gnawed away the flanks. The defending soldiers began to chant vengefully "Fredericksburg! Fredericksburg!" as they gunned down Pickett's men, and it didn't take a military strategist like a Meade or a Hancock to recognize the stupidity and hubris of the gamble Lee had made, one that would result in his defeat and Pickett's utter destruction.

I was trailing a few steps behind Lucas Harlow as he vaulted over the low stone wall. He crouched into a kneeling position on its far side. His hands were angled as if he carried an imaginary rifle, which he pointed at me playfully. Breathing heavily from the walk, I threw up my hands in surrender.

"Bang!" he said.

I clutched my chest.

Then the two of us sat, a pair of mismatched friends. When I checked my watch, it was twenty minutes past two o'clock. On July 3, 1863, Pickett's Charge had run between two and two thirty that afternoon. Thirty minutes, that's all it'd taken. The last ten minutes proved most intense and comprised hand-to-hand fighting on the wall where we now sat. The defeated remnants of the Southern assault had then retreated across the field, back into the woods on Seminary Ridge, where Lee had met them, mounted on Traveller, telling his troops that this failure wasn't theirs but his, that "It's all my fault." We sat facing those woods.

I had made this walk countless times; but, perched on the wall, I realized I'd never crossed this ground with Lucas Harlow despite our years of friendship (strained though it had often been). "No, we haven't," he said in firm response to my observation as though this were a detail he had more carefully tracked. Then, gazing across the field, he pointed a mile away, to where the demolition crew had nearly completed the jackhammering of the granite pedestal. We'd wait until they finished before crossing back.

As we caught our breath Lucas Harlow again asked me about Ableson. What would he do if the judge revoked his will? I tried to answer, but couldn't say how Ableson might react to such a verdict, which would wipe out his heirs.

Lucas Harlow stared in the direction of Pickett's retreat. "Can you take back an inheritance?" he asked. I tried to explain the mechanics by which Ableson's children would forfeit their wealth in the event the judge invalidated his will. I was tripping over certain details when he interrupted me: "If some ancestor of yours had crossed this field with Pickett, you could never change that."

"No," I said. "I suppose you couldn't."

"You couldn't," he answered definitively. "Some inheritances you can't give back." For the first time, I understood why Lucas Harlow and I had never before walked Pickett's Charge together, despite having both toured so much of this battlefield. I understood why he'd chosen to teach at Gettysburg College among the many other institutions that might have employed him. This Mississippi football player turned scholar, this son of the South who made his life in the North and who wanted to tear down the monuments to his ancestors; he too was troubled by an inheritance. His inheritance was this field. I could read Shelby Foote, learn the details of the Civil War, and understand the history of the nation my ancestors had adopted; but I could do it all objectively, which is to say abstractly, devoid of emotion. Lucas Harlow had no such luxury. Some ancient member of his bloodline had charged across this field. Like the redheaded boy at the gas station, his blood was literally in this soil, and he had committed himself to the impossible task of erasing the mistake of spilled blood.

"Right there," he said. "That's the marker." He gestured behind his shoulder, to a knee-high granite square. He remained sitting on the wall as I wandered over and read the brass plaque affixed to its top:

JULY 3, 1863. THE 11TH MISSISSIPPI INFANTRY REGIMENT, WITH ITS RANKS GROWING THINNER AT EVERY STEP, ADVANCED WITH THE COLORS TO THE STONE WALL NEAR BRIAN BARN.

THE REGIMENT WAS HERE "SUBJECTED TO A MOST GALLING FIRE OF MUSKETRY AND ARTILLERY THAT SO REDUCED THE ALREADY THINNED RANKS THAT

ANY FURTHER EFFORT TO CARRY THE POSITION WAS
HOPELESS, AND THERE WAS NOTHING LEFT BUT TO
RETIRE."

—REPORT OF BRIG. GEN. JOSEPH R. DAVIS

That was it. Only the specifics of what had happened.

No Lee on his horse.

No seven Confederate soldiers gallantly posed.

Staring down at the marker, so much of my friendship with
Lucas Harlow came into relief. I thought of the evening decades
before, when we'd heard Shelby Foote lecture and Lucas had chosen dinner with Annette over meeting our once-shared hero. I had
judged Lucas harshly then. Now I understood that he couldn't hide
himself from Foote, a fellow Mississippian. Foote would've known
his family, perhaps even the name of his ancestor; Foote would've
known that the 11th Mississippi Infantry regiment—the famously
doomed University Grays—sustained more than one hundred per-
cent casualties; and Foote would have known the exact position of
the marker where I stood, and Lucas Harlow hadn't been ready
for that. It was only now, after demolishing the largest monument
on the battlefield, that he would acknowledge his inheritance. And,
because we shared a past, he acknowledged it to me.

I sat beside him on the low stone wall, the two of us dipped in
that communal silence unique to old battlefields. Then Lucas Harlow and I walked back the way we came. The demolition crew had
finished its work and the view looked different. The trees along
Seminary Ridge appeared larger without General Lee presiding
among them and I had never before noticed the way in which his
presence had diminished them for these many long years. When
Lucas Harlow and I returned, nothing remained of the Virginia
Monument except for a large square of upturned dirt that the Park
Service would cover with a patch of fresh sod.

We said goodbye. We promised to see each other more often and left that day as what we had always been to one another: friends. When I pulled out of the parking lot, Lucas Harlow wasn't yet to his car. Something compelled him to linger for a few moments on his own. Before pulling onto the road that would take me to Halcyon, I saw him bend over and pick a stone out from the grass. It was a shard of white granite from General Lee's pedestal. He tucked it in his pocket. It seemed he couldn't resist taking a part of the monument with him.

Public radio carried that evening's presidential debate as I drove back to Halcyon. The broadcaster called the event with a low, smooth monotone as if with her voice she was recreating every drive, putt, or chip in a round of PGA golf: the two candidates take the stage and meet in its well-lit center. Gore extends his hand first. Bush shakes it, but he grasps Gore by the bicep as well, controlling their exchange. He's cheerful, his shoulders hiccupping when he laughs in that inimitable way, the way that makes so many Americans feel as though they could have a beer with him. Gore now reaches for Bush's bicep, but it's an after-the-fact gesture, and before he can complete it the handshake is over and Gore is left grasping at nothing.

One at a time, the two of them approach the moderator and shake his hand. Tonight's questions will be asked by esteemed reporter Jim Lehrer of *PBS NewsHour*. They take their places, Gore barricaded behind his lectern, stage left, and Bush behind his lectern, stage right. Each has a single glass of water. A single pen. A pad of paper. Gore sips from his water. Bush waves at the crowd. The debate is scheduled for one and a half hours, nearly the exact remainder of my drive between Gettysburg and Halcyon. Lehrer explains the ground rules, which presumably both candidates have already heard, so this is more for the audience of 43.6 million Americans. Then the questions begin.

Foreign policy comes first. After the September 11 attacks, Gore had faced criticism from Republicans, Bush included, for not fully investigating the potential role played by Saddam Hussein's regime. If granted a second full term as president how would he deal with the Iraqi leader? Gore begins his response by telling Mr. Lehrer that he's glad he asked the question. After a minor preamble, in which Gore affirms the horrors of 9/11, he reminds listeners of all his administration has done to keep the nation safe in the three years since. Let's not forget it was his administration that by that very same Christmas had hunted down and killed Osama bin Laden, the mastermind of the attacks. But there's something about the way Gore speaks, how he feels he must remind us who bin Laden was—"the mastermind of the attacks"—as if we'd forgotten. His critics often indict him with the term *professorial* as it relates to his communications style, and this is on display now. He explains that his administration has found no evidence of a connection between Saddam Hussein and September 11. When it comes to Iraq, he says the United States lacks a *casus belli* (and Bush ticks an eyebrow skyward when he hears the Latin).

Mr. Lehrer asks Bush if he agrees.

With a high-noon swagger, Bush shakes his head. No, Jim, can't say that I do. This is a man, Bush explains, who tried to kill my father, our president. This is a man, he adds, who on "nina-leven" made common cause with the terrorists. And he holds the *r* in the word, revving the letter like an engine. This is a man, Bush says once more, having now created a refrain, who wishes this great nation harm and has the resources at his disposal to do it. Then Bush turns to Gore and he says, Al, I just don't think you've done your homework on this one.

Al . . . homework . . .

Bush creates a moment.

Mr. Lehrer moves on to the next question but Gore is beside himself, choking on his response to Bush's accusation. When the follow-up question is directed to Bush, Gore raises his hand. But instead Mr. Lehrer finishes his question and the president is left standing behind his lectern, with his hand raised like a child who will not be called upon in class . . . This image creates another moment.

The question Lehrer asks is about education, school vouchers and whether Bush supports such programs. Four years before, the issue formed a centerpiece of his campaign. Among his supporters, school choice remains popular, it polls well, and the question allows Bush to launch into an aria about *compassionate conservatism*, buzzwords focus-grouped to target crossover voters. On this issue, Gore gives as good as he gets. He discusses the primacy of public schools in our communities and the importance of teachers and their unions. He decries Bush's efforts to privatize education. The word "privatize" is one he presses down on hard.

But it's the only blood Gore will draw that night.

The debate careens from one issue to the next as Mr. Lehrer ticks off his list of questions. When Bush outlines a plan for corporate tax cuts, Mr. Lehrer pushes him on how he'll pay for this. Bush then accuses Gore of being hesitant to reinvest in America. Gore explains that his predecessor passed a balanced budget on to him and he has every intention of keeping the nation out of the red. But the issue of budgets quickly loses people's attention and Mr. Lehrer knows this. At the mention of Gore's predecessor, he asks a question about the Clinton pardon, which every poll shows as Gore's greatest political liability. He is, of course, prepared for the question. But there is no level of preparation that will absolve him of his sin, which isn't the pardon per se but the hypocrisy it speaks to. And, listening, I was reminded of Ableson and what he'd said to me months before, how it is time itself that makes hypocrites of us all. But that's not an answer for a nationally televised debate and Gore stumbles through a response.

The table is set for Bush. He embarks on an obviously well

rehearsed but up to this point undeployed line of rhetoric. This is the moment, he says, for moral leadership. The tired dogmas of the past two administrations are insufficient to meet the challenges facing the country. Equivocation is not leadership, he says, evoking the Clinton pardon. Appeasement is not leadership, he says, evoking the possible invasion of Iraq. And science is no replacement for the spirituality of this, our one nation under God, he says, evoking the breakthroughs that placed Ableson among the living.

Mr. Lehrer's next question is obvious. Gore drinks from his glass of water to ready himself. He must defend his funding of cryoregeneration and the controversial genetic restructuring that has upended the once impermeable barrier between life and death. When he sets his glass on the lectern, it is empty. Gore explains his vision of progress: he believes that frontiers are designed to be broken; that societies must travel forward or perish; he misquotes Martin Luther King Jr.: the *bend* of the moral universe is long and it *arcs* toward justice, confusing the placement of those two words. Harvard-educated man that he is, he even dips into some of the technical aspects of cryoregeneration, losing me and I imagine most of America in the arcana of scientific detail. Mr. Lehrer interrupts him, but he isn't quite ready to concede the floor.

Gore insists on one last point, as though this will take his argument over the finish line and convince every American, no matter how skeptical, that the future of the nation exists in the scientific breakthroughs supported by his administration. But Gore's throat is dry and his glass of water is empty. He begins to cough. He swallows desperately but the coughing gets worse. Soon he can't speak. Red-faced, with one hand pressed to his chest and the other gripping the lectern, he drowns in this coughing fit. There's a minor commotion, as for a moment it seems as though Gore might be suffering a true medical emergency.

Bush rushes stage left. He's first there and carries his own glass of water. He offers it to Gore, who reluctantly drinks, regaining a modicum of composure. Bush asks if he's all right. When Gore tries to answer, he again descends into a coughing fit and this exchange is picked up and broadcast nationally through Gore's microphone. Eventually, Bush returns to his lectern across the stage and Mr. Lehrer invites him to formulate a rebuttal. Bush's remarks are familiar. He speaks about the sanctity of life, his Christian values, and God's plan for us all. He doesn't engage on the science of the issue but rather on its morality, dishing out a mélange of scripture that reinforces his personal belief that the pathway to everlasting life is only found through Jesus Christ, Son of God, Savior of mankind.

The debate is down to its last minute. Gore's lackeys have now placed an absurdly large carafe of water beside him. Mr. Lehrer grants Gore the stage. He has his final point to make, the summation of his argument for why the American people should embrace the controversial science pioneered by his administration. When Gore opens his mouth, his voice remains choked. He speaks in a weak, imploring whisper. Intermittently, he again succumbs to fits of coughing. While driving I had to lean in toward my radio but could make out at best only every other word. Gore must have known how with each squeaky, unintelligible phrase he spoke—or tried to speak—he was digging the grave of his own campaign. Whether it was Nixon sweating profusely under the television lights against Kennedy, or Reagan turning to Carter and saying "Oh, there you go again," many a presidential ambition has floundered and died on the debate stage. This type of political death was, after all, an American tradition. Gore arguing that science could overcome death while he couldn't overcome a simple fit of coughing would enter into this pantheon of American political catastrophes.

In those final moments of the debate, I pulled up to the guest cottage at Halcyon. I wanted to see Gore and Bush onstage to have a clearer image of the drama I'd listened to over this hour and a half, so I rushed inside and turned on the television. The pair of candidates still stood behind their lecterns. Gore had just finished speaking and his face was red as though he'd blown up several dozen balloons. He poured himself yet another glass of water. The camera reoriented on Jim Lehrer, who thanked the audience and viewers at home for joining him. Then he thanked the candidates. A close-up held on Bush, who took the opportunity not only to thank Mr. Lehrer, but also to thank the American people for allowing him to share with them his vision for the country. The close-up shifted to Gore, who had a similar opportunity. When he thanked Mr. Lehrer and the American people his voice had returned to him, full and clear. His expression was a mix of surprise and pure regret. If only his voice had returned a few moments before. With a little extra time, he could have said so much more.

A pounding on my front door woke me that night.

It was Boose.

"My God! Get up! Get up!"

When I turned the doorknob, it was snatched from my grip as she barreled over the threshold. She crossed the den in her night-gown, heading straight for the phone that hung on the kitchen wall. She jabbed her finger at the receiver, dialing 9-1-1, as I faced outside watching with utter disbelief as the flames rose from behind the partition of trees that divided the guest cottage from Halcyon. I could hear the crackle and fizz of the blaze and could feel the warm glow against my face even though it was hundreds of yards off. Behind me, Boose pleaded with a dispatcher for help. "He's still in there! . . . My father is still in there! . . ." and then a pause, followed by "Right now! . . . You have to send them now!" and when I turned inside I noticed the dustings of burnt hair on the backs of Boose's arms as she clutched the phone with both hands and how the hem of her haircut was uneven where the fire had singed it too.

"I'm going up there," I said, and she stared back at me as if in a dream when I ran out the door with my bare feet stuffed into my untied shoes.

I didn't make it far, not even to the end of the driveway. The wall of heat was too intense. Boose joined me. She seemed more confused than upset, stupefied at the speed and scope of destruction. When I muttered something about it being safer if we went back inside to wait for the fire department, she sat down in the driveway. It was as if she needed to watch Halcyon burn.

"I tried to get to his room . . . I couldn't."

"What happened?"

Her voice collapsed into a string of *I don't knows*, repeating the phrase in a cadence as if beating a set of oars against a ceaseless current, so I didn't ask her anything more. The trucks arrived and worked all through the night, dousing the property with their hoses so that the driveway turned to mud beneath us. Gradually, as the fire was put out, the night turned cold again. I went into the guest cottage and returned with a blanket for Boose to wrap herself in while I put on my coat. Hours passed, whole systems of stars traversed overhead as we waited in the driveway, and when the morning's light could be distinguished from the glow of the fire, all that remained of Halcyon were its chimneys in rubble, the charred outline of its foundation, and its largely unscathed garden. The fire chief—a woman compact like a gymnast and stern like a principal—had throughout the night intermittently checked in with Boose, asking her questions about the layout of the house and, early on, when a rescue of her father seemed plausible, asking for Robert Ableson's whereabouts inside.

"We're still looking," said the chief. "But when a house goes up like this it burns pretty hot; often, there's little if anything left to recover."

Boose drew silent.

The chief turned to me. "This isn't definite, but based on how the fire spread, it doesn't seem like it started inside the house."

"Where did it start?" I asked.

"Outside, likely on the portico," said the chief, who then asked whether anything flammable was stored there, anything that could've gone up quickly. Immediately, I thought of Boose and her cigarettes plus the few cans of paint and thinner I'd noticed before; however, I didn't say anything and Boose continued staring off in that dreamy, shell-shocked way. As if to anchor Boose, the chief said, "We did find this," and in her gloved hand was the pendant with the Mercury dime. "It was in the room where you said your father had been sleeping."

Boose flinched when the chief placed the pendant in her outstretched hand; it was still hot from the flames.

I abandoned the writing of my book. I couldn't say exactly when I made this decision. Perhaps I made it when I saw how despite Lucas Harlow's tenacious activism, he still couldn't resist pocketing a piece of General Lee's pedestal; or perhaps it was witnessing Halcyon burn to the ground and the noxious smell of its stubborn ashes that lingered in the air. The more I pondered the dissolution of my own work and its rosy hypothesis that a spirit of compromise underwrote American life, the more I felt like Gore in the debate, unable to string a coherent sentence together, even if that sentence might have changed the very trajectory of our existence.

I had decided to leave Halcyon once and for all and to return to an uncertain future at Virginia College without a completed book manuscript and so with little prospect of achieving tenure there, or anywhere else for that matter. As I was packing up my things shortly after the fire, Ginny unexpectedly arrived at my door. Along with Dr. Shields, she had traveled down from Philadelphia to help Boose attend to the end-of-life minutia surrounding

Ableson's death. She revealed that before the fire (while I had been at Gettysburg with Lucas Harlow, as I calculated it) the judge had ruled on the validity of Ableson's will.

The parties to the dispute had gathered on a conference call: Susan Templeton and her daughter, Ableson and his family, along with Dr. Shields and Ginny. The judge had read the ruling from a prepared document. It began with a preamble, noting the "exceptional nature of Mr. Robert Ableson's circumstances" and the lack of preexisting case law. Nevertheless, the judge had to rule on the validity of the will itself. Before doing this a definition of death was required. The judge, a self-proclaimed textualist, had referred to his copy of Merriam-Webster: "a permanent cessation of all vital functions: the end of life." If permanence was an enduring characteristic of death, the impermanence of Ableson's death meant that he had never really died. If he'd never really died that meant he had always been alive. If he had always been alive then the transfer of his assets in trust to his inheritors was illegitimate. Those assets now reverted back to him and could be subject to damages depending on the court's decision in the upcoming harassment suit *Templeton v. Ableson*. That was it.

The ruling had elicited a variety of reactions on the call:

Janet Templeton, speaking for both herself and her mother, had brandished her voice like a long-concealed weapon, asking the judge a number of tactical questions as to the trial's progression, the method of discovery, the criteria for introducing evidence, to include fact witnesses and expert testimony. Initially, the judge answered these questions with patience but increasingly that patience grew thin. This ruling was a gift to the Templetons and when Janet's eagerness matched that of a spoiled child tearing through a Christmas morning's worth of presents, it was only her mother who had restrained her and said they'd have time to answer those questions later. Doug and Bobby had reacted to the news by hanging up immediately. Ginny imagined they'd hopped off the call to get on another call with their respective accountants and brokers to figure out what, if any, portion of their inheritance they might salvage. Boose had taken her father's hand. She'd told him not to worry, while Dr. Shields had watched Robert Ableson from across the table, trying to ascertain what he might do next.

"Dr. Shields is at the main house with Boose," said Ginny. "They've got something they want to show you." The two of us traveled in silence the short distance from the guest cottage to the ashy remains of Halcyon, where Boose in her desire not to abandon her family's home had chosen to stay in a trailer lent to her by the builder who'd overseen the renovation. When we arrived, Boose and Dr. Shields were gathered around a table on what had been the portico. The fire had hardly touched the garden, which with summer waning had spent its flowers, so only a few stubborn blooms remained. The weather would soon turn, and months would pass before it was again warm enough to sit outside. Ginny and I joined Boose and Dr. Shields, who held a manila folder, similar to the one that had contained the article about Ableson and his father on Saipan. He handed the folder to me, saying, "This letter arrived yesterday at my office."

Inside was a handwritten note from Ableson. He had addressed it *To my loved ones*, and only a few lines followed, in which he said he'd made a mistake by *coming back*, that not enough existed here for him, and that he no longer wished to be a burden on anyone. *Life*, he concluded, *must resume its natural course*. Then he requested that they accept his choice.

"Have you phoned the police?" I asked.

Boose averted her eyes and Ginny glanced at Dr. Shields. It was clear that he was making the decisions. "We haven't yet," he said. "We wanted to talk to you first. When did Robert last pay you a visit?" Dr. Shields spoke with an utter lack of urgency, without any pretense of wanting to circumvent Ableson's desire to have life *resume its natural course*, which evidently included the fire that had consumed both him and Halcyon. Nevertheless, I explained how not quite two weeks before, Ableson and I had enjoyed a drink at the guest cottage together. "Did he say anything to you during that drink that you think the authorities should know?" And, as Dr. Shields asked, it became clear to me that the four of us were gathered around this table not so much in an effort to account for Ableson but rather in an effort to get our story straight before the authorities became involved, at which point I mentioned the bottle of Scotch. "Bowmore, I think it was. He said he'd bought the bottle when Elizabeth was born and that he'd been saving it for a special occasion."

Dr. Shields glanced at Boose. "It's important," he said, "that when the authorities arrive you mention he'd come by to drink that bottle with you. Did he give a reason why he'd finally chosen to open it?"

"No, no reason. He said now seemed as good a time as any."

"What else?" asked Dr. Shields. The question wasn't only posed to me, but also to Boose and Ginny as he glanced at the three of us around the table. When we shook our heads, he excused himself and went into the house to phone the authorities and thus set in motion the investigation into Robert Ableson's suicide.

Later that day, a half-dozen local and state police congregated at Halcyon, along with the two Drs. Jones. One by one they questioned the four of us. They asked about the note, about Ableson's state of mind before and after the judge's ruling, and, as Dr. Shields had predicted, when questioning me they showed particular interest in the bottle of Bowmore. During my interview on the portico, the Drs. Jones hovered behind the police, feeding them questions with an expression of mild panic frozen onto their faces. Throughout this ordeal, which stretched into hours, Dr. Shields was the picture of calm.

He had a story he needed to tell on Ableson's behalf. Without a body, it wasn't immediately clear that this was a suicide, although many of the signs were there: the note, the bottle of Scotch, and, most importantly, the motive. I wasn't certain what Dr. Shields said in his interview with the authorities, but I imagined this was a conversation he had long been preparing to have, perhaps ever since Ableson had first told him the carefully curated story of his own father's death. Now Dr. Shields had an opportunity to return the favor.

Of course, Ableson's suicide eliminated the Templetons as a concern. Their complaint of ongoing harassment would vanish as quickly as it had appeared. The law couldn't hold the dead to account in the same way it could the living. Ginny needed only to notify the judge, which she did as the authorities drew their questioning of Dr. Shields to a close late that afternoon. While Ginny and Dr. Shields remained occupied, Boose and I sat on the far end of the portico watching the sun set through a gray haze that hung over her property. For a woman who had twice endured the death of her father, as well as that of her mother, she seemed remarkably sanguine and in complete self-possession, as if she had always known it would come to this—which, if you think about it, makes perfect sense. How else would it go? Parents die. Children survive them. What remains is passed on. There is, as Ableson wrote, a natural order to things. Still, I felt myself in awe of her ability to endure that order.

"Janet Templeton won't take this well," she said with her gaze fixed over her garden. When I asked Boose whether she thought the Templetons might continue to cause her problems, she notched her eyes upward as if solving an algebraic equation; then, conclusively, she answered no, saying "Susan Templeton never really wanted to file a complaint against my father. Her daughter pressured her into it. Sure, Janet will be upset, at least for a while. But she's young . . . Every day that a person wakes up on this earth, think of all they have to forget just to get themselves together and keep going. The younger you are the less there is to forget, so it's easier. Janet will move on, finish her degree, maybe even discover some new galaxy in the cold, dark reaches of the universe. Also, her mother's petition succeeded in the end, so that helps too. I read in the paper a few days ago that the Gettysburg Park Service had torn down the Virginia Monument."

"I know. I was there."

"You were?" When she asked what that was like, I considered telling her about Lucas Harlow's complicated family history, the way we'd walked Pickett's Charge together, the grass brushing against our ankles, the gradual rise up toward the stone wall, and the marker dedicated to the 11th Mississippi Infantry. Ultimately, I chose not to mention any of it. That history wasn't mine. Lucas Harlow would have to decide what it meant to him, whether to teach it or to hide it. Now that he'd destroyed his monument, I hoped he would choose the former but the choice was his. To answer Boose's question of what it was like to see the Virginia Monument toppled, I simply answered, "It was time to let it go."

A beat of silence passed. "What's next for you?" she wanted to know.

"Head back to school, I guess. I have to teach next term."

"Will you finish your book there?" I told her, no; that I wouldn't be finishing my book at all. This confused her. When she asked why, I didn't have a satisfactory answer, except to say, "It just never came together in the end." She was very sorry to hear that and knew what a distraction her family could be. She hoped it wasn't their fault my work hadn't progressed. Maybe if I just gave it a little more time? When I told her that I'd decided to take a break from writing altogether, she again apologized, saying how she wished I'd had a better experience at Halcyon. "No," I said. "Don't be sorry. If anything, this place has given me a fresh start."

The two of us sat quietly. We watched the light change as it filtered through the grove of pear trees and fell on the last of the hydrangeas, aster, and Mary's old bed of peonies. Parts of the garden remained dug up in places. There was a bit more planting left to do but, despite the fire, it would soon be finished, and the house eventually rebuilt. In a year, or maybe two, Halcyon would be exactly as she'd always remembered it.

EIGHT

HALCYON

George W. Bush lost the popular vote that November but won in the Electoral College. On Thursday, January 20, 2005, he became the 44th president of the United States. Gore's supporters decried the antiquated system that delivered this result. Between the election and the inauguration, they demanded reforms, but once Bush took office, those calls for reform subsided until, eventually, everyone accepted things the way they'd always been.

Quieter, more considered voices hadn't blamed the Electoral College for Gore's defeat; instead, they had blamed his administration's failed scientific policies. Bush had carried the election with razor-thin margins and, had Gore stayed away from controversial programs like cryoregeneration, many believed he could have succeeded to a second term. Only days before the election, a spate of newspaper articles reported a series of suicides among those who had participated in Gore's programs, including Robert Ableson. Within Bush's first hundred days in office, he cut all federal funding for these programs and placed restrictions on any future research.

In the years that followed, I couldn't help but imagine alternate histories. What if Ableson had made a different set of choices? If he hadn't taken his own life, if he hadn't provoked Susan Templeton's harassment suit, would the scientific advances sponsored by the Gore administration have further advanced mankind's understanding of life, death, and the permeability between the two? They would have at least swung the election back in Gore's favor. But it wasn't only scientific policy and electoral outcomes I wondered about. During those first hundred days of Bush's administration, while he was quietly shutting down Gore's scientific initiatives, he was also laying the groundwork for an invasion of Iraq. This required his administration to educate the American people on a different science, one that involved theories about yellow cake, its uses, as well as the uses of certain aluminum tubes and the possibilities of uranium enrichment.

After that war started, it seemed as though the Bush administration ricocheted between crises, whether it was the president's failed response to Hurricane Katrina in 2005 or his administration's inability to predict the devastating financial crisis of 2008. Polling as low as he was, Bush proved no match for his challenger, whom I'd first heard of during those months I'd spent at Halcyon, when the idea of an African American president, elected by this country, had seemed a prospect as far-fetched among the electorate as resurrection once had been among the scientific community. In the lead-up to that election, I was glad that I was no longer teaching at Virginia College because our nation's long, complicated history with the Civil War again took center stage— although, due to the efforts of individuals like Lucas Harlow, who had made a name for himself as the country's leading advocate for the removal of Confederate monuments, much of the iconography of that period had been displaced from public view and consigned to a constellation of underfunded and poorly attended museums across the country.

Despite my continued affinity for Shelby Foote and my belief that compromise was the spirit that underwrote this country— even if I'd failed to coherently prove this point in a book—I had by this time made a career shift. I still taught, but not at the university level and not history. I had, instead, earned a certificate to teach elementary school math. With a bit of help from Ginny (who had handled the divorce of the superintendent of the Philadelphia schools) I had secured a job in the city and had resumed my life not far from the apartment where she and I had first lived when married. Unlike history, math was objective and defied interpretation. As for my students, they were ten- and eleven-year-old kids. As long as you taught the material, there was no wrong way to do it. Also, I'd met someone.

Amélie taught French. Dark-haired and dusky-eyed, she'd come from the gritty port city of Toulon on a two-year work visa, part of an exchange program to deliver more foreign-language instruction to inner-city public schools. Her English was shaky, my French nonexistent, but during her first semester our class schedules conspired to make us the only teachers in the faculty lounge for one fifty-minute period each day. She bore an uncanny resemblance to Ginny, which was perhaps part of the attraction, and the age difference between us was similar to that of Robert and Mary Ableson. Also, she wore her dark hair like Mary, tied back in a chignon that revealed her long neck. I fell for her instantly, and with me putting a little effort into my French-English dictionary she fell for me. Because of her youth, whole possibilities stretched before us, a new life, a family. Which left me equally excited and terrified.

Over a decade had passed since that summer at Halcyon, but I'd kept up with Dr. Shields and often went to him for advice. A few times a year, I would meet him at his office at the Abramson Cancer Center and we would grab a bite around the corner at the same greasy spoon diner where we'd first taken a meal together. His obligations at the hospital had slowed as he approached retirement and he'd used this increased allowance of time to participate in overseas medical missions. He'd traveled extensively on these missions, to Africa, to eastern Europe, to Central America, but the one place he'd returned to repeatedly was the island of

Saipan. The first time he went, he'd visited the airfield. Not long after returning from that trip, the two of us had met at the diner and, leaning over his plate, he'd told me how meaningful it'd been "to stand right where I lost my father."

When I spoke to him about my life, he was patient and listened closely. Amélie had no long-term desire to remain in the United States. She wanted to return home and wanted me to return home with her. "If you leave, what will you do?" Dr. Shields asked. To which I answered, "Teach math, I guess." He nodded and listened as I sketched an approximation of what life might look like for me outside this country. "When would you come back?" he asked, and I told him that I didn't know. "What does Ginny think?" and this last question was hardest of all. Ginny knew about my workplace romance and that the woman was younger, but nothing else. She and Amélie had never met. I'd kept them apart because of my embarrassment; when they saw how closely they resembled one another what would each think? Dr. Shields laughed when I explained this. "You worry too much," he said. "You're a young man. You have your entire life ahead of you."

For the rest of dinner, Dr. Shields and I talked politics. Neither of us could believe how quickly President Obama's eight years in office had passed. Our reservations notwithstanding, we agreed he'd done a good enough job. As unlikely as it might have seemed during the darkest hours of Bill Clinton's impeachment and conviction, the Democratic Party had now crowned Hillary the presumptive nominee. Based on every poll, she seemed poised to return to the White House in triumphant style. Both Dr. Shields and I thought the masterful handling of her ex-husband had proven key to her political success. She had very publicly divorced him but then also very publicly forgiven him, praising his accomplishments as president at every turn, building a reputation for magnanimity that led her to the Senate, to the

State Department, and on to her current trajectory toward the highest office in the land. If I spoke with such certainty about her victory, it was because of the disarray in the Republican field. Ever since Bush's single term, the party had no sense of itself, allowing its populist wing to war openly with its establishment wing. While a disciplined Democratic Party coalesced around Hillary, the Republicans had literally dozens of candidates vying for their nomination in a debate that was no debate at all but veered toward incoherence. "She's bound to win," I concluded.

At first, Dr. Shields didn't say anything. He sat studiously across from me calculating his half of our bill. Then, with that calculation complete, he paid in cash, shrugged his shoulders, and answered, "Maybe so." When I asked if he really thought a Republican could defeat Hillary, he said that he didn't know. It depended on who they nominated. But he added, "This might be a good time to head abroad."

The week after my dinner with Dr. Shields, I decided to return to France with Amélie. When I told her she began to cry. A tremble seized her voice when she confessed that she'd never expected I would come. I chose to interpret her tears as a sign of her love and imagined that if everything went well, we'd be married within the year. I then told her that I needed her to do one thing for me before we left. "Anything," she said, leaning toward me and cupping both of my hands in hers. And I asked if she would meet my ex-wife. That started her crying again.

Our plans were set. A frenzy of last things animated each day before our departure. By the end of May, I had let our school's principal know that I wouldn't be returning in the fall. I had yet to find a job in France but was actively searching, having emailed my resume widely. Amélie assured me something would come along, but I was worried about money and became doubly worried when she snuck out one afternoon to the nearest Zales and returned

with a gift for Ginny. Inside the little gray box was a charm bracelet cast in white gold. When I explained to Amélie that we could
only afford the essentials—at least until I found work—she apologized. She said she thought she understood why I wanted her to
meet Ginny, that Ginny had once been the most important person
in my life and that I didn't want to have to hide one chapter of
my life from another, that I wanted my past reconciled with my
present. Amélie was, of course, correct. I told her as much and
then she told me that an exchange of gifts was always a nice way
to begin a friendship.

That meeting occurred a few days later, at the bar of the Four
Seasons Hotel. I had, foolishly, allowed Ginny to pick the venue,
and so would not only have to absorb the cost of the gift Amélie had bought her but also the eighteen-dollar drinks—that is,
unless I permitted Ginny to pay for the three of us, a prospect
too demeaning to consider. When we arrived, Ginny was already
waiting at a corner table. Years had passed since I'd been at this bar.
Ginny, it seemed, continued to come here often and the hostess
took us right to her.

When Amélie and Ginny saw one another, my humiliation
was complete. "Oh my," said Ginny, and Amélie paused a step
short from our table. For her, it must have been like staring at a
photograph of herself twenty years into the future. Ginny immediately assumed the role of an elder and gestured for Amélie to
sit. I pulled out her chair. The two of them were now looking at
me, their expressions mimicking each other's in a sort of shared
wonder that I had managed to find two virtually identical versions
of the same woman. Like a coward, I buried my gaze in my menu,
and was pondering aloud our drink order when Ginny reached
across the table, placed her hand on my arm, and, mercifully, said,
"She is lovely, Martin," and then, turning to Amélie added, "It is
so good to finally meet you."

This put Amélie at ease. Which in turn put me at ease. Ginny ordered us an overpriced bottle of wine and asked about our plans. While Amélie explained the logistics of our move, I couldn't help but notice how this bar had changed in the intervening years since I'd last had a drink here with Ginny and her then-boyfriend Daryl. The bar wasn't run-down, but it certainly lacked its onetime luster and I noted the several vacant tables that surrounded ours. The clientele had cleared out gradually, over a period of years, like the emptying of a stubborn party, and I thought of Ginny, who despite the proximity of other, more chic venues chose to frequent her regular booth here.

Amélie, who was laying out our plans, had gotten to the part where I would drive my car down to South Carolina, to a gentleman who had offered to buy it for a good price, and then fly from Charleston through JFK and on to Charles de Gaulle, after which I'd take the train south to Toulon, where she'd be waiting.

"You're selling the Volvo?" Ginny asked incredulously.

"What else am I going to do with it?"

Ginny shrugged. "That's the end of an era."

Amélie had only ever referred to the Volvo as "that horrible car of yours," and she struggled to understand this flash of nostalgia. She changed the subject by reaching into her purse and producing the little wrapped box, making a few preemptory remarks about being so pleased to finally meet Ginny and her hope that the two of them could remain friends. If I needed any reminder of how acutely Amélie craved Ginny's approval, I noticed the slightest nervous tremble in her hand as she placed the gift on the white tablecloth. Ginny reciprocated with a gift of her own in a turquoise Tiffany's box, which, to my chagrin, she boldly called "an early engagement present." Inside was a very elegant and clearly expensive watch.

Amélie fastened the watch around her wrist and sat mesmerized, staring at its face. She turned weepy and mustered a string of thanks before excusing herself to the restroom.

"Was the gift too much?" asked Ginny.

"No, she's fine," I said. "Just a bit sentimental sometimes."

"Unlike me."

"You're sentimental," I said and reached across the table, to help Ginny with the clasp of her new bracelet. "Just in a different way." While I held Ginny's wrist, she asked when I planned to drive down to South Carolina. "Next month," I answered. "When school lets out."

"You'll drive right by Halcyon," she said. Ginny had kept up with the Ablesons. I knew from her that Boose had used the insurance money as well as her inheritance to rebuild the vast estate and that aside from her stepbrothers, who visited only on occasion, she had led a decidedly solitary life. One of her only consistent visitors through the years had been Susan Templeton. After the fire, she had ensured the smooth passage of Robert Ableson's death certificate at the records office and this went a long way in reconciling her and Boose. However, a couple of years ago Susan Templeton had passed away, only further isolating Boose, which was why Ginny now suggested that I pay her a visit on my journey south.

I was noncommittal and said that if I had time I'd try.

Ginny ran her fingers over her new charm bracelet.

School let out. Amélie and I packed our things. The night before her flight home, I helped her loosen the stubborn bevel on her new watch so she could reset it to Paris time. After that, we watched her first-ever Fourth of July fireworks celebration from the grounds around Independence Hall. Assuming my flight landed on schedule, we would watch my first-ever Bastille Day fireworks ten days later from her home in Toulon. When I dropped her at the airport there were no tears, only the anticipation of our happy reunion. I left the departures terminal and immediately turned my car around, heading south. Without a job, I was living on my savings, budgeting both money and time.

Traffic north of Baltimore proved heavy and only got worse as I skirted around Washington. Whatever hopes I had of completing the ten-plus-hour trip to Charleston in a single day vanished as I sat stalled in Beltway gridlock. By late afternoon, I had resigned myself to finding a hotel someplace and waking up early to finish the drive the following morning. I was just south of Richmond as I reached this conclusion and, looking for a place to pull off the interstate, recognized I wasn't far from Oak Ridge Cemetery, to which, impelled by curiosity and a dash of nostalgia, I diverted.

After pulling into the parking lot, I sat in my car for a long while. Maybe five minutes, maybe fifteen. I stared tentatively up the long, headstone-studded slope, toward the crest of the ridge and the Ablesons' shared grave. I considered getting back on the road—and very well might have—if a groundskeeper hadn't crept up behind me, knocking on my window. He asked what I was doing sitting in the lot. If there was someone I wanted to visit, I needed to get on my way as he'd soon be shutting the gates. I thanked him, stepped out of the car, and plodded up the ridge, hands jammed in my pants pockets.

As I walked, I searched for a pair of pebbles I might leave on the Ablesons' headstone, nosing the toe of my shoe around in the grass. The manicured grounds yielded nothing, and by the time I'd arrived up on the crest, beside the single grave, I remained empty-handed. I was, however, heartened to see evidence of a recent visitor. A half-dozen different color peonies rested at the base of the headstone, the petals browning at the edges. I wanted to leave some memento of my own. In my pocket I had a bit of change, to include a pair of dimes. I placed them on the headstone, one for Mary and beside it one for Robert.

Golden light carpeted the valley floor. The Ablesons' grave looked out on that view, which I enjoyed before descending the reverse side of the ridge toward the parking lot. At this hour, the light on the backslope cast drab shadows that caused the colors of a matching bouquet of peonies to stand out among the headstones. When I approached this grave, I was surprised to find it belonged to Susan Templeton. Although I'd known of her death, I hadn't known of her choice to be buried in this cemetery, so close to the Ablesons, even if her resting place afforded a less spectacular view.

It would soon be entirely dark and I imagined the groundskeeper was growing impatient; still, I had one last thing to do. I marched back up the ridge and snatched one of my two dimes off the Ablesons' grave. I placed it on Susan Templeton's headstone instead and then returned to my car.

I knew who'd left the matching bouquets; or at least I suspected I knew and now felt determined to know for certain. Half an hour later, at the end of that dark gravel driveway, Halcyon appeared, rebuilt exactly as I'd remembered it. Light poured from its windows, causing its blemishless white façade to glow warmly. You could have told me that a decade had passed or a day and I wouldn't have been able to determine the difference. After the fire, Boose could have constructed a new home, with a vision entirely of her own; but she hadn't. Time eroded into a useless unit of measure as I knocked at the threshold of this old house turned new.

When Boose arrived at the door, she appeared equally unchanged, except around her eyes; here, the faintest of crow's feet had spread as if she had spent the intervening years squinting out into great distances. What she wore was also familiar to me, a variation on the white hostess dress she'd put on and seemingly never taken off after first inheriting Halcyon. "Martin," she said. "What a lovely surprise."

Except she hardly seemed surprised. I surmised that Ginny had phoned and mentioned that I might show up. And here I was, further proof of my predictability to the women who knew me best, of which I supposed I could now count Boose even if I hadn't seen her in over a decade. She led me through a string of familiar rooms, replete with candles and little silver dishes of candy set out on every console table. We then arrived in the kitchen, where she'd set the dinner table for one but had cooked enough for two. She uncorked a bottle of wine and laid down a second place setting, and we sat with what in the daytime would have been a view of her property; instead, in the night-dark windows we could see only our reflections.

She said congratulations were in order, that she'd heard about my impending move abroad through Ginny and that she was happy for me. She listened with interest as I told her about my career shift and the simple satisfaction I'd found in teaching a subject as straightforward as elementary school mathematics. I listened with equal interest as she updated me about her stepbrothers, each of whom was approaching retirement, and her many nieces and nephews, whom she saw once or perhaps twice a year and who were off at college. She carried on at length about the house, its reconstruction and her constant battle to preserve it in this immaculate condition. "Each year," she said, "it becomes a little more difficult," as though her work at Halcyon had devolved into a struggle against time itself.

It was only after she cleared our plates that I mentioned my visit to Oak Ridge Cemetery earlier that day. "It surprised me," I said, "to find Susan Templeton buried so close to your father."

Boose considered the observation, swishing the dregs of wine in the bottom of her glass. "Well, her daughter hadn't approved. After my father passed, Susan's relationship with Janet became increasingly distant." When I asked why, Boose ran the tip of her finger around the edge of her empty crystal glass, so it made a hollow sound while she considered her answer, settling on "Some people want to stay wronged. Their entire lives are defined by being in opposition to someone or to something. Janet is one of those people. Her mother wasn't. Ultimately, my father had helped

Susan more than he'd harmed her. She'd forgiven him his faults and wanted to acknowledge that. I suppose that's why she chose a grave near his."

"Except he's not buried in that grave."

Boose glanced up at me harshly. "No," she said, "I suppose he isn't. I prefer to remember him in other places." She went on at length about Richmond, where he'd practiced law, and of course Halcyon, its garden and specific spots on the grounds where she had recollections of her father even if the fire had burned his body to ash. "To be honest," she said, "I never visit the cemetery." Boose began to clear our plates, taking them to the sink.

"Whatever happened to that monument?" I asked.

She didn't seem to hear my question, so I asked her again if she knew where the monument was. She said, "It's stored in some museum in South Carolina, I think," and then she turned on the garbage disposal, cutting off the rest of our conversation.

Once we finished cleaning up, I brought my bag in from the car. Boose had invited me to stay the night and led me upstairs to the guest room, which wasn't really a guest room at all but a reconstruction of the old master suite. Boose explained how she'd never felt comfortable moving into what would've been her parents' room and so used it for visitors instead. When I asked if she often had visitors stay with her, she laughed. "Aside from family," she said, "you might be the first." She had set a bottle of water on my bedside table and placed fresh flowers from her garden around the room. She asked if there was anything else that I needed. I told her there wasn't and mentioned that I planned to leave early the next morning, right at sunrise. I didn't want her to wake up on my account. So we said our goodbyes.

Tucked into a replica of her parents' bed that night, I couldn't sleep. I was curious to know exactly where the Virginia Monument had wound up. Who knew, if it was in South Carolina perhaps I could pay it a last visit before heading abroad? Lying on my back, I could feel an impression in the mattress, as if Boose did in fact have visitors and someone had regularly used this bed. Eventually, I got comfortable and began a search on my phone. This led to a local news story that mentioned the Virginia Monument's acquisition by the Museum of Southern Heritage, not a twenty-minute drive from the address where I was scheduled to drop my Volvo off the next day.

That night I didn't sleep but rode that liminal barrier between dreams and waking thoughts. I knew that the Virginia Monument hadn't vanished from the earth, but in the years since watching its removal with Lucas Harlow, I had given little thought to its ultimate fate, in much the same way I'd given little thought to Ableson's ultimate fate and what had become of his vanished remains apart from an empty grave at Oak Ridge Cemetery. An hour before dawn, I couldn't lie in bed any longer. I got up, dressed, and went back downstairs. I sat with a cup of coffee outside on the portico, where I'd once enjoyed afternoon lemonade with Ableson and Boose.

The peaks of the distant Blue Ridge lightened, suggesting the rising sun. Points of birdsong picked up in the many trees, including the pear grove at the distant edge of Boose's garden. The morning slowly revealed its details, and I could see the fountain at the garden's center, with its border of purple aster and surface that glistened in the dawn like a mirror. I could see the hydrangeas that hung heavily on their stems. There were new plantings, too. Lilies of the valley. Sunflowers. Giant clusters of forget-me-nots. But when the sun rose entirely and I could see the garden properly, what drew my eye was the bed of peonies. Boose had once said that she'd wanted to dig them up because they reminded her too much of her mother. Boose had once said that her father made her promise to keep them so long as he was alive. That's what she had said. I remembered it clearly.

I got in my car and drove south.

. . .

By lunch I had arrived outside of Charleston, at the address given to me by the man who'd bought my car, a man who seemed born to this new era: a middle-aged bachelor whose Facebook profile was tiled with CrossFit pictures and whose job status was "self-employed." We stood in his driveway as he gave the Volvo a once-over, checking beneath its hood and marveling at its excellent condition despite a high odometer reading. He sat in the front seat and made out a check on the steering wheel. He handed it to me and that was it, the car was his. My flight wasn't until that evening and he offered a ride wherever I wanted to go to pass the time. When I mentioned the Museum of Southern Heritage, his eyebrows knit together. "If you say so," he muttered, but when I went to climb into the Volvo, he stopped me. "I'd rather we take my car. I'm planning to sell yours for parts, so the fewer miles on it the better." He clicked his garage-door opener and inside was a Tesla. I climbed into the passenger seat.

The drive was smooth and silent. The disembodied voice of the Tesla's onboard navigation system couldn't find the museum; the software it relied on didn't seem to acknowledge its existence and so we navigated to a nearby address instead. When we arrived, there was no sign out front. We pulled into the parking lot and found the museum's address on the side of a multistoried warehouse. From the driver's seat, my ride leaned over his steering wheel, craning his neck upward, as he said that he'd always heard about this place but had never thought to visit. When I invited him inside, he shook his head in a mild panic. "That's okay," he said. "I'd rather not," and his Tesla was out of the parking lot and back on the road before I had reached the front door.

Inside, a ticket counter stood to my front and the glassed-in façade of a gift shop to my right. A stand near the counter offered brochures and a map of the museum. My flight that night departed at a little after eight o'clock and the museum shut at six. This gave me a couple of hours to wander around. A large book was spread open next to the cash register, which I recognized immediately. It was the final volume of Shelby Foote's *The Civil War: A Narrative*. Whoever was reading it would soon return, and after a few moments a door opened from what appeared to be the gift shop stockroom.

"My apologies," said a young man who stepped behind the counter. Clear-eyed, square-jawed, with shoulders built sturdy and wide as rafter beams, he was college-aged, wore an open-collared shirt and linen sports coat. He appeared convinced of himself, assured, and in this manner of conviction and assurance he very much reminded me of Lucas Harlow. He tucked his marker into the volume of Shelby Foote and offered to sell me a ticket. I asked him about the book, and he mentioned that he was enrolled in a graduate program in American history. When I mentioned how glad I was to learn that they still assigned Shelby Foote, he shook his head. "They don't," he said. "I'm reading it on my own." He issued me a ticket and then removed a map of the museum from the stand. His knowledge of the relics inside proved encyclopedic as he recommended certain exhibits. "How long have you worked here?" I asked, tucking my ticket stub into my pocket. He explained that it was simply a summer job; next year, he'd receive his degree and after that he planned to teach. I made a comment about summer jobs being difficult to find and mentioned some of the horrible ones I'd once held as a graduate student. To which he replied that working at this museum had been, in fact, his first choice. "What type of a historian would I be," he said, "if I refused to understand every side of an issue, no matter how odious." He glanced over his shoulder, into the cavernous maw of Confederate regalia behind him. "By the way, it's just me around here," he added. "So please make sure you're out by six." When he finished speaking, I couldn't help but think—with a mix of satisfaction and also grim resignation—that nothing has been settled, that no enduring conclusion has been reached, that Lucas Harlow would, at some later date, have to contend with this doppelgänger of his, with this future self that tended to the monuments he had torn down. Then the young man disappeared, withdrawing back into the stockroom to continue whatever inventory I had so clearly interrupted.

I advanced into the dim-lit depths of the museum, where I wandered among the displays of rifles, glinting cavalry sabers, tattered regimental flags, uniformed mannikins, and dioramas of famous battles—Chickamauga, Fort Donelson, Big Bethel, the Siege of Corinth—all entombed in glass. To save power, motion sensors controlled the lights so that my progress illuminated the path. Speakers clamped to the rigging in the ceiling played "The Bonnie Blue Flag" on a loop, the volume set to a low background murmur. Several times, I grew disoriented, unable to situate my place on the map among the labyrinthine and seemingly endless corridors that housed this collection, which was arrayed in no discernible order aside from the order in which the museum had acquired it. Marked on a far corner of my map was the Virginia Monument.

The motion sensors above the monument triggered when I stepped inside the four-story bay that housed its bronze edifice. A cluster of lights shined down on General Lee, Traveller, and the seven soldiers gathered at the monument's base. The museum had needed something to place the monument on and so had commissioned a replica of the original pedestal, except instead of granite it was cast in far less expensive poured concrete. Around the monument the museum had also erected a four-story scaffold. The result was quite democratic, allowing visitors to view the statue from every angle, not just from the ground staring up.

I climbed the scaffold to its fourth story. The higher I went, the closer I came to the overhead lights, which cast a gloomy halo over Lee, and soon I was standing face-to-face with the old general.

He appeared different from this angle, not like the venerated Lee, but more like any man who I might recognize in a crowd. When I leaned on the scaffolding's railing, the two of us were separated by such a minor distance that it seemed as if I were leaning forward to hear him better as we shared a table at a crowded restaurant. While I considered his bronze face, I wondered what other expressions it had been capable of. How often had it formed into laughter, into rage, or even into apology? That was what he'd done after all, when the survivors of Pickett's Charge had crossed back over the field; he'd apologized, telling them, "It's all my fault," and he'd spent the five short years of his life that remained after the war uttering a string of similar apologies. It was Lee himself who'd argued against erecting any monuments to his misbegotten cause. And yet here he was, preserved in bronze.

On the scaffolding's landing was a bench. I sat on it, resting the back of my head against the railing. I had hardly slept the night before and, in the last two days, had traveled hundreds of miles by car and still had an ocean to cross. Exhaustion set in when I thought of the overnight flight ahead of me. "The Bonnie Blue Flag" played on its incessant loop from the speakers above and, just for a moment, I decided to shut my eyes . . .

When I awoke, it was to a vast darkness and silence. Four stories beneath me, at the base of the scaffolding, I heard the metallic clatter of wheels. A noise like a mop bucket proceeded in my direction. When whoever was below triggered a motion sensor, the glaring overhead light that hung above me shined down, reilluminating the bronze contours of Lee's face. His expression no longer seemed apologetic but accusatory as I blinked my eyes, struggling to adjust them out of the darkness.

Footsteps ascended the scaffolding. With them came the hollow sound of whistling, the same song that had looped all day across the speakers, "The Bonnie Blue Flag," a tune engineered to get in your head and stay there. The whistling grew closer. In a burst of panic, I checked my watch. The museum had closed thirty minutes ago. If I left now I could—maybe and with a bit of luck—still make my eight o'clock flight. I stood from the bench but hadn't taken a single step before the janitor appeared on the fourth-story landing, clutching his bucket with one hand and his mop handle with the other. He set both down clumsily, a splash of water spilling across the stairs.

When he saw me, he startled and took a step back, his ring of keys jangling on his hip. I apologized, explaining my mistake and that I wasn't a burglar or any kind of criminal but that I'd simply fallen asleep. He was an older man in coveralls with a thick but well-groomed beard, much like Lee's, and with a similar dignity in posture, though I did notice how his eyes refused mine at every glance. Frozen to his spot atop the scaffold, he blocked my way. I fished around in my pocket, hunting for my ticket stub, as if this might convince him of the sincerity of my mistake. When I produced it, his eyes finally met mine; they looked as though they had seen a battle and in them, I recognized the cold gaze of Robert Ableson.

"You're alive . . . ?"

Whether it was the beard or simple proximity to the statue, the man's resemblance to both Abelson and Lee was uncanny. Like the old general, the man's gaze proved equally perplexing, a mix of rage, defeat, defiance, and also apology.

"I visited Boose . . . and Mary . . . and Susan. I saw the peonies . . . I knew you'd left them on their graves . . . I knew it was you . . ." I spoke in a stammer, each word tripping over the other like those of a madman as I hoped to prod some response out of him, some acknowledgment that what I suspected was true: that he'd never died and, perhaps, never would. "You're living down here . . . ? How long have you worked here . . . ? How often do you visit Halcyon . . . ?"

The janitor threw down his mop handle, tipping over his bucket so that it blocked my path. With this head start he sprinted down the scaffolding, taking the steps two at a time.

"Wait!" I shouted, chasing after him.

With water pouring over the stairs, I also took them two at a time and soon slipped, landing painfully on my side. When I arrived at the scaffold's bottom, the janitor had already vanished into the depths of the museum. I followed him but quickly became turned around and then lost entirely among this endless accumulation of memorabilia. Down a nearby corridor, I heard what sounded like a door flung open. Then, out of the silence, an alarm thundered from every speaker in the museum. When I eventually made it to the emergency exit, the janitor was nowhere to be found.

I stepped through the door he'd left open, out the back of the museum and into the heat of a stifling night. Off in the distance, I could see clusters of orbiting siren lights already traveling both ends of the road in my direction. I would miss my flight and would, likely, miss my celebration of the Bastille Day fireworks with Amélie, which I had so long anticipated, and had hoped might prove my first memory of a different life made in a new country. All those plans seemed suddenly quite foolish.

I had no car, no means of escape, so I sat on the curb and waited for the police to arrive. I wondered what crime, if any, they would charge me with.

My thanks, as ever, to PJ Mark,
and to Diana Miller,
and, of course, to Lea Carpenter.

A NOTE ABOUT THE AUTHOR

Elliot Ackerman is the *New York Times* best-selling author of the novels *2034, Red Dress in Black and White, Waiting for Eden, Dark at the Crossing,* and *Green on Blue,* as well as the memoirs *The Fifth Act: America's End in Afghanistan* and *Places and Names: On War, Revolution, and Returning.* His books have been nominated for the National Book Award, the Andrew Carnegie Medal in both fiction and nonfiction, and the Dayton Literary Peace Prize, among others. He is a contributing writer at *The Atlantic* and a Marine veteran, having served five tours of duty in Iraq and Afghanistan, where he received the Silver Star, the Bronze Star for Valor, and the Purple Heart. He divides his time between New York City and Washington, D.C.

A NOTE ON THE TYPE

The text of this book was set in Ehrhardt, a typeface based on
the specimens of "Dutch" types found at the Ehrhardt foundry
in Leipzig. The original design of the face was the work of
Nicholas Kis, a Hungarian punch cutter known to have worked in
Amsterdam from 1680 to 1689. The modern version of Ehrhardt
was cut by the Monotype Corporation of London in 1937.

TYPESET BY SCRIBE,
PHILADELPHIA, PENNSYLVANIA

PRINTED AND BOUND BY FRIESENS,
ALTONA, MANITOBA

DESIGNED BY BETTY LEW